What Are Friends for?

SARAH SUTTON

Golden Crown Publishing, LLC

To those who encouraged me to fly.

One

I squinted at the crooked display of underwear in front of me, the colors and patterns making my eyes ache. The tier had been picked over by the hordes of people milling about, the midwinter half-off sale drawing in the crazies desperate for a good deal. Crazies like me, apparently.

I lifted two pairs of panties in each hand, holding them side by side and inspecting them closely. They were the same price, both floral, both the cotton boyshort style that I loved. However, one pair was blue with daisies, the other purple with lace accents and sunflowers, and I couldn't decide which I liked best.

Life-or-death decisions were made in the underwear store.

"Okay, you choose." I turned around to face the boy behind me and lifted the pairs of underwear, shaking them to catch his attention. His gaze, however, looked over my shoulder at the wall, unfocused. "Earth to Eli."

His dark eyes snapped to mine. They were brown—not hazel, not chocolate, just brown. As dark as the morning coffee he drank, but depthless. "What?"

"Pick: blue daisies or purple sunflowers with a lace band?"

"Oh." Elijah looked between the two panties, analyzing them. "Isn't the lace itchy?"

I smiled, placing the purple pair back. "See, this is why I bring you. You think about the logistics of shopping more than Eloise. She just goes 'oh, that's cute' and adds it to her pile."

Elijah's eyes roamed over the tiers of lacy clothing items without fixating on one place for more than a few seconds. Our winter jackets were thrown over his arm, my puffy red mixing with his denim, allowing me an unobstructed shopping experience. What a gentleman. "Please do not try to tell me I have better taste in women's underwear than your best friend."

"You do. You should put it on your résumé. And anyway, *you* are my best friend," I told him seriously, nudging his shoulder. "My list goes chronologically. I've known you way longer than her."

Elijah Greybeck and I had been best friends since third grade when his parents packed him and his brother up and hauled them nearly 200 miles across the country. The best decision of the Greybecks' lives. It was, at least, the best thing that had happened to mine.

Cue the *aww* sound effect.

"And you need to say it," I said, lifting my eyes to his. "*Panties.*"

"Never. I'm never going to say it." He mock-shuddered, following me as I moved to the next tier of clothing. I opened one of the drawers that held bralettes and sifted through the different patterns. One had a smattering of pink polka dots on a white background, and I added it to the pile I'd started, balanced in one hand. "You know, it was fine walking around with you when we were in the activewear section. But looking at underwear with you is a little freaky, Remi."

"It's not freaky," I told him, tilting my head at the tier. "Just pretend that I'm looking at bathing suits. Or just close your eyes."

In all honesty, I couldn't explain *why* I liked it when Elijah came with me to the store. Maybe because I liked torturing him, my best friend since childhood. I liked watching him squirm. Or hey, maybe because carting him around with me made it seem like I had a boyfriend, even though I was as single as the last cookie in the cookie jar.

What did my mom say that was again? Oh yeah: *picky*. I was picky.

I'd started to move to the next display when Elijah's voice stopped me. "That's not your size."

"Uh, what?"

He gestured to my pile, and even from here, I could see grayish smudges of clay stuck underneath his fingernails, a chalky dust near his cuticles. "You grabbed that from the B shelf and you...you usually grab the C."

I glanced at the tag and, sure enough, it read B instead of my normal C. I pressed a hand over my heart, unable to fight a grin. "Elijah Greybeck, after all these years of friendship and mall trips, did you actually *memorize* my bra size?"

Elijah couldn't keep his gaze neutral either, his eyes crinkling at the corners. "Sav would have a heart attack."

Sav, or Savannah, and Elijah had been dating for the past month and a half, but hearing her name fall from his lips still surprised me. She seemed fine enough, but we weren't really around each other for me to know otherwise. Elijah said I'd like her more when I got to know her, but as far as initial reactions went, I wasn't too impressed.

As of late, there weren't many opportunities for us to hang out together. Too much had gone on in Elijah's life this past week and a half.

I instantly sobered as I thought of what happened, cutting a glance his way. He seemed normal enough. One hand was in his pocket, and his gaze settled on me.

Elijah raised an eyebrow. "What's that face for?"

"How's your mom been?" I asked, feeling like I needed to mind my own business, but I couldn't *not* ask. "My mom's been trying to call her so they can get lunch."

"Oh, *that's* what the face is for," he said with a sigh. "She's fine. Dad's fine. I'm fine. We're all fine."

"And how's Terry?"

Elijah looked away from me, but I caught his scowl.

The fabric of the underwear in my hand slid as I curled my fingers, trying to stare at him as seriously as I could. "You can't pretend like it didn't happen."

"I know I can't," he snapped, "because everyone brings it up all the time. 'Hey, was it your brother that robbed those gas stations last week? Did he shoot anybody? How long is he in jail for?'"

I winced, an icy feeling spreading through my stomach.

Almost a week and a half ago now, on New Year's Day, the Greybeck family had received a phone call from the Greenville County Police Department at 12:45 in the morning. Five minutes after that, my cell phone rang, Elijah's name flashing on the screen. I got to his house and found him in his room, surrounded by broken bits of clay.

The newspaper reported the crime as an armed robbery at one of the 24-hour drug stores over in Bayview, almost an hour away from where we lived, as well as a gas station. The article listed four people as culprits—one of them being Terrance Greybeck, Elijah's older brother.

Biting my tongue, I made my way to the perfume section, stepping around a girl with her arms full. This wasn't a fancy store by any means, so the bottles of perfume weren't name-brand, but their glass containers were still pretty. I reached for one.

"Remi," Elijah said quietly, trailing after me. "Beanie, I'm sorry. I just don't want to talk about it, okay?"

Beanie. My childhood nickname, since I used to collect those bean-filled dolls. I didn't have a creative nickname for him, just Eli. But he didn't let anyone else call him that. Only me.

Though it was hard for me to accept, I understood where he was coming from. With everyone bugging him about his brother, he probably hoped he could find peace with his best friend.

His very curious best friend. Because though he'd called me the night Terry was arrested, I never got the full details. Like my classmates, I was in the dark. And since I was a super curious girl, I hated being in the dark.

"It's okay, Eli," I told him, reaching around and squeezing the arm that held our coats. "But when you do want to talk about it, know that I'm here, okay?"

Elijah didn't smile, but his face did soften, the lines around his mouth looking less pronounced. "I know."

I turned back to the clearance display, swiping up a glass bottle in the shape of an ice cream cone, the amber liquid swirling inside. The scent was sharp and fruity, enough to make me cough. "What do you think of this one?"

"You literally just gagged sniffing it," Elijah said, but humored me, leaning in so that I could hover the bottle underneath his nose. "It's nice. Wait, why do you need a new perfume anyway?" I sniffed yet another glass bottle. This one was shaped more like a flower, with a curved glass petal. This one smelled sugary-sweet, one of my favorite scents. "Didn't Eloise just buy you one the last time we were out? In that amber-colored bottle?"

"You never smelled it," I told him, spritzing the liquid onto my neck, the scent immediately strengthening. "The one she bought literally smells like I bathed myself in oregano. It's disgusting. I need something new. Here, sniff me."

"What? No. I'm not sniffing you, Rem."

I angled my neck closer to his face, and I had to stand on my tiptoes to even reach halfway. "Sniff me. Perfumes always smell different when mixing with people's body chemistry— or whatever. Sniff me. Tell me what you think."

His lips parted as another tortured sigh came from him, and he leaned close enough that I could feel his breath tickle my skin. Our jackets crinkled with the movement. "Smells good, but I liked the other one better."

I wasn't sure I agreed with him on that but set the flower bottle back regardless. "I'm sorry for dragging you along to this. I know it's not your favorite thing in the world, shopping with me. If I had a car—"

He gently cut me off. "Stop. I know I'm being a pain, but what are best friends for? And it's not that I absolutely hate it or anything—it can just be weird."

I raised an eyebrow at the perfume. "Weird?"

"You know, the shopping for underwear part. Shopping for that stuff with a girl that I'm not dating is...weird."

Ooh, this is a cute bottle, I thought, swiping up a rainbow-colored perfume in the shape of a hair-bow. It had a fainter fruity scent than the other one, but enough to remind me of those gummy candies. Or maybe the smell was mixing with the fragrance I'd sprayed a second ago. Not a clue.

"No offense," Elijah hurried to add, misunderstanding my silence. "I mean, I'm sure you look great in panties—ugh, I mean underwear—who the heck says panties anymore?"

I tried to fight a laugh. "You've said it twice now."

"*Anyway*, I just don't like imagining you...you know..."

"Butt-naked?"

Elijah squeezed his eyes shut, as if trying to chase away that image. "You're terrible. *Terrible.*"

I snorted a little. Why did a little part of me feel offended that he couldn't imagine me naked? Honestly, I should've been relieved. This was Elijah. I'd seen him go through puberty, the strange phase when he only wore blue clothes, and even the time he tried to grow a mustache. We still had nicknames for each other. It'd be weird if he *could* imagine me naked. I mean, I didn't go around imagining *him* naked.

Elijah groaned, rubbing his hand over his eyes. "See, this is why I can't come here with you. All the girly perfumes and bright patterns completely kill my brain cells."

I decided to save him from his stupidity. "Careful, dude," I said, punching him in the arm. "You don't have many brain cells left to be wasting them on girly perfume and panties."

"Yeah," he scoffed, tugging our jackets closer to his chest as we made our way to the cash register. "No kidding."

two

Greenville High wasn't the biggest school in the county—it didn't compare to Bayview or Northside Prep by any means—so even though everyone was buddy-buddy for the most part, Elijah and I were closer than most. Partners in crime, two peas in a pod. All that cliché crap. We even made friendship bracelets with each other's names once. He still kept his on his key ring, though mine had broken years ago.

A lot of girls at school thought Elijah was "sweet cute." Cute without being a jerk about it. In an objective way, I guess he *was* sort of cute, if you were into the whole wavy-haired, narrow-boned, artsy kind of thing. His eyebrows were several shades darker than his blond hair, which almost looked bleached. His features were fine, apart from the slight curve that bent his nose from when I'd accidentally broken it in fifth grade.

I'd tried to pressure him into playing softball with me, tossing the ball at him and solidly connecting with his nose.

We learned then that hand-eye coordination wasn't exactly his thing. But art was. Give him a pencil and he could draw the entire map of the world, line for line, from memory. He was currently working on an art project to enter it into a county-hosted art contest in a couple weeks with the theme "Family." Though he refused to tell me what exactly he was going to enter—painting, drawing, sculpture—I wondered if it had something to do with his brother.

But I knew one thing—Elijah was a pottery guy at heart. No doubt his project would be made of clay.

"So what happened today that made you want to go shopping?" Elijah asked around his chocolate ice cream cone, periodically licking any drips. Elijah had this *thing*. Everyone has a thing that makes them unique, and Elijah had this. Thirty-three degrees outside, snowing like mad, and he had to have ice cream. I teased him all the time that he's probably the reason why Freezing Fred's opens in winter, the only ice cream parlor in the county that does so. "I know you. You only ever like to shop when something bad happens. What's wrong?"

I slouched a little in my seat, goosebumps covering my skin as I stirred the vanilla and blue raspberry ice cream. "Nothing. I was just in the mood for a good sale."

"Liar."

Fine, I was lying, but I also wasn't admitting anything. I reached up and rubbed my hand over my mouth, feeling the stickiness of the blue raspberry syrup.

Elijah fanned a napkin in front of me, seeming to pull it from nowhere. "You do this every time. You never get a napkin, but always need one."

I snatched it from his grasp, sticking my tongue out. "You should start reminding me."

"Did you finish the assignment for art yet?"

Ugh, I didn't want to be reminded about *that*. Didn't want to think about art or about Mrs. Keller, our art teacher and, as of a few hours ago, my mortal enemy. I could still hear her voice echoing in my head, like a villain in some bad movie. *You have a fifty-six in my class, Remi.*

I shoved the words down, pushing a huge bite of ice cream into my mouth.

"It's due tomorrow," Elijah said in his prodding, fatherly voice. "A papier-mâché of any object in your home. Pretty easy stuff."

Sure, easy-peasy if you were an art god like Mr. Pottery Hands over here. "I can start it tonight."

Elijah blinked, lowering his cone. "Wait, wait, back it up —you haven't even *started* it?"

Shaking my head, I pulled my spoon to my mouth.

People had coping mechanisms when it came to stress, right? People might overeat, might take naps. My coping mechanism, from self-examination, was shopping. And Mrs. Keller totally was the reason for this impromptu trip, given she'd sent my stress levels through the roof. *If you don't pull up your grade, you're not going to pass this semester. You may have forgotten, but two art credits are a requirement for gradu-ation. Not passing this semester means no graduation, Remi. Are you listening?*

"You're not listening to me," Elijah said.

"I'm listening." Sort of. "Hey, switch."

Elijah made a face as he offered his ice cream cone to me.

I swiped my tongue along its edge, the rich chocolate coating my tongue.

I closed my eyes. "Mmm. I should've gotten chocolate."

"You say that every time." Elijah opened his mouth, and I grabbed a nice spoonful of blue raspberry flavoring and slipped my spoon into his mouth. Immediately, his face screwed up. "Ugh," he said, shuddering around the mouthful. "Nasty."

"And you say *that* every time." I laughed and licked off the remainder from the spoon. "Did you hear Jeremy's having a party tonight?"

Elijah leaned back in his seat, causing it to squeak. "I wondered when you were going to bring it up."

"I thought about going."

"Mostly because it's an excuse to flirt with Jeremy about something other than homework, right?"

No reason in denying my mega crush on Jeremy Rivera, but we'd come to a pathetic standstill. We talked, flirted here and there, but our torrid love affair extended no further. Elijah was right; asking about homework didn't count as a conversation. But we didn't need words to communicate. We were on a level where just eye contact conveyed attraction.

Did I say kind of pathetic? I meant a freaking sob story.

"Earth to Beanie, do you copy? Or are you lost in your head, imagining Jer's abs?"

"They're nice abs." I tried to kick him under the table, but my foot didn't connect. "Are we going tonight, then?"

"I don't know." He sighed with a twist to his mouth. "It's Thursday. Who parties on a school night?"

"Jeremy, apparently. And whoever else shows up." I

glanced out the ice cream shop's window, where the snow fell at its even pace. It was only half-past five and the sky was already darkening, gray snow clouds eclipsing the slivers of sun. "The forecast says we're supposed to get a lot of snow tonight. Everyone's expecting a snow day."

"Have you looked outside? We've been getting a lot of snow all week and we haven't even delayed. Greenville High is ruthless."

I set down the cup of ice cream on the table, leveling my gaze with his. "When did you stop being fun?"

"I literally just went shopping with you, Remi," he said, finally allowing his irritation to shine through his words. "I helped pick out something. I even sniffed your perfumes. That's fun. Besides, you've got your papier-mâché to do."

Ah, that reminder didn't feel great. In fact, it almost felt like a punch to the gut.

Though I wanted to, I couldn't tell him about my failing grade. There wasn't much he could do about it, anyway. In art, we were graded more on participation than actual quality, and I knew already what he'd say. *Remi, you should be applying yourself more. How could you have let this happen?* Disappointment from my parents was bearable. Dad wouldn't do much—the cold shoulder for an hour or two would be the extent of his discipline—and Mom might threaten no technology, though she'd never enforce it. But Elijah disappointed in me?

The mere idea made me feel icky, like my insides were covered in mud.

And besides, he had enough going on in his own life.

Between his family, the sculpture competition, and his new girlfriend, no way did he have time for my art drama.

Elijah's phone started ringing from his pocket before I had a chance to respond, a lively tune that I faintly recognized. He leaned further back in his seat to fish it out, glancing at the screen before pressing it to his ear. "Hey, Sav." A pause. "I'm with Remi right now, but we can hang out afterward. No. I'll come when we're finished."

Inwardly, I cringed at the mention of my name. I knew I should've been the good best friend and volunteered to leave, to respect some kind of girl code and forfeit the man when requested, but I didn't. Bitterly, I took another bite.

"I get it. Yes, I do. I'll text you when I'm on my way. Okay. Bye." When Elijah pulled the cell away from his ear, he fumbled a little to press the end button.

"Did you two have plans?"

"No, she just wanted to hang." He slipped the phone back into his pocket. "You should just go tonight without me. Can't you hitch a ride with Eloise or something? Surely she wouldn't miss it."

In all honesty, I *could've* hitched a ride from Eloise or even asked my mom to borrow her car. The latter, though, posed its own problems—mostly revolving around the question of where I would tell her I'd be going. A study group? Mom went to bed early on weeknights since she had to get up at the crack of dawn for her consults—"an interior designer should be the first person to the job site in the morning" was her motto—so sneaking back in wouldn't be too hard.

But I didn't want Eloise to drive me, and I didn't want to borrow Mom's car.

I channeled my puppy-dog face. A hook, line, and sinker move, and I hated that I was using it to my advantage, but it was too late.

Elijah held my gaze for a moment before he shut his eyes. "What do I get if I go?"

Immediately, I broke into a grin. "Drunk?"

His unamused expression wasn't what I'd hoped for.

"Ah, don't listen to me, Eli," I relented, stuffing my napkin into my now-empty ice cream cup. "Just promise me you'll think about it. I always have more fun when you're there. We rock at beer pong and you know it."

He'd finished his own ice cream, leaving only the cone in his hand. It was funny—he always got cones but never ate them. "I'll see what Savannah wants to do," he said finally.

That response would have to do. I got to my feet and grabbed my coat. "Let's head out, then. Maybe if you get some extra alone time in before the party, Savannah will want to go. Maybe you can talk her into it."

Elijah pushed away from the table and tossed his cone into the trash, eyes flicking to mine. "I make no promises."

Back in the third grade, my parents sat me down and declared the impending apocalyptic doom of something called a "divorce." Or at least it had seemed doom-worthy, judging by the dual expressions they wore that day. "Mommy and Daddy are going to live in different houses," they'd said, "but they still care about each other. Do you understand?"

And that was it. No huge blowout. No yelling or scream-ing. "Irreconcilable differences" in my parents' case meant "falling out of love." Like a snowflake falling from the sky, slowly fluttering before it hit the ground. It almost sounded whimsical.

But even though their separation hadn't been dramatic or world-ending, I never wanted to do that in my life. The idea of falling out of love with someone was enough to break my heart. If I was being honest, that was the reason I was picky with guys, settled with harmlessly flirting when it didn't matter so much. I didn't want to give my heart away, only to have them fall out of love with me later on. I didn't want that kind of wishy-washy love story. I wasn't naïve enough to think that all high school relationships lasted forever, but I couldn't bear the idea of falling in love with someone and then falling out of love with them.

"Mom," I called into the house, juggling my backpack and my shopping bags with one arm, tugging on the door with my other hand. The dampness of winter agitated the springs or the jamb or something, and the door felt like it fractured more and more each time it opened. I made a mental note to ask Elijah to come over and check it. Mr. Pottery Hands knew a thing or two about tools—at least more than Mom and I did. "Mom, you home?"

"In my office," she answered, her smoky voice trailing down the hallway. "Don't forget to take your snow boots off before you come in, Remi."

With a grunt, I finally slammed the door shut. Clumps of ice and snow covered the bottoms of my boots, and it was hard to toe them off in the cluttered entryway.

One thing about Mom: ever since Dad left, she collected junk. Really useless, cumbersome things. Mirrors of all shapes and sizes hung on nearly every wall. Glass vases, some empty and some filled with fake flowers, on almost every flat surface. There were even three shoe racks in the foyer, and the two of us barely filled one. "They're for decoration," she'd tell me in her superior voice. "Who's the interior designer here, Remi?"

Her, technically, but I'd never seen anyone on TV decorate with three shoe racks.

After hanging my coat and putting my boots on the stand,

I carried my bags into the house, dumping everything in my bedroom before going to find Mom.

She sat poised in front of her office computer, probably peering at a Pinterest collage of bathrooms.

"I'm home," I said, waiting for her eyes to lift.

People said Mom and I looked alike, but I didn't see it. Mom had a sharp jawline and high cheekbones, and I had none of those things. In comparison, my face was as round as a basketball and, as far as I was concerned, my cheekbones were made of rubber. Her eyes were a light brown, accentuated by a thick line of kohl. Her hair was so dark it could've been considered black, cropped in a sharp bob at the middle of her neck. My blonde hair and blue eyes were a gift from my father. Looking at her professional cut made me think of my at-home barber job on my straight-across bangs. The first time I'd ever done it, Elijah made fun of me for a week because I'd cut them too short.

Hey, I'd at least gotten my height from Mom—a squat five-two.

"It's a little after five o'clock," Mom said. She didn't sound disapproving, just curious. "Don't tell me you had detention again."

Honestly, her little jab hurt. I hadn't had detention in at least two weeks. "I went shopping with Eli after school."

She raised a pointed eyebrow. "Against his will, I'm sure."

"It was mutually beneficial. He got his ice cream."

Mom's lips twitched, but they slanted downward. "How has everything been with him?"

They were loaded words, and she knew it. My thoughts

went back to the way he'd acted today, the scowl across his face. "He's been fine."

"Are his parents doing okay? I've been trying to reach out to Kathleen, but she hasn't been taking my calls, and—"

"We don't talk about it." I cut her off, not wanting to think about his mom. "Eli...he doesn't like to talk about it."

"Well, maybe that's a sign that he should."

Mom might've been right about him needing to 'fess up, but I hadn't exactly been successful trying to pry information from him earlier. Instead, I had to trust Elijah and hold onto the belief that he would talk about it when he was ready.

However, Mom's sympathy for him sparked an idea, and I perked up. "Elijah actually wanted me to come over tonight," I told her. "To work on a project for art class."

Mom's eyes fell back to her computer screen, giving up on her previous line of questioning. "How late will you be out?"

"His house is literally across the street." That was always our go-to excuse, and it worked to our advantage almost always. Probably because I could throw a stone from my front door to his driveway. "It's not like I'm driving across town or anything." *Is my fake smile realistic enough?*

"Ten at the latest," Mom said finally. "It's a school night."

I rapped my knuckles on the edge of the doorjamb again, trying not to feel guilty for yet another manipulation tactic. How many did that make today? No matter. Everything would work out in the end.

. . .

After dinner, I sent Elijah a text along the lines of *yo, you gonna be my chauffeur for the night?* Irritatingly enough, he didn't answer. Several options went through my head. I couldn't ask Mom to borrow her car because she thought I was going to Elijah's. Eloise had probably already arrived at the party. That left Elijah. I just had to go across the street and pry him away from his sketchbook, sweet-talk him a little. Maybe incorporate some blackmail. Should be easy enough, right?

Just before I ducked out of my bedroom, I grabbed ahold of the perfume Eloise bought me the other day. A quick sniff of the nozzle clued me in that the scent didn't change—it still smelled like strong spices. Without thinking about it, though, I spritzed some across my throat, trying not to gag. I could show Elijah just how strong this stuff was, and he'd agree that I'd need a new perfume.

"I'm heading out, Mom," I told her from the doorway, the perfect vantage point to see her lounging on the couch. I made sure my coat was buttoned all the way, hiding my top.

She'd already dressed for bed and now had a book in her hands, feet propped on a pillow. "Have fun with your art assignment. Maybe he'll inspire you to do something pretty for once."

"Hey, what's that supposed to mean?" I demanded as I wrapped my scarf around my neck.

"Oh, don't pretend you have an artistic cell in your body," Mom teased. "There's a reason I never pinned any of your drawings on the fridge."

I slipped my foot into my snow boot, still wet on the

bottom, and held it over the hardwood floors. "Don't make me."

Mom took an extra pillow and threw it in my direction; it bounced off the wall of the living room, not even making it into the hallway. "Not too late. Don't make me come over there and get you."

An empty threat, since we both knew she'd be asleep by nine.

The snow had stopped falling sometime between when I got home from shopping and now, leaving the air feeling stagnant. I saw the weather for what it meant—there would probably be school tomorrow.

Which meant my papier-mâché would still be due tomorrow, and yet I was still going out.

I liked to torture myself, apparently.

A truck sat in the gravel driveway in front of Elijah's garage. So Elijah *was* home, just not answering my texts.

The 2006 pickup had actually been a purchase of his brother's after he graduated high school, but in the week since Terry's arrest, Elijah had been using it to drive to school instead of taking the bus. Sometimes I rode with him, but that meant waking up earlier so he could pick up Savannah, who lived on the other side of town. Most of the time, I couldn't be bothered. Given the choice of anything and sleep, I'd almost always choose the latter.

I stepped onto Elijah's porch, rubbing my boots along the snow-covered doormat.

This was the first time I'd been to Elijah's house since that night, and I stared up at the siding with a heavy thumping in my chest. Normally, I wouldn't have rung the doorbell or even knocked; I would've walked right in. But now it felt intrusive to open the door on my own. Ringing the doorbell seemed like the only logical way to respect their privacy.

It took only a moment for the door to pull inward, revealing a short man with a smudge of a five o'clock shadow. Dark circles hung underneath his eyes, making them look hollow. "Remi," he greeted. "Oh, it's so good to see you, dear. Are you here to see Elijah?"

"Hi, Mr. Greybeck. And I am, if that's okay. I can head up to his room—"

"No, no, I can grab him. The house is just a mess right now, and I'd rather you not see it in its full glory." Mr. Greybeck took a little step back into the house. "Kathleen's in the kitchen if you wanted to say hello. I did the dishes earlier, so the kitchen should be clean enough."

I thought about how Mrs. Greybeck kept ignoring Mom's calls and wondered how she was holding up. Even though the idea of speaking with her one-on-one made me uneasy, it'd be rude to decline. "I think I will."

Mr. Greybeck turned to head up the staircase as I toed off my boots, making my way inside. I tried to think of all the times I'd made this same trek, Elijah's mother somewhere in the house, father at work, older brother upstairs. Calling it my second home thing sounded a little cliché, but I knew the house's layout like the back of my hand.

Or my third home, if Dad's apartment counted.

Though the rest of Elijah's house hadn't been renovated, giving off mid-century vibes, their kitchen sat newly redone. Mom had helped Mrs. Greybeck go through the motions of designing it last May, and they managed to do it themselves during the summer—of course, with their kids' help. And though they'd decorated it light and airy, the lights were turned down very dim now, making the room feel small.

Mrs. Greybeck sat at the breakfast bar with her laptop open in front of her, the glow of it covering her skin. "Hi, Mrs. Greybeck. It's Remi."

"Hi, Remi." She didn't turn.

She slowly scrolled through the open webpage, one that contained a whole lot of text and not a lot of pictures. I stepped closer, subtly attempting to read it over her shoulder. "I wanted to come and say hi."

"Mmm" was all she said—or mumbled—not averting her eyes. I was familiar with that sound. Mom made that sound when she really engrossed herself in what she was reading, barely aware of what was happening around her.

I came close enough behind her to see the title of the webpage: *Laws and Penalties in Your State.* My fingers picked at the fabric of the scarf at my throat, pulling it away from my skin. "My mom's been meaning to stop over," I told her, one last attempt to gain her attention. "Something about going ice-skating sometime soon, over at Gallice Rink. You two used to do that every winter, remember?"

I almost convinced myself I hadn't spoken. The lines of her shoulders didn't even twitch. Her eyes continued to seek the webpage, but instead of feeling offended, I felt a tight twinge of pain.

"Well, it was nice seeing you," I said, curling my fingers into tight fists.

"You too, Remi. Say hello to your mom for me."

Cue my exit. I made my way back to the foyer, feeling a little put-off of my party mood, trying to shake off the weight that rolled over me. It was this house. I couldn't even begin to explain it. The free-spirit vibe that had once existed here had fled as if on fire, replaced by a heaviness. I knew that Mrs. Greybeck had to be taking the arrest hard—she'd always had high hopes for Terry, her golden boy. And now...

"Remi?"

I looked toward the sound of my name, the weight lifting a bit. "Hey."

Elijah stood in the middle of the staircase, staring at me. He still wore the jeans from school today, still wore his graphic tee. His blond hair stuck up in some places, as if he'd just run his fingers through it. His face, I noticed, appeared a little red. "What are you doing here?"

I glanced around, but didn't see his dad. "You weren't answering my texts."

He blinked a little. "I must've put my phone down somewhere."

I pulled the edges of my coat away from my body, exposing my sparkly sequin top. When I shifted, the light reflected off of the fabric. "It's party time."

Elijah let out a harsh breath. "Remi—"

"Before you say no," I hurried to interrupt, starting up the first two steps, "I won't ask anything of you again. I won't ask you to go shopping with me in the underwear section anymore, even though you get rewarded with ice cream."

He opened his mouth to say something just as a face formed over his shoulder, and my brain registered it as the face of his girlfriend. And it was...pinchy.

Oh, she was here? *Oops.*

"You went underwear shopping with her?" Savannah demanded, coming down a few steps to meet Elijah in the middle. Her haircut looked similar to mine, with straight-across blonde bangs and a longer bob, her own blue eyes a shade or two darker than mine. "Are you serious, Elijah?"

Elijah's gaze lifted to the ceiling.

"It's not his fault," I told her, trying to diffuse the situation and the bomb-like energy that radiated from her. "I had a *really* crappy day, and I just needed a stress reliever. That's it. He just gave me a ride, and I asked him earlier if he wanted to go to Jer's party—"

"Party?" Mr. Greybeck asked, his face appearing over Savannah's shoulder.

You have got to be kidding me.

Elijah's face conveyed my thoughts perfectly, offering that disbelieving smile to no one in particular. Seeing it on his face made my sequin top and the idea of a party a whole lot less exciting. "Beanie, just go, okay? You'll have to have fun by yourself."

"But—"

"Go, Remi," he repeated firmly. He didn't look at me, but I *so* didn't blame him. I had barged into his house and gotten him in trouble left and right. If not with Savannah, then with his father. "I'll see you at school tomorrow."

Savannah crossed her arms over her chest, staring at me like I had just kicked her puppy or something equally despicable. In her eyes, kicking puppies and taking someone's boyfriend underwear shopping probably evened to the same severity.

But honestly, why was she mad at *me?* He had chosen to stay with her instead of going with me. Total win on her part.

"See you in homeroom," I said uneasily, tucking my hands back into my jacket and turning to put on my shoes. No doubt everyone's eyes were still on me—everyone's but Elijah's. I turned as I opened the door. "Bye, Mr. Greybeck."

He lifted a hand over Savannah's shoulder. "Oh—good-night, Remi."

Savannah didn't offer any parting words, and I didn't supply any. No sense in poking an angry bear.

Finally, I caught Elijah's eyes. He didn't look mad, but there was also no shaking the uneasy feeling between us.

I pulled myself from the house and into the night air, shutting the door as quickly as possible.

four

"And then his dad came out from behind Savannah and was like, 'Party? What party?'" I buried my face in my free hand, letting out a groan. My fingers had finally lost the chill they held from walking all the way over here. Twenty minutes separated my street from Jeremy's, leaving me shivering, teeth chattering. The lengths I'd go to for crappy music. "It was so awkward."

Eloise leaned against the wall opposite of me, holding a plastic cup loosely. She'd twisted her long dark hair over her shoulder for tonight, securing it with a bow. Her almond eyes looked down into mine as she spoke. "It probably wasn't as bad as you think. I'm sure they have a lot of other stuff on their minds."

No kidding. I took a sip of my drink, feeling the warmth spread slowly through my stomach. "You're probably right."

"I mean, I doubt Mr. Greybeck thought anything of it. And as for Savannah, well...yeah, I've got nothing."

"It's not like I'm trying to steal her boyfriend," I said irritably, glancing around the room. Tucked between the house's walls, I counted fifteen people pooling into the space, talking, drinking, and dancing. I had to give it to Greenville High—there weren't as many people here as normal. Maybe everyone feared there'd be school tomorrow, or maybe they had to finish their art projects, too. *Not thinking about it.* "But if we're going to play that card, I knew Elijah first."

"I'm just going to play devil's advocate here, okay? Don't hit me. But, I mean, would you want your boyfriend shopping for lingerie with his girl best friend? You know, if you had one."

I nearly choked on my sip of alcohol. "Eloise, we weren't *lingerie* shopping!" Though Elijah did correct me on my cup size. Maybe *that* was a little weird. "We just wandered over to that side of the store. It couldn't have been more than five minutes tops."

Eloise lifted her shoulder, drawing her cup to her lips.

Up until freshman year, it had just been me and Elijah, the two of us against the world. Or, well, against the beginning of high school. Then I met Eloise Xiang, a transfer from Bayview. Quirky, funny, *female.* My first actual girl friend. Eloise had taught me just how great a tube of mascara could be, as well as the beauty in a bottle of nail polish. She also took me to get my first real bra, with a clasp and everything. A true gem, that Eloise.

Eloise and I weren't as close as Elijah and I were, but I valued our friendship so much. The three of us didn't hang out as much as I would've liked, but that was okay.

"You wore that new perfume I bought you," she said with

a soft smile, drawing in a breath through her nose. "I like it. It smells sugary."

"What? It does not," I said, making a face. "I don't smell sugar. I smell spice. It smells spicy to me. Totally different."

"Let me smell," a deep voice said from over my shoulder, prompting me to turn—and falter as my heart did a little jump in my chest. Jeremy Rivera stood behind me, holding a plastic cup, confident smile on. He came close to my neck, inhaling deep. "Oh, I agree with Eloise; you smell incredible. It's a nice surprise to see you here, Remi."

It took me a moment to summon the nonchalance that I normally used when flirting with guys. That sort of loose gaze, shrugged shoulder, light laugh. Not too engaging, but a leave-them-wanting-more kind of vibe. Or at least that was what Eloise called it. I'd gotten good at implementing it with Jeremy.

"Are you saying you didn't throw this party secretly hoping I'd come?" I asked.

The level of Jeremy's attractiveness was seriously unfair. His curly brown hair, a few shades darker than his skin tone, hung long enough to hold the wave but short enough that it wouldn't get in his eyes, which were a pretty hazel. "Man, am I that obvious?"

"Maybe just a little."

Jeremy flashed me a smirk. "I've got to kick my game into high gear with you, huh?"

See, this? Totally worth bailing on my stupid project and probably failing my senior year. I mean, this was why they had summer school, right? For cases like me, a love-struck girl, bailing on homework to flirt with a cute boy.

And man, he was so cute. It almost made my brain hurt.

"Can I get you a refill, Remi?" he asked.

I looked down at my near-empty cup. "I'm good. I have to walk home after this, so I'll have to settle for being slightly buzzed." And that buzz felt good so far. Especially with Jeremy to look at.

"Anyone playing Lip Locker?" Eloise asked, her eyes darting my way as if she were trying to be sneaky.

Lip Locker—a mouthful when you were a little tipsy— was kind of like Seven Minutes in Heaven, where a couple went into the closet and got their freak on, except Greenville played it with blindfolds. So you couldn't see—only feel. I'd only played once freshman year, paired with senior quarterback Julian Castleroy. It could've been hot, and I could've used it as a total popularity boost, but he'd had the most chapped lips ever, and he'd been too drunk much to remember it. Romantic.

"Not yet, I don't think." Jeremy shifted, drawing my eyes down to the neon orange basketball shorts he wore. They definitely didn't match his red shirt, but who cared about one small fashion faux pas? "But I wouldn't be opposed to the idea."

This time, his eyes snapped to me. I tipped the contents of my cup back, swallowing the rest and passing the empty cup to Jeremy. "I'm going to run to the bathroom," I said to the both of them, utilizing the leave-them-wanting-more card. "Don't talk about anything interesting without me."

Jeremy revealed a set of white teeth. "You're taking all the interesting with you, Remi."

Swoon. Eloise lifted her own plastic cup to her lips, and even over the rim, I could see her smile. "We'll be here."

I turned down the hallway, making sure to add just the right amount of swing to my step. Elijah was right—I had to have fun without him. And I was. I didn't need him to come tonight. We were both perfectly happy where we were.

I hadn't dried my hands enough to get all the water droplets off, so I rubbed my palms along my jeans before pulling the bathroom door open. It felt like I'd been away for hours. The line in front of the bathroom trailed atrociously long, and I had to wait behind seven people. *Seven.* Ridiculous. It was like everyone decided to pee at the same time. Five people still stood in line at the door, and I edged out of the way so the next could pass.

The party carried on in my absence, bass pumping from the crappy speakers in the living room. When you were drunk enough, though, anything sounded good. More people had shown up since I was gone—either that or I miscounted earlier.

"Remi!" Eloise appeared around the corner before me, an excited look on her face. She gripped my shoulders. "Deem me a better friend than Elijah, please. Because I rock. It's official."

Immediately, my guard went up. "What did you do?"

She tipped her dark eyebrows toward her hairline, dropping her voice suggestively. "Oh, just convinced Jeremy to meet you in the guest bedroom closet for Lip Locker."

My stomach shifted as I glanced down the hallway,

recalling our conversation minutes before. Had my flirting worked that well? "Is he in there now?"

Eloise took that question as agreement and steered me down the corridor. "Probably. He ran off to find a breath mint, but you can wait for him. I mean, it's *Jeremy*."

We opened the guest bedroom door to darkness, and I immediately pressed a hand to the wall to orient myself. The lights were off, the window coverings drawn. "Here's the blindfold," Eloise said as she fitted it over my eyes, fingers careful when they moved around my hair. "This is the sash off Kelsey's dress, so don't lose it."

"This is silly," I declared as she tied off the knot, but I couldn't ignore the anticipation building within my stomach. I honestly didn't even need the blindfold; the darkness was so thick I couldn't see two feet in front of me. "If Jeremy wants to kiss me, why does he have to do it in a closet? Isn't this for blind hookups?"

"No, this is *sexy*," Eloise corrected. "You can't see—your sense of touch is heightened. *Sex-y*."

"Yeah, tell that to my hair. Are you even trying to put this thing on right?" I took a deep breath through my nose, taking stock of everything. My lips didn't feel too chapped, despite the jaunt I'd taken in the cold to get here. I didn't think my breath smelled bad—but really, was it ever possible to know if your own breath smelled bad? My palms were still a little wet from washing them—or was that sweat?

"I'll come check on you in five minutes," Eloise said, oblivious to my mental freak-out. She grabbed my hand and laid it on the closet door handle. "I'm walking away now. Remember, just be yourself. With more tongue."

I cringed, stiffening my spine. "I'm not using—"

I heard the bedroom door shut.

With my heart beating fast in my chest, like horse hooves pounding against the ground, I pulled the closet door open. The hinges creaked horribly, announcing my presence at once. I took a step in, my hands out to steady myself. They landed on something solid and firm.

Jeremy's chest.

His hands immediately rose to steady me, falling awkwardly on my sequined sides. The contact made my heart jump before resuming its frantic, nervous beat.

"Sorry," I said, my nervousness making my voice lower. It also sounded obnoxiously loud in this claustrophobic space.

This was such a stupid idea. And awkward. And embarrassing.

One of Jeremy's hands pushed the hair back from my face, a gesture so affectionate that it surprised me. I tried to inhale, but my nose was still stuffed from the cold outside, prevented his familiar scent from hitting my senses. I could feel each of his calloused fingertips against the skin on my cheek, gentle and warm.

I was definitely, definitely overthinking this. I just needed to go for it.

Drawing in a brave breath, I stood on my tiptoes and sought his mouth out with mine, trying to imagine where it'd be in the darkness. It took a moment before our mouths aligned perfectly, my top lip hitting his nose at first, and my breath caught.

His soft, warm lips pressed against my own with a firmness that caused something inside me to stir. I had to tilt my head back farther than I thought I would've; he loomed taller up close.

At first, our mouths just pressed together, like two second graders stealing a kiss behind the teacher's back, neither one of us moving. And then—

Jeremy pulled me flush against his chest, and I had to clutch his narrow shoulders for support. I reached up and curled my fingers into his hair, the silky locks coiling against my skin. I tugged a little, trying to angle his mouth closer, and he made a muffled sound in response. It echoed through me, drawing an army goosebumps. It was a dance move of a kiss, a choreographed song of perfectness in this tiny closet space. I swayed into every step wholeheartedly, never thinking of myself as a dancer but now desperate for the beat to continue. One of his hands still pressed against my waist, five fingers curving delicately against the fabric of my shirt. His other hand settled against the back of my neck, leaning my head back, back, my hair tangling in his light touch.

And oh. My. Gosh. He was a *fantastic* kisser. It could've been because I hadn't been kissed in literally forever, or my last Lip Locker kiss had sucked. Either way, every single time his lips broke from mine and realigned, I was shocked by tiny electrodes, all stuttering my brain activity. Shuttering, leaving me wondering if this was even real, if this was even happening. My mind spun, pulse raced.

I reached my hands around his waist, meaning to just touch the waistband of his shorts, but my fingers caught against the material of belt loops. I hooked my fingers through them, pulling him closer.

He gasped a breath against my lips, shooting a shiver

down my spine. Using my grip on his jeans, I tugged him backward, wanting my back to find the wall, wanting him closer, wanting *something*—

My head cracked on a low shelf, banging off the edge with enough force that I stumbled forward into Jeremy, white stars tearing across my vision. I swayed into him unevenly, nearly gagging from the pain splintering against my skull. Biting back a moan of pain, I tore my blindfold off.

"Are you okay?" he asked, one hand still on my waist. "Did you hit your head?"

We were close together, one of my hands pressed to his chest. I leaned against him as my equilibrium tried to balance itself. In the darkness, I could just make out the sharp angle of his chin. "Yeah," I huffed, cautiously pressing my fingers to my head, fearing for blood. Nothing felt wet, but the sensation sent another roll of nausea through me. "That's embarrassing."

"It's because it's so dark," he said as he let go of me. "It's life-threatening, apparently. I know we thought this would be fun and exciting, but it just seems dangerous."

For a single moment, my heart stopped. Totally and completely just stopped. I rocked again in the darkness, but not because of the pain.

That voice...didn't sound right.

In a bit of a panic, I scrambled for my cell in my back pocket, dizziness reaching its peak as a strange feeling washed over me. The home screen caught my attention momentarily. I had missed a call nearly a half-hour ago from Elijah. Why had he tried to call me? Had he changed his mind and wanted to come? No—that could wait.

When I clicked the button, the small space filled with blue light, illuminating the boy in front of me. If I thought I had frozen before, now I was a statue.

It *wasn't* Jeremy standing in front of me.

Almost as if conjured by his name on my phone, Elijah leaned against me, a blindfold still fully covering his eyes. "Savannah?"

five

"Savannah?" Elijah repeated, concerned. His voice sounded so obvious now, and I couldn't believe I hadn't placed it before. Pain radiated through my head, and I gaped at him in a strange sort of horror. "You hit that pretty hard. I could hear your head crack against it. Are you good?"

Was I hallucinating? Had I hit my head so hard enough that I'd actually imagined this moment? Imagined *Elijah?* No, that was impossible. There was no mistaking the blond hair tucked over his ears, nor the worn graphic t-shirt. All the air stalled in my lungs as his face moved in the LED light.

I'd kissed Elijah. I'd been kissing *Elijah.* The nausea I'd been feeling before came back in full force, and threatened to come back all over his shirt. "I'm okay," I said, trying my hardest to use my best Savannah voice. Deep, throaty, flippant. Instead it came shaky, nervous, shocked. "I'm...okay."

Elijah didn't buy it, but my screen went dark before I could see his face. "Here, let me see."

Without thinking twice, I slapped my hands over his eyes, his eyelashes brushing my palms.

"Okay," he said with a quizzical chuckle, fingers wrapping around my wrists. "Now I know you're concussed. What are you doing?"

Oh, what was I doing? Kissing my best friend in a closet, apparently. No, more than kissing. We were *making out*. With tongue. Oh gosh, there was *tongue...*

Something strange and heady flipped over inside me, warming my blood to a searing degree. My body hummed as I stared at him, my hands over his eyes. I could barely make out his pink lips, slightly swollen from how fiercely I'd been kissing him, parted as he waited for my response. *Savannah's* response. I felt hot and cold all over as I searched for an explanation.

But every time I tried to imagine an excuse, my mind latched onto the desire I'd had pull his mouth back to mine, to feel his hands exploring my skin again, in a way that felt both strange and thrilling.

No, it's wrong, I told myself firmly, shaking my head a little to get rid of the thought. The movement elicited a sharp pain in the back of my skull. *He's like your brother. Definitely wrong.*

And yet...

"Savannah?"

"Y-You can't look at me," I told him, my voice shaking with the effort to remain calm, but with the lights still off, my dizziness only worsened. I needed an aspirin. Or a strong drink. This situation was definitely starting to warrant it. "I—it—there's blood."

"*Blood?*" Definitely the wrong thing to say. One of his hands closed over my sequined shoulder, as if ready to pull me away. "How much blood? Sav, let me see."

"I just need to go to the bathroom," I said immediately, losing the grasp I had on my sliver of sanity. I didn't even think I sounded like Savannah anymore. "I don't want you to look."

"But if you're hurt—"

"*Elijah.*" I couldn't breathe. "Promise you'll keep your eyes closed."

I felt his fingers on my shoulder twitch before he responded. "Okay, I promise."

It took me a moment to trust him, to gather my courage and remove my hands from his eyes. Darkness still hung between us, and I stood still for a moment, waiting for his eyes to open. Which they didn't. I could see that his lashes still rested on his pale cheekbones. And I didn't waste any time before he changed his mind; I pried the closet door open just enough to fit through and ran out.

No one lingered in the hallway when I burst from the guest room, but the blaring music of the party still thumped, too loud for my throbbing ears. I made a beeline for the bathroom door, bypassing the person who stood in front of it, tugging on the handle. When it didn't budge, I banged my fist against it. And again. I clamped my jaw shut, but I knew I couldn't keep it that way for long. With my free hand, I clutched the back of my head, almost sure it'd crack open.

I had raised my fist to knock one more time when the door gave in, a figure filling the threshold. Horror and recognition swamped through me at the same time.

"Jeez," Savannah grumbled, her eyes wide. She glanced at where I held my head. "What's your problem, Remi?"

Looking at her made me feel even more panicked, as if she'd be able to read my mind by the look on my face. It also freaked me out, seeing how much we looked alike. It almost felt like I was looking at my doppelgänger.

Another wave of pain swiped across my eyes, and I cut in front of the two people in line, slamming the door shut in their faces. My vision began dotting with black spots, and I braced my hands on my knees, dragging in breath after breath of warm air. The throbbing in the back of my skull felt so intense that I was afraid of blacking out.

I'd been kissing Elijah. My breathing stuttered now for an entirely different reason, my heartbeat unable to find its normal beat. My lips still tingled from the pressure, and I could feel the way his chest had pressed against mine. Or the way he tenderly swept the hair from my face. I couldn't shake it from my mind.

And why...why did I not want to? Why did I want to replay it over and over?

Man, how hard did I hit my head?

I stumbled toward the sink, intending to splash cold water on my face. Maybe that would calm my hot blood, orient my dizzy world. When I glanced in the mirror, swallowing the feeling of sticky saliva, I noticed that my pupils were two different sizes.

There was only a second of warning, but it was enough for me to turn and kneel in front of the toilet before I threw up.

Six

"I can't believe you fell *up* the stairs," Mom said for the hundredth time, tucking the blankets tighter around me. "Only you, sweetie. Only you."

Don't ask me how I managed to convince my mother that I fell going up Elijah's staircase last night, resulting in my "mild concussion," but I did it. Though I didn't know exactly how much she bought, or if she just decided to not ask any questions.

"Don't blame me, blame the stairs," I said. "They were evil stairs. *Possessed* stairs. I barely escaped with my life."

"That's why we don't have any, huh?" she teased, bending down and kissing my forehead. I cringed away from the contact, wondering if she'd left lipstick on my skin. Mom had already dressed for the day, even though today she'd be working from home Her blazer was even ironed. "Do you need anything else? More hot cocoa? A heating pad? Dr. Armada said that you need plenty of rest, so I'll get you anything you need."

Dr. Armada had entirely convinced Mom he was doctor royalty or something, hence why Mom cocooned me on the living room couch, tucked so tightly that I started to lose circulation in my arms. Anything he said, she ate it up.

"I'm okay. Can you turn on the TV for me?"

She pursed her lips. "Dr. Armada said no extended amounts of screen time."

"Then can you grab me a magazine from my bedroom?"

"This website I looked at said you shouldn't do anything that could cause strain. Reading strains your eyes."

I closed my unstrained eyes. "So I'm just supposed to lie here and stare at the ceiling?"

"Well—"

"But not intensely," I amended. "Wouldn't want to strain my eyes."

Mom ran a hand over my hair. "You should feel lucky. You got out of going to school today."

Right, because school *hadn't* been canceled today. A part of me felt relieved that I'd hit my head, since I hadn't even started my papier-mâché project.

I closed my eyes, pushing the image out of my mind that threatened to surface. Elijah had texted me last night around nine-thirty—probably ten minutes after the *incident*—asking where I was. There were four messages. *Hey, I'm at Jeremy's. Where are you? Remi? Did you leave early?* They were all sent within minutes of each other and I, a chicken, hadn't responded to them. *Ugh.*

He probably knew the truth by now. As soon as he found Savannah at the party, she'd have revealed that it wasn't her in the closet. When he asked about her head, the truth would come out. It was only a matter of time before he realized it was me. *Double ugh.*

"Are you okay?" Mom asked, pulling me from my thoughts. "Are you in pain? Why is your face pinched up?"

"I'm just dandy," I told her, trying to draw in a steady breath. "Go. Get your work done, I'll be here. If I need anything—like, you know, being freed from my restraints to go to the bathroom—I'll call."

She tried to kiss me again, this time on my hair. "I love you, Remi."

Why did she have to be so mushy-gushy? "Okay, okay. I'm not dying, just concussed, and mildly at that. Now shoo."

Thankfully, she rose to her full height without trying to kiss me again. "I'll break again around four. That should give you plenty of time for communing with the ceiling." She headed out of the living room, flipping off the lights.

All things considered, Mom's hovering wasn't the worst thing. Her sweetness regarding this entire situation made me feel like a horrible daughter for lying to her. If she knew the truth about last night, she'd definitely be treating me differently. As much as the coddling irritated me, I'd take that over the passive-aggressive cold shoulder.

Even after taking the medication, I had a headache, a constant pain behind my eyes. Dr. Armada said it would fade with time, along with the weird haze that still hovered across my vision, but conveniently left out how *much* time.

In all honesty, I wanted nothing more than to text Elijah, but all the weirdness from last night still coated me, leaving everything feeling...well, *weird.* If he found out it was me, would he ever talk to me again? Here I was, obsessing over that kiss—how could we go back to our normal nonchalance if he knew?

I just had to apologize. That was all I had to do. Tell him I'd thought he was Jeremy. That was the fix-all, right? He'd thought I was Savannah. And really, it was his fault. Who played Lip Locker with their significant other? What was the point?

The house phone started to ring loudly in my ear, and I realized it sat on the side table behind my head. Wiggling an arm out of my cocoon, I pulled on the cordless handset. "Beaufort residence."

"That sounded so professional," said the voice on the other end, sounding amused. "Are you practicing to be a desk clerk, Remikins?"

Despite the craziness filling my head, I relaxed at the sound of his voice. "Hey, Dad. And I prefer 'receptionist.' Sounds much more professional."

"I agree." There was a pause as something shifted on the other line. "How are you feeling? Your mom called me last night, saying that you'd hit your head. Falling *up* the stairs?"

I balanced the phone between my ear and my shoulder as I pushed to a sitting position. Since this was Dad, I knew the details didn't matter so much. "Yeah...well. More or less."

"I'm thinking less, but maybe that's just because I know you. Your middle name is Grace for a reason."

A part of me felt tempted to tell Dad the truth, but I knew better. No doubt he'd immediately tell Mom and I'd be busted. So even though I wanted to spill the beans to *somebody*, I kept my mouth shut. "How's Harmony?"

Dad laughed a little. "Oh, she's good. Not as graceful as

you, but we're working on it. Clarabelle and I are thinking she'll take her first steps soon."

Dad had remarried almost three years ago to Clarabelle, a woman he had met at work. She was nice. Southern, if her name hadn't hinted at it. She said things like "bless your little heart" and "I reckon," which made her that much sweeter. They'd had a daughter last year, Harmony Blythe Beaufort, and she came out as probably the ugliest baby ever. With a rattail of hair and one eye larger than the other, she looked like a little alien. Now that her hair had grown out to a normal length, though, and her eyes matched in size, her cuteness was unrivaled.

"You better record it," I told him sternly. "I want to see it happen."

"I'm sure Clara will catch it. She's always got her camera out."

I gazed up at the ceiling, imagining Harmony's pudgy little legs moving in tandem. She was growing up so fast. "Did you call just to check in, or...?"

"I just wanted to call quick from the office and tell your mother that I can take you next weekend, if that's all right with her. You were supposed to come up for the weekend, but you should just take it easy."

Right. I'd totally forgotten that I planned to go to his house. I alternated each weekend at Mom's or Dad's, since Dad lived nearly an hour away in Biscayne Park and I couldn't go see him during the week. "Are you sure? Because I can come over and be an invalid on your couch, though the leather isn't as comfy."

He laughed on the other end, a sound that made my

insides feel calm for the first time for the past day. From the whole art class debacle to Jeremy's party, everything has been a whirlwind. "I'm sure. Besides, your mom is better at the whole coddling thing than I am."

I tried not to let my sour expression show, though no one witnessed it. "You're right about that."

"Just rest up and feel better, okay, Remikins? We don't need any more traumatic brain injuries at the Beaufort residence."

I smiled at the ceiling, though it felt a little wobbly. "No kidding, Dad. I'll see you next weekend. Love you."

"Love you too, Rem."

He ended the call first. I hunkered back down in my blankets, getting my head comfortable on the pillow.

I thought for a moment about Dad and Clarabelle, remembering the day he'd introduced me to her over dinner. It was a few years after he'd separated from Mom, and it threw me off guard that he was seeing someone new. I wasn't mad, just surprised. I'd thought that falling out of love with someone meant there was never a possibility of falling in love with someone else.

It made me realize then that I knew almost nothing about love, and as I lay on the couch now, staring at the ceiling with strange thoughts running through my head, I figured that was probably still the case.

Five fingers nudged my shoulder, jarring me awake from the quasi-sleep I'd been in and out of for the past few hours. I blinked the grogginess from my eyes, trying to focus on the face looming over me. "I'm fine, Mom. You don't have to wake me up every half-hour."

Mom made a mocking face at me, looking comical. "I know, I know. I'm waking you to tell you that a boy named Jeremy is at the door."

Despite having been asleep a few moments before—and dreaming about a pretty yummy taco, if I remembered correctly—I felt everything in my body snap to attention. I looked down the hallway toward the door, but the haze over my eyes made everything a little blurry. "Jeremy?"

"He's asking for you. He's got some homework from today."

I kicked the blankets off my legs, tripping on the tangle of fabric. The sudden movement ratcheted my headache higher on the pain scale, and I winced. "Did it look like he had a lot of it?"

"He just had a few papers." Mom helped me stand from the blanket burrito and wrapped it around my shoulders. "Why don't you invite him in and you come back to the couch? You two can talk while you sit and rest."

The idea of Jeremy in my house made something turn in my stomach, in a way that felt similar to a stomachache. A side effect of the concussion, surely. "He probably won't stay long," I said.

I rounded the corner into the hallway, finding Jeremy standing awkwardly in the doorway. He held papers in both hands and glanced around the walls. The front door was left open, the screen door the only buffer between him and the cold. He looked almost the same as he had on Thursday, wearing a pair of basketball shorts in the wintertime and a megawatt grin, especially when his eyes landed on me. "Hey, Remi."

"What are you doing here?" I asked in dumb surprise, not even remotely channeling my inner flirt. Probably because I had no makeup on, my knotty hair draped over my shoulder, and I was still in my duckling pajama bottoms. Did I even wash my face today? *Cringe.*

"I'm bringing you some history homework," he said, waving the papers in the air. "It's just a take-home quiz, nothing huge."

I took the papers from him, studying the first page before huddling deeper in my blanket burrito. "That was sweet of you."

He did a scoff/chuckle combo. "Oh, no, Mr. Valdez actually asked me to drop them off. It's kind of like an extra credit opportunity for me, actually. I should be thanking you." Jeremy leaned a little closer to me, close enough that I could see the flecks of gold in his eyes. "So, I don't know whether or not to bring up the fact that you stood me up on Thursday. For that closet game? I sat in my bedroom closet for probably a half-hour."

I felt my eyes widen. In the mess of everything that happened, I'd forgotten about meeting Jeremy for Lip Locker. I mean, yes, I was supposed to meet up with Jeremy, but after everything with Elijah, I never stopped to wonder what happened to him.

For a moment, I gaped at him, unable to think of a response. "I—Eloise thought you meant the guest bedroom closet."

"Really? So you were waiting for me there the whole time

too?" Jeremy let out a breath. "Well, that mends my broken ego. Though I'm probably lucky, huh? You would've given me your sick-person cooties."

I let out a nervous laugh and found myself looking past him, past the open screen door, at movement across the street. Elijah was heading down his porch steps quickly, shoving his arms through his jacket and heading toward the truck. His pace was quick, obviously agitated. Normally, I would've called out to him, some harassing comment that would've made him smile or roll his eyes. But now the sight of him caused every muscle in my body to lock up, freezing me in place. It turned out, though, that I didn't have to say a word.

Elijah's gaze inexplicably lifted to mine a moment after he pulled his truck door open. A dark expression hovered on his face from whatever had just happened, but it softened as we looked at each other. My mouth suddenly ran dry, lips tingling as I remembered his breath against them. The same shiver ran down my spine now as it had the night before, and that shiver totally wasn't from the outside air. Not one bit.

"What do you say, Remi?"

I looked back to Jeremy, startled by the mention of my name. It took me more than a moment to shake myself from the memory, to extract myself from the ghost sensation of Elijah's fingertips. "Uh, a-about what, exactly?"

"To a movie. I can't this weekend, but how about Monday? After school, of course."

"A date?" The fog in my head felt a little more than mind-numbing, the throbbing at my temples more than distracting. That had to be by why my insides weren't doing all sorts of happy dances. Because this was *Jeremy*. Jeremy was asking me out on a date—finally! After how long of this back-and-forth flirting? This was huge. Where were my stinking butterflies?

My eyes darted back to Elijah, but he'd already climbed inside his truck and started it up.

I smiled at Jeremy, convincing myself that the turning in my stomach was only from my headache. "I'd love to."

Seven

During my weekend of forced bed rest, I tried to pretend that Thursday night had never happened. That the night itself had just been entirely deleted from my catalog of memory. Because thinking about Elijah and those things his mouth did elicited a cascade of heat to crash through me, one that threatened to swamp me and swallow me whole. I couldn't think about his face without feeling his soft, warm lips pressing against mine. I couldn't think about his hands without feeling each individual finger exploring my body. And thinking about all of those things made me feel...*something*. Everywhere.

Which was bad.

So I couldn't think about it. I wasn't allowed to.

But how did you just stop thinking about your best friend? How was I supposed to pretend nothing had changed when every single time I thought about him, all the other stuff came to mind, making my face hot, my mouth dry?

It had to be because of my concussion. Concussions

could make people think differently, act differently. They affected emotions, caused mood swings—right? Maybe this was all a result of it. Some crazy side-effect that made my stomach jumbled and my heart confused. And maybe I was overthinking everything. It was just a kiss.

But it wasn't just a kiss. No, we were *making out*.

Ugh, ugh, ugh, I needed to stop. Stop thinking about that kiss, his mouth, any of it. I needed to sear it from my brain. This was *Elijah*. My best friend with the crooked nose and a love for sculpting. This should've been funny. Accidentally kissing my best friend? That was hilarious. Except that it was singlehandedly the best kiss I'd ever had, and that killed my humor.

I wanted to bash my head against the wall, but Mom and Dr. Armada probably wouldn't appreciate that.

I decided right then and there, hiding underneath my covers, that when I went back to school on Monday, this would be over. Never to be thought of again. Who kissed Elijah? Not me. Besides, I was supposed to like Jeremy Rivera. I *did* like Jeremy Rivera. Heck, I had enjoyed the kiss when I thought it was Jeremy, and when I saw Elijah, I distinctly remembered feeling horrified. Crushing on Elijah was a result of thinking that he was Jeremy mixed with my concussion.

By Monday, things would be back to the way they were before. Like the kiss had never even happened.

Sunday morning came without anything exciting. Mom still held my phone hostage, saying it would strain my eyes—if I never heard that freaking phrase again, it'd be too soon—so the temptation to text Elijah was well out of reach.

Okay, so I kind of hated myself for being a bad friend, but sometimes being selfish was better for everyone.

I was sitting on the couch, spending my allotted thirty minutes of TV time watching some bad sitcom, when the doorbell chimed. "I can get it," I called out to the air, unsure if Mom was in the kitchen or in her office. Regardless, she didn't answer or emerge.

I pushed to my feet and hurried down the hallway. It took me a minute to fight with the front door, but I finally got it open with a huff, a flash of cold air greeting me. "Eloise?"

She was all bundled up in a puffy pink jacket, black scarf wrapped up to her chin, almond eyes curving as she smiled. "You can ignore my texts all you want, but you can't ignore me now."

I stepped back into the foyer to allow her to enter, feeling ten times lighter. "Mom has my cell phone."

"Are you grounded?" she asked as she unwound her scarf. "Even from school on Friday? Can your mom adopt me?"

"I think your parents wouldn't appreciate that," I told her, kicking the door shut. It shuddered as it tried to click into place. "And I'm not grounded, just concussed. Mom says no phones."

"Concussed? Like brain trauma? Seriously?"

"Unless my doctor was joking, and if so, he needs to let my insurance company know."

She hung up her stuff on one of the hooks near the door and toed off her shoes. The path to my bedroom was familiar to her, and she showed herself inside, plopping down in the butterfly chair by the window. My bedroom was a hodge-podge of styles—bohemian, pastels, minimalistic. Mom hated coming in here because she said it overloaded her brain. But personally, I loved it.

"How did you get a concussion?" Eloise asked.

I bit my bottom lip as I sat down on my bed, the duvet cover wrinkling. "Well, I—"

"Was it at the party?"

I wanted to tell her the truth so badly, but panic clamped down on my chest as soon as the words settled on my tongue. Telling her was totally not the way to pretend like it had never happened. In fact, telling her would be the opposite. I'd be *acknowledging* that it happened, and that was a definite no-no. "Yeah, I—I fell on the stairs," I said slowly, immediately cursing myself. Jeremy didn't have any stairs in his house; it was a single level.

"You mean on his steps? The porch steps?"

It was like a light bulb went off over my head. "Yes! His porch steps." My voice probably sounded too relieved, and I probably nodded too much, but I couldn't stop. "I slipped on them. With all the snow and stuff, they were just super slippery. I went outside to get some fresh air, and I just went down. Cracked my head on them. It was...crazy."

"After Lip Locker?"

Breathe. Don't think about it, don't think about it. "Yeah, a-after."

Eloise shifted in her seat, pulling her legs up to her chest. "Can we talk about that? Lip Locker, I mean."

I pressed my face into my hands, pushing hard enough that stars popped up behind my eyelids. "I don't want to. Not right now. Next time someone has a party, make sure I don't go, okay?" I should've just stayed home, worked on my papier-mâché project, been a good girl—oh, freak.

My papier-mâché project.

Freak, freak, freak.

"Elijah."

I moved my hands from my face, looking up. "What?"

Eloise was peering out the window by her side, the one that faced the street. "Elijah's walking across the street. He's coming over."

Without another thought, I flung myself off my bed, falling to crouch on the floor. The window wasn't even angled so he could see me, but I couldn't take any chances.

"Uh, what are you doing?"

My heart beat fast, and I hated myself for it. "I'm not here," I whispered.

"You're...not?"

The doorbell rang, which was somewhat of a relief. Usually Elijah just walked into the house.

"Are you going to go answer it?" Eloise asked, ducking down out of view from the window.

I wanted to. Man, so badly did I want to. I couldn't remember the last time I'd purposefully ignored Elijah like this, but the idea of facing him nearly had me breaking into hives. "No, I'm going to just wait until he walks away. He'll assume I'm not home."

Eloise looked at me like I'd lost my mind. Maybe I had. "Remi, my car is parked out front. He knows we're here."

Freak, freak, freak.

She stood from the butterfly chair, moving to the

doorway of my bedroom. "What are you doing?" I hissed after her, but she'd already turned into the hallway, and a minute later, I heard her struggle to open the front door.

And then I heard Elijah's voice, low and soft. I had to close my eyes, trying to tip the thoughts from my mind like a bowl of water, dumping them out. "Jeez, is their door broken?"

"Must be," came Eloise's quiet response. As silently as I could, I crawled close to the doorway and leaned against the wall, straining my ears. "Remi's not feeling good."

"No? I wondered. I thought she was mad at me. She hasn't been answering my texts all weekend, so I thought I'd swing by."

He was so thoughtful. So thoughtful.

Wait. Stop. I pinched my thigh, trying to clear my head.

"Do you know what's wrong with her?"

"She has a concussion," Eloise said, and I couldn't stop myself from cringing. *No, no, Eloise, no.* He hadn't known. He hadn't known I had a concussion; he hadn't known it was me in the closet. But now it had to be obvious. I squeezed my eyes shut, almost afraid to hear his response.

It felt like it took him a long time to reply. "A concussion?"

"She fell at Jer's party, out on his porch steps." I heard Eloise cough. "Anyway, I can tell her you stopped by, but she's not feeling up for company."

"You're here," he pointed out.

"Yeah, well, I'm pushy."

I knocked my head softly against the wall, hating this stupid situation. I should've just been a bigger, better person and confronted him. He'd been concerned—he *cared*. And yet I was letting some stupid kiss come between our friendship? We'd both mistaken each other for other people, and I'd been a little bit tipsy. Sure, my stomach fluttered weirdly whenever I thought about it, and the memory would play itself over in my mind without my permission, but that was just my body reacting. It didn't mean anything.

Just as I was about to push myself into a standing position, Elijah spoke again. "You don't have to tell her I stopped by. I'll see her tomorrow."

"Say hi to Savannah for me," Eloise said, and after a moment, I heard the door slam shut. "Remi, you've got to get that door fixed. It felt like it was going to break apart."

I sat still, trying to keep my breathing normal. There was a certain pain in my chest that came with knowing I'd just willfully blown off Elijah for the first time in my life. It was a funny thing, kissing him. I'd kissed *Elijah*. My best friend. And all I wanted to do was tell him and laugh it off, but I couldn't. Maybe I would have the courage tomorrow.

"Remi?" Eloise came into the doorway, looking at me. "Are you okay?"

"I don't want to talk about the party anymore," I said quietly, rubbing my forehead. "Can we talk about something else?"

Eloise hesitated above me, but I couldn't bring myself to look her in the eye, afraid she'd be able to see everything on my face. She ended up letting the conversation go, but that didn't mean my thoughts were so quick to follow suit. In fact, I wasn't sure I'd be able to push the events from the party totally from my mind.

The next morning, about ten minutes before I headed to the bus stop, a text dinged on my phone. Mom had given it back to me the night before so I could set my alarms for school, and indeed my phone had been blown up with texts and calls from both Elijah and Eloise, both asking if I was okay and why I wasn't answering the phone. Safe to say, I didn't answer the former.

The text this morning, though, wasn't one I'd been expecting.

Elijah: Want a ride 2 school?

Me: Aren't you picking up Sav?

Elijah: Yeah, but I figured it beats the bus. Up 2 you. I miss you.

It wasn't that I didn't want the ride—because, c'mon, a senior riding the bus was kind of lame—but I hesitated to say yes. *I miss you.* It was a completely normal thing for him to say after we hadn't seen each other all weekend, and yet it didn't feel normal.

Me: Do I get shotgun?

Elijah: I pick you up 1st, so I'd say yes.

Me: ...deal. :)

I stared at the unsent text for a moment before deleting the smiley face, overthinking everything. He replied that I could come out in five minutes, and I hurried to twist my hair up. With the short notice, I had no time to throw a small wave in it with the curling iron, but I did take a minute to fluff my bangs out so they didn't hang low in my eyes.

After grabbing the strap of my backpack, I headed out of my room. "Mom?" I called, finding her sitting on the couch, sipping her morning coffee. "I'm going to go."

"So soon?" She glanced down at her watch. "Don't you have a few minutes for breakfast?"

"I'll get a banana when I get to school," I promised. "Elijah's giving me a ride, and he leaves a little early to pick up his girlfriend."

"Today's a long day onsite for me over in Addison. They're putting in cabinets today, and I want to make sure everything looks right in the space. I probably won't be home until six-ish."

"Well, see, that works, because I was going to go out tonight."

A worried expression crossed Mom's features, and I could've guessed what she said next word for word. "Honey, don't overdo it, okay? It's your first day out since your head trauma. Take it easy."

I tried to hide my annoyance. "It's a *mild concussion,* Mom. Doctor said I was given a clean bill of health as of today." I had woken up with a slight headache, but I definitely wasn't going to tell her that. She probably would've made me stay home. "I'll be fine."

"Text me if you need anything," she said as I turned away. "Or just text me throughout the day anyway. Give me some peace of mind."

Calling out an affirmative, I hurried down the hall and slipped on my snow boots, tucking my sneakers into the big compartment of my bag before tugging the door open. My puffy jacket hung on one of the hooks by the door, and I grabbed it, pulling it on as I tried to coax the door shut.

Elijah's truck was already running across the street, the taillights dim in the dark. I pulled my scarf from my coat pocket, winding it around my throat as I carefully crossed the street. It hadn't snowed since Saturday night, but Greenville tended to under-salt the side streets, leaving it slick.

Though it was cold outside, my hands felt slick with sweat. *No reason for nerves*, I told myself, drawing in a sharp breath of winter air. *It's going to be a good day. A normal day. Last Thursday never happened.*

Elijah had exited his house by the time I got to the tailgate of his truck, tumbler of coffee in hand, giving me a tired look. "Hey, kid. You've risen from the dead, huh?"

Okay, he sounded normal. From what I could tell, his facial expression was normal. Now it was my turn to act normal. I held my breath, sternly telling my body not to react. It didn't listen; it sent a rush of warmth over my cooled fingertips instead, spreading to the center of my body. "Thanks for driving me. I promise this can be a one-time thing."

His eyes lingered on me. "I don't mind at all, Beanie. This can be an everyday thing."

Beanie. For some reason, hearing the nickname fall from his lips created a strange pressure behind my ribs. I drew in a breath to squash the feeling. "But Sav—"

"If Savannah has a problem with it, *she* can ride the bus." He gestured to the cab. "Hop in."

Once we were safely in the truck, all buckled in, Elijah put it in reverse. A mix of smells tickled my nose, hitting me all at once. It smelled a little like Elijah, clay and pottery glaze, but I could also still smell Terry, body wash and the faintest trace of cologne.

I hadn't ridden in the truck with Elijah since he'd taken temporary ownership, afraid that it'd feel too strange. But really, it was strange for a whole other reason.

"You should let me drive sometime," I told him, trying to channel the normal nonchalance between us. "I doubt Terry would mind."

Elijah just smiled a little in response, the corners of his soft lips tipping up. I'd never paid much attention to his smile before, not really. I'd never noticed it wasn't totally perfect, one corner a bit tighter than the other, a tiny dimple in one cheek and not the other. I could still imagine the pressure of his mouth curving around mine, recollected with perfect clarity, especially when that mouth was only a few inches from me. Perfectly in reach.

I was knee-deep in crap.

"Why did you ignore me all weekend?" he asked, glancing sideways at me. "Eloise said you hit your head. Did you have some memory loss and forget that I was your best friend?"

I forced myself to laugh, because normal me would've

laughed at that, but it came out shaky. "No cell phones for concussed people. At least not under Mom's watch."

"Terry got a concussion once. Fell off a friend's motorcycle. He had a headache for weeks."

The mere mention of his brother's name made me hesitate. After his reaction last Thursday, hearing him bring up his brother again came as a shock. I noticed, though, that it wasn't an invitation to start talking about it. It was merely a statement of a fact.

"Yeah, my head feels like it's going to fall off." I refused to look at him as he turned off our street, struggling to keep my voice normal. "So how was your night? Thursday night, I mean. After I left. Your, uh, house." *Gosh, can you be any more awkward, Remi?*

"Oh, right." He shook his head a little. "I didn't tell you. Savannah and I ended up going to the party. Just a little while after you left the house. I called you to tell you, but you didn't answer."

That's why he called me that night.

"I tried to find you at Jeremy's, but I guess you left before I got there," he continued. "Which is okay, because we didn't end up staying long. Savannah hit her head too, actually. Playing that stupid closet game. Crazy coincidence, huh?"

My mind slowed as everything he said registered. *Playing that stupid closet game.* I felt frozen, trying to think but each thought getting stuck. So he *did* think it was Savannah he'd been kissing? He hadn't connected the dots between me and the closet. That was good. But he had to have seen Savannah afterward, had to have asked about her head. Did she lie? Wouldn't Savannah had told him that it wasn't her?

She knew. It was the only explanation. Unless she actually did hit her head on something.

"So." He drew out the word, reaching for his coffee tumbler, and I realized I hadn't responded. I'd been too lost in my thoughts, consumed by the turmoil that was my life. "I saw Jeremy over at your house yesterday."

I shifted in the passenger seat, knocking my boots together and watching the snow clumps fall. "He brought over homework."

Elijah slowed down for a stop sign, brakes squeaking as the truck came to a halt. "How sweet of him."

I didn't tell him that he'd only done it because Mr. Valdez asked. I wanted to look away, to not see his expression, but my eyes were magnetized to him. His pale eyelashes caught the light, cute and wispy—wait, no. What? Ridiculous. *Not cute*, normal. Totally normal eyelashes.

"He asked me out on a date, too," I said.

I waited for any instance of surprise, annoyance, agitation —something to prove that he cared about what I said—but Elijah only tapped his fingers on the steering wheel. "And you said...?"

"We're going to see a movie after school today," I said.

"That's great, Bean."

Was it? Then why did I feel like throwing up all over my boots?

"We tell each other everything, don't we?" he asked immediately, turning to glance at me. His mouth formed a firm line. "We're best friends. You said so yourself: we're best friends. We're honest with each other."

Am I going to forever live in this constant state of anxiety? "I—I guess so. Yes."

"I think you and Jeremy are a great fit. I know you've been crushing on him for a while, but I think you two would be great." He hesitated, still drumming his fingers. "Mr. Valdez actually gave me the homework."

My eyebrows pulled together. "He gave it to *you?*"

"And I gave it to Jer. And I may...or may not have told him you have a crush on him. But it's obvious he likes you too, so I thought I would move things along." Elijah hunched his shoulders up, like he expected me to punch him. "I know, I know, I'm a jerk who broke friendship code."

The fabric of my scarf felt choking at my throat, but I didn't move to loosen it. "It's okay," I said, because it was. Everything had worked out. The pressure on my chest had nothing to do with the fact that Elijah had pushed us together, orchestrated the start of a relationship. It was just my too-tight scarf. "I should be thanking you, then. For being our matchmaker."

"Exactly. Hey, speaking of being a matchmaker, I've always thought Casper Renner and Julia Ferrand would be cute together. What do you think?" Elijah looked over at me. "You okay, Remi? Awfully quiet this morning."

"Yeah," I said immediately, knocking my boots together again and looking out the window. The sun hadn't begun to crest the horizon yet, leaving the world in a state of darkness. "Just have a little bit of a headache."

Savannah lived on the higher end of Greenville, where houses were all three stories with gated backyards and frozen animal-shaped shrubbery. Elijah eased the truck into her paved driveway, turning to me. "I'll go get her."

You mean, you'll go warn her I'm here. "Okay."

I took the time to glance around the interior of the cab after he hopped out, moving across the snow-covered lawn. No trace of Terry remained—no gas station receipts, no cigarette lighters. There were a few art pencils rolling around, but I knew those were from Elijah. The smell of coffee from his mug hung in the air, warm and familiar.

I hugged my backpack closer on my lap, leaning my chin against it as I thought about this afternoon. When was the last time I'd been on a date? And how long had I been dreaming of going out with Jeremy? Hottie Jeremy. Guy I'd been crushing on forever. So why were there no butterflies at the idea of going out this afternoon, no thrill of anticipation? Why was there...nothing?

The driver's side door popped open, as well as the door behind me, the interior lights glowing. Elijah climbed into the seat and immediately brought his seatbelt over his lap, cutting a glance my way. It seemed to linger, and I took it as my cue.

"Good morning, Savannah," I said.

The girl in question poked her head between the seats, giving me a face-full of her freckles. I tried not to look at her expression too closely, afraid she'd be able to read my mind. "Morning, Remi. Oh, your makeup looks so good today. You must've woken up super early to do it."

There was something passive-aggressive about her state-ment; I was sure of it. "It's just mascara."

"Well, it looks really good."

Elijah put the truck in reverse, hooking his hand on the

back of my seat to watch as he backed out. Five fingers, just inches away from the back of my head. Those same five fingers had pressed against the back of my neck before, gentle and— "Did we have a quiz today in physics?" I blurted out, desperate for any onslaught of conversation to distract myself. "I can't remember."

The rest of the ride, we talked about school, boring and unexciting, and I couldn't help but notice the way Elijah's hand kept twitching on the gearshift. While their words passed through my ears, I imagined what it'd be like to slip my fingers into his, and wondered whether his grip would be warm or cold.

By the time fourth period rolled around, I had my story down. I hadn't completed my papier-mâché project, but I did have a great excuse and alibi ready, rehearsed and memorized.

Greenville High's art teacher wasn't as much of a free spirit as one might've thought. Her love for art was all internal, apparently, but none of it spilled into her outward appearance. She wore blazers, wide glasses and pencil skirts, and kept her hair slicked back into a tight bun. Definitely not artistic-looking at all. Elijah said that her personality was where her creativity stemmed from, but from her hostile words on Thursday, I didn't think that was the case.

She sat at her desk as she looked up at me, no trace of happiness on her face. "Remi, I wanted to talk to you about your papier-mâché project."

I looked at her innocently. "Mrs. Keller, did you hear that I had a concussion? This weekend was mandatory bed rest. Doctor's orders. I can give you his number if you need it."

"I did hear, and I also heard that it happened Thursday night. Plenty of time for your project to be finished." Mrs. Keller blinked patiently at me, holding onto a pause. She put her hands on the desk, crossing her fingers and looking at me expectantly. With that devious glint in her eye, she looked more like a lawyer than an art teacher, or maybe a detective. "But you did good by asking Elijah to turn it in for you."

Turn it in for—*huh?*

"He dropped it off before school Friday morning. But I was curious as to why you chose to paint it."

"Um, painted...*what* exactly?"

Mrs. Keller's expression remained neutral. "Your papier-mâché."

Back up the bus. Elijah actually turned in a fake assignment? *For me?* He risked his own grade *for me.* Something in me just...melted. Like a bar of chocolate left in a hot car, it spread into a puddle of warmth. My stomach turned ever so slightly as the butterflies' wings brushed alongside it, flipping it over.

I tried to squash the feeling, stamp it out like a flame beginning to form, and harness my poker face. "Um, you're asking me why I was being creative...in an art class?"

"The assignment was to create something out of papier-mâché with only newspaper clippings. Not to paint it or add any sort of color. Yours was the only one that'd been painted. I'm asking you why you took an extra step that you didn't have to, when all semester you've barely done the bare minimum."

I flattened my palms along the surface of the desk, entering her space. "Listen, Mrs. K. I get that it's kind of suspicious. But papier-mâché is really interesting to me, with the whole glue and newspaper technique. *Super* cool. Peeling the glue off my hands was practically my favorite part. I just felt…inspired."

Mrs. Keller's lips twitched a bit at that, and she leaned back, reaching for something underneath her desk. "I wasn't suspicious until Elijah turned in his assignment." In one swift movement, she set a medium-sized papier-mâché bowl on the surface of her desk. It wobbled from its uneven base. The words on the newspaper were smudged and see-through, only enough layers pasted on to keep the shape. "As you can see, not his best work."

I stared at the crappy bowl with tunnel vision. "He did *that*?"

"Yes, and this was yours." She placed another project beside the bowl, and it completely blew the dish out of the water. It was a mask, resembling the kind one would find at a party supply store, with a newspaper skin tone and dark holes for eyes and a mouth. But a river of paint cascaded down the cheeks from the eyes, beginning with a pastel blue before blending into a bloodred. The surface of the mask had been smoothed out perfectly, unlike the bowl's, and it rested flat on the desk. "You can see why I'm curious, can't you?"

A spark of irritation lit inside me, like a match kissing a candle, and I welcomed it with open arms. Irritation was good. "What are you saying?"

"I think you're claiming Elijah's work as your own to boost your grade. It's very interesting that you turn in something at this level after I told you that if you failed this semester, you wouldn't graduate."

I tried to imagine what she'd say if she knew Elijah had made the crappy bowl too.

But seriously, what the freak was he thinking? Didn't he think she'd question it? Sure, he didn't know about my grade predicament, but this definitely didn't do me any favors.

My answer was a psychologist's approach. "Why would Elijah let me claim his project?"

"I'm assuming you told him about our conversation on Thursday."

I glanced around at the room behind me, making sure no one tried to listen in. They all seemed to be engrossed in a new assignment. It was something to do with pottery, but I hadn't listened when someone tried to relay to me the project's requirements earlier. "Elijah doesn't know I'm failing. No one does. I—I painted it because I thought it would give me extra points. Your speech scared me, Mrs. Keller. I have to graduate."

See, here's the thing with Mrs. Keller: she could kind of see through my bullcrap. I mean, I'm not that great at it anyway, but with her, it was like I didn't even try. She had a detector for it or something.

So I had no idea why she didn't call me out. She just leaned back in her seat, eyeing me the entire time. For a long moment, we had a stare-down. On the surface of her desk, my fingers trembled.

"The semester ends next Friday," Mrs. Keller said finally.

"Nine days to bring your fifty-six to a sixty. Which is very unlikely, Remi, since there is only one assignment left."

Raising my grade four percentage points in less than two weeks would've been a sight to see, especially since it had taken me the entire semester to tank it.

Whoa, wait. Wait a second. Was she really saying that it was impossible I'd pass this semester—pass my *senior year? Fine Art* was going to keep me from graduating? "What about the papier-mâché grade?"

"Remi. Let's cut it out. I may not have proof, but we both know you didn't do that mask."

My heart started to beat faster as desperation set in. "Is there a bonus assignment I could do? Extra credit? Anything?" Heck, I'd even donate my piggy bank to the art department if it meant it could save my grade.

"I can't give you any extra opportunities that I'm not giving to any of the other students," she said simply, cold-heartedly, evilly. "It would be unfair."

Everything around me dimmed for a moment as my blood pumped hard, emotion starting to tickle my throat and tear ducts. "So, what? You're saying I'm going to fail this semester and that's that?"

"You need to pass two semesters worth of Fine Art credits your senior year. This semester counts as one credit, and the spring semester counts as the second. Since you can't take two classes of Fine Art in one semester, if you fail the one, it's over."

My brain hung on her words. Mrs. Keller was saying there was no way I could make up this class if I failed it. *No way.*

She was quiet for another long moment, drawing out my agony for as long as possible. Did teachers learn that in college, how to make their students almost pee their pants at the edge of their desks? Maybe she went to a different kind of teacher school, one that wrote grades down in students' blood. "The student council is throwing the annual Snowflake Dance next Saturday night. Have you heard about that?"

Uh, hello, what senior hadn't heard of the Snowflake Dance?

"Due to budget cuts, the art department and student council are in charge of making the displays and decorations this year, instead of going out and purchasing banners and decorations. That's a lot of snow and ice for a handful of people to do in a short period of time. I've taken a list of volunteers, and those who choose to help are given two percentage points toward their semester grade."

"But two percentage points—"

"The sculpture assignment we're working on now counts for two points, since it's essentially your final exam for this class. That will be due as well. I'm willing to bring your grade to a sixty if you're willing to put in the work, Remi." Mrs. Keller gave me a stern look behind her glasses. "*Without* cheating."

"Deal," I said immediately, nearly gasping the word out. "One hundred percent. What do I have to do?"

Mrs. Keller glanced at the clock on the wall. "The bell is about to ring. Meet me after last period and we'll talk about what you can be in charge of."

I nodded so fast that my ponytail shook, whipping around

my head. A chance existed. I'd be able to bring up my grade just enough to graduate. It would totally wreck my GPA, but who cared? I would graduate.

I turned my back on her and headed back to my seat, doing a quick once-over and making sure that no one was paying attention to our conversation.

I used the cover of my hoodie to pull my cell from my pocket, trying to keep it hidden from Mrs. K, and shot out a quick text. **You are so dead.**

nine

After last period, I swung back by Mrs. Keller's room to pick up the templates she had prepared for me. I, Remi Grace Beaufort, was on snowflake patrol for the Snowflake Dance. Such an honor. It didn't seem like a big deal until Mrs. Keller said that I needed to have 150 done by the dance. One hundred and fifty blue snowflakes needed to be cut out and covered in white glitter. She gave me the address to the craft store she frequented, as well as a couple of coupons for the glitter and the construction paper.

I didn't know what I was going to do. One hundred fifty handmade snowflakes by next Saturday? It didn't *sound* like a big deal—only thirteen snowflakes a day—but that was on top of other homework and midterms and the sculpture project we were working on now. And they were big snowflakes, twelve by twelve inches, that I had to cut out by hand.

Mrs. Keller had said no cheating, but would she really know? And what did cheating mean? Did that mean no help at all, or just don't let anyone do them *all* for me?

I hooked my lock on the side of my locker and pulled out my backpack, sliding my math book inside. My teachers had been pretty accommodating, not loading me up with homework and giving me some extended deadlines. My headache worsened after fourth period—probably from all the stress. Not enough to have me call home, but enough that focusing was troublesome.

A shadow dropped over the edge of my locker, and I felt my stomach shift in a way that almost made me nauseous. I tried to take in a discreet breath, coaching myself to speak—

"Are you going to pretend I'm not here?"

Yeah, my stomach dropped again, but for a whole new reason. "I didn't realize it was you," I said finally, glancing up from the depths of my locker to stare him in the eye.

Elijah's expression appeared strangely somber as he looked down at me, light blond hair curling into his eyes. I never noticed how much of a wave his hair held before, but a hot flash of a memory worked its way over me. My fingers tightened instinctively as I remembered how his locks felt against my skin, how I tugged on the ends to bring his mouth closer to mine. And the noise he made in response...

"Who did you think I was?" he asked.

I didn't answer that question. Instead, I faced my locker, trying to convince myself that my fingers weren't shaking. "I'm mad at you."

"I figured, since I got a death threat during fourth hour." He leaned against the lockers, smiling a little. "I'm assuming Mrs. Keller talked to you about your papier-mâché."

"Yeah, the stupid papier-mâché I didn't even know that I did. Why on earth would you give me *yours*?" I demanded, my voice pitching high as I turned and slapped him on the shoulder. "Of course she would question it—were you not using your brain?"

"I thought she'd just think I coached you to perfection is all."

"Yeah, except the piece you said was yours was absolute garbage."

His eyes crinkled at the corners as he watched me. "Yeah, fine, I didn't think that through."

"No kidding. It's not funny." I tried to hold onto that annoyance, I really did, but as I looked at him, the first thing I focused on was his mouth. He bit the edge of his bottom lip, eyes flicking down the hallway with an attentive gaze. I wanted to say something like, *if you keep biting your lips, Savannah's not going to want to kiss them*, but what would've once been an easy sarcastic comment now felt entirely different. "Are you looking for your girlfriend?"

Elijah's teeth left his lip. "No. Why?"

Because I need to remind myself that this is wrong, and you have a girlfriend. Because I need to remind myself that my Elijah detox worked, and any leftover feelings are some sort of weird transference attraction meant for Jeremy. That's all. "No reason. How's your entry for the county contest coming? The deadline's almost here."

Elijah seemed to relax a little, the tension seeping from his shoulders. "It's coming along. Slowly but surely."

"And you're not going to tell me what it is? A drawing? A self-portrait, maybe?"

That had been Elijah's thing ever since Mrs. Keller told him about this contest. The county announced the competition back in December, and Elijah figured out what he was going to do not long after. But did he tell me? No. Of course not. Because it had to be a *secret*.

"My lips are sealed," he said simply, looking smug. "You're just going to have to wait and see. A week from tomorrow."

Right. Next Thursday they were to present their projects at the district library. "I'm not sure I can wait that long," I said. "Maybe I'll just sneak up to your room and watch you."

One of Elijah's eyebrows rose, a corner of his lips tugging up.

"I mean, I'll watch you *work on it*. Because you have that pottery wheel in your room? Not like, *watch you*, watch you. Not, like, watch you sleep or anything super creepy like that."

"Are you okay?" he asked, words laced with amusement. "Or should I just write off your weirdness as a side effect of hitting your head?"

"Yes, do that," I said with a sigh, head throbbing sympathetically. "Please."

I tried to hide my face in my locker, hide the heat that began to creep up my neck, but my ears snagged on a whispering voice just getting out, "*...that was his brother.*"

The heat on my skin no longer resembled embarrassment as the words registered. Immediately, my eyes flashed to my left, finding a cluster of freshmen girls at an open locker. They were too busy looking at Elijah with their snooping gazes to notice me.

Anger poured through me, so much that my fists clenched into little balls at my sides. "Stare much?" I demanded, shooting them my most scathing glare. I wasn't sure if it was scary or not, but my face felt pinchy and red, like I was a dragon about to breathe fire. "Get lost."

The three girls looked at me wide-eyed, cheeks pinking from getting caught. "S-Sorry," one of them said, hastily grabbing her things. "We didn't mean anything."

"It's fine," Elijah said quickly, cutting off whatever was going to come out of my mouth.

Not even I knew what I'd been about to say, but it sure as freak wasn't going to be something nice. "It's definitely *not* fine!"

"What are you going to do about it?" The two girls hurried away as Elijah turned to me, lips thinning. "Fight them in the hallway? Cause *more* talk? I don't know about you, but I'd prefer to fly under the radar. People talk. There's no stopping them."

"That doesn't mean they have to do it five feet from you," I threw back. "So, what, you yell at just me about it then? Everyone else can run their mouths but you don't care. Only I can't talk about him?"

Amazingly, his lips grew thinner. "It's different."

I turned my back to him and rummaged through my locker, searching for where I sat my lock. Different, right. Everything was different. "Listen, I should go find Jeremy."

"Are you excited for your date?" His voice sounded flat.

I snorted, trying to stop myself from rolling my eyes. But eye-rolling was good—much better than going gaga at his stupid face. Annoyance was good. "You're pretty invested, huh?"

"My duty as matchmaker requires me to be invested." A glint of metal shone from the corner of my eye, and I turned to find Elijah with my lock balanced on the tip of his finger. He held it out to me. I grabbed it, not making eye contact. "You know you can call me if you need to, right? In case anything happens and you want me to pick you up."

"It's just Jeremy."

"What's just Jeremy?" a voice inquired, and a second later, I felt a hand drop over my shoulders, heavy enough to make me wobbly. "Also, don't put emphasis on the *just* part."

I glanced up at the boy in question, finding his pleasant expression focused on me. "We were just saying how it was going to be just you and me going out. No third wheels."

Jeremy threw a pointed look at Elijah, whose face still looked stiff from our argument. "We could double sometime if you wanted to, bro. But first dates are sacred."

"I can see if Sav would be up for it sometime this week." Elijah's voice was at odds with his appearance, eyes flicking to me meaningfully. "My offer always stands, okay?"

"Okay, *Dad*."

That seemed to crack the strange atmosphere between the two of us. Elijah's eyes regained their normal light humor and he moved to brush past us. At the last minute, he stopped and leaned in to whisper something to Jeremy, something I didn't catch due to the perfectly timed slam of a locker door.

Before I could ask what had happened, Elijah strode away.

"Here, I'll carry your pack," Jeremy said, swiping my backpack away before I had the chance to object. He had it up and over his bicep in a moment. "So you know, I was thinking. I know I originally said a movie, but I'm starving, aren't you? We could go to Mary's Place over on Fifth Street. You know, that diner?"

"Okay," I said distractedly, glancing over my shoulder to watch Elijah's retreating figure. His backpack bounced with his casual gait, and I kept wishing he'd turn around, meet my gaze one last time. I could just imagine the tortured look he'd pass me, the idea of me going on a date with another guy tearing him apart.

But he didn't turn. His green backpack just rounded the corner and dropped out of sight, the nonexistent tortured look going with him.

Jeremy took his arm from me to hold the door open, and I slipped through. "Look, the snow's melting. Finally. I know winter just started and all, but I am already sick of this season. Once Christmas is gone, I'm over it."

As the cold ghosted over my arms, I realized I'd left my coat in my locker. I paused, ready to turn back. "Oh, my jacket—"

"Don't sweat it, Rem." In an expert move, Jeremy slipped his varsity jacket off his shoulders and laid it over mine. A gust of his cologne hit my nose, and I hardly stopped myself from gagging over the intensity. "Come on, my car's this way."

He'd double-parked at the very edge of the student parking lot so the silver sedan was in no danger of being dinged by another car door, he said. He bumped into me in his haste to open the passenger side door, so I stepped aside to let him pass. "Can you try and knock off as much of the snow from your boots as you can before you get in? I have all-weather floor mats, but I've got a thing about dirt, and the snow out in the parking lot is filled with all sorts of crap."

"Of course," I answered at once, tapping my toe against the slippery asphalt. I pried the edge of the door back so I could slip past him and ducked into the car.

Once I settled in, I reached for the door handle to tug it shut, but Jeremy just smiled down at me, pressing his hand against the outside glass. "I've got it, Remi. Luxury treatment. Just make sure your feet are in."

Despite the slight strangeness of it, I was touched by the gesture, and I tucked my boots back so he could slam the door. He was trying a little too hard, that much was obvious, but maybe our outing wouldn't be so bad. Maybe I was stressing over nothing.

There weren't many places to eat in Greenville—in fact, there were only two. Mary's Place, an amazing diner that offered the best strawberry crepes in the county, and a steakhouse so expensive that I'd never even been to it before. Mom and Dad used to go there sometimes for date nights and would bring back leftovers, but that was the closest I'd come to eating there.

The diner, though, was as familiar as Freezing Fred's Ice Cream Parlor. Dad and I used to go to Mary's every Sunday when I was little, and after he'd gone, Elijah and I continued the tradition about once a month. Always sitting in the same booth, swapping bites. He'd always get chocolate-chip pancakes and I'd get my crepes. Every single time.

I'd never gone there for dinner before, and I stared at the other side of the menu like it spoke a different language.

"Their burgers are to die for," Jeremy said from across the table, already sitting with his menu folded. "I come here all the time with friends and it's the only thing I ever get. Well, that and their steak fries. Man, those are seasoned to perfection. Have you ever had them?"

I rubbed my fingers against my left temple, trying to keep track of his quick voice. "I haven't, actually."

"They're good. Savannah—you know, Sav, Eli's girlfriend? I used to come here with her sometimes and she'd always steal some of mine. Not like a date or anything, just as friends who hang out. I mean, we *did* date before, so it's not like it's weird or anything. We haven't hung out since she started hanging with Eli, though, so don't worry."

"It's Elijah," I told him, tracing my fingers over the greasy menu. "I mean, he doesn't like anyone using the nickname Eli." *Anyone except me.*

"Oh. Okay."

I gritted my teeth, wishing I'd kept my mouth shut, and focused on the words in front of me. I wasn't much of a burger eater, and nothing on the menu sounded good. Yes, their breakfast was good, but dinner? I wasn't sure. "So I should get a burger and fries?"

Jeremy shrugged. "I mean, if you want to. Their mac and cheese is good, but that's really a side. Savannah always used to get their country-fried steak, but to me, it's kind of gross. Gravy isn't supposed to be milky white, you know?"

The waitress came back to the table with her pad of paper in hand, pen poised and ready to begin writing. She looked about our age, flawless makeup, and her pretty blonde hair wrapped in a bun on top of her head. Her orange and white dress had her nametag pinned by her collarbone, *Sienna.* "Have you two decided yet?"

"I have. Just waiting on her. Did you figure it out yet, Remi?"

I closed the menu, reaching for my napkin. "I'll just have a side of mashed potatoes."

The waitress and Jeremy both blinked. "*Just* mashed potatoes?"

"I'm not feeling that hungry," I told them, passing over my menu. The throbbing between my temples hadn't subsided yet; in fact, it felt like it was getting worse. "No gravy, please."

Jeremy placed his long order—"burger well done with lettuce and tomato but *no* mayonnaise with steak fries and extra seasoning"—and Sienna disappeared with a quick smile. Then we were alone.

Something I realized about Jeremy that I'd never noticed before? He was a *talker*. As we waited for our meal, he talked about the parties he threw—"only occasionally, I'm not really a partier, you know?"—and about graduation—"I just can't wait to get out of this godforsaken town"—and he also touched a little bit on bones he'd broken when he was younger—"my left collarbone, my humerus, and two of my fingers."

After our meal was delivered, he kept talking. At least he didn't talk with his mouth full. "So, do you watch basketball?" he asked, popping a steak fry into his mouth.

"I don't, not really." Sometimes I went to school games, but not often. Elijah and I usually stayed home and watched movies. "Do you?"

"I'm on the team," he said with a chuckle. "Have been since I was little. Like those little league baseball teams?

That's actually how I broke both of my fingers, playing basketball. Sophomore year and junior year. Still have time left to break one my senior year."

I stirred my spoon through my mashed potatoes, giving him a tired smile. "That doesn't sound like a fun tradition."

"Sports are just a big part of my life. Football, basketball, golf. Except baseball—yeah, I'm not a baseball fan one bit. Watching it is fine, but playing is so not my thing."

"I've never been into sports," I said.

"I wish our school had lacrosse," Jeremy said, picking up his burger with one hand, a fry in the other. "That would be sweet. Or golf. Yeah, golf would be so cool. Why doesn't Greenville have a program like that?"

I watched as he took a big bite of his burger, something not sitting right with me. Maybe it was just the throbbing headache, the jackhammer to my brain. Not even my warm, very tasty mashed potatoes made me feel better. We went on for a little while, him talking my ear off, me interjecting here and there.

And then I realized what exactly felt off. Every time I spoke to Jeremy, it was like my words went in one ear and out the other. Not registering. Or maybe they were registering, and he just didn't want to hear them.

Jeremy slowly pulled into my driveway just a little bit after five, and by slowly, I mean *slowly*. He'd barely broken thirty-five the entire drive, even in the fifty-five zones. I'd tried to casually make a comment about it, but he said that going slower in these weather conditions was a way to stay safe.

"I'm sorry about your headache," Jeremy said as he slid the gearshift into park, turning to look over at me. "I would've loved to keep this night going with a movie. There's a great one out right now that's said to have the most explosions in one movie ever. Who doesn't love explosions?"

"Next time," I replied in a light voice, my forehead propped against the cool glass window. Mom's car wasn't in the driveway, so at least I could stumble inside without a barrage of questions.

Jeremy's spine straightened. "I'll walk you to the door."

I pressed my hand against his arm the second he reached for his seatbelt. "You don't have to do that," I said. "I can manage the walk. You've been gentleman enough for the entire night."

His face pinched as he tried to smile. "I overdid it, didn't I?"

"Maybe just a smidge."

"Elijah told me I needed to be on my best behavior," he said, releasing a breathy chuckle of relief. "I figured you were only into charming guys. I didn't know how long I could keep it up, honestly. Good to know you thought it was lame too."

I blinked at him. "Wait, what?"

"The whole opening the door, giving you my jacket—I don't know how guys do that all the time."

"Do what?" I asked with a frown. "Be thoughtful?"

"Yes! I was exhausted the entire time, trying to think of what I needed to do next." Jeremy adjusted the collar of his jacket against my neck, fingers lingering. "I'm glad you're not the kind of girl that expects that. A bit unrealistic, yeah?"

I looked into his hazel eyes, thoroughly confused. Was he

saying being a gentleman was lame? I mean, yeah, he went a little overboard with everything, but that hadn't been what annoyed me this evening.

Unrealistic. And Elijah had prompted him to act this way? What was that about?

I pressed my fingertips to my temple, their chill soothing the heat there. "Well, the next time we get together, just be yourself."

"Next time," he murmured, fingers by the base of my throat. "I like how that sounds."

I popped the car door open before he got any ideas. "I'll see you tomorrow."

"Remi?" Jeremy called once I got my feet. "My jacket?"

"Oh. Yeah." I pulled my arms from the sleeves and set it on the passenger seat. Goosebumps swept across my skin in a moment, and I crossed my arms. "See ya."

Jeremy waved at me as he backed out onto the roadway, and I'd just stuck my key in the lock when he started down the street, still at full-on turtle speed. Well, at least he'd been genuine about his cautious driving.

The door jammed, of course. I kicked it in the corner, but it didn't budge. Ugh, seriously not what I needed.

I turned around, planning to go for the back door, and saw a car backing into Elijah's driveway, running lights on and brightening a section of my snow-covered front lawn. I wouldn't have thought anything of it, but it was Savannah's car, and there were people inside. It really wasn't hard to guess who.

Since it was the middle of winter, the sun went down a lot earlier, and though it wasn't completely vacant from the sky just yet, I was able to hide in the shadows of my porch. My heart pounded fast, and I reached complete creeper status, standing out there with my breath fogging and my arms freezing. I wanted to lie to myself and say that I didn't know why I was watching them, but I knew.

Elijah popped his door open, causing light to fill the interior, fully illuminating their faces. Fully illuminating how they were pressed together, close enough to kiss.

And then they were kissing, Savannah's hand cupping Elijah's cheek, her lips landing on his. My stomach twisted painfully, and then my chest followed suit in a way that it never had before. All the air flew from my lungs. I started moving. Down, off the porch, out of the shadows, and into the glare of Savannah's stupid headlights. The snow crunched as I hurried across it, desperate to escape the scene before me. The rapid breaths that my lungs demanded didn't feel too good, the air like knives on my insides, burning my throat. My brain was about to start oozing out my ears.

I'd seen Elijah and Savannah kiss before. Not too often, since they were just starting to get their footing in their relationship, but it'd happened before. But there was no explaining the violent way my stomach seized when I saw them tonight. Her hand cupping his cheek. His hand touching her hair. Maybe because I could still feel those fingers in my hair, his lips on my lips, and it threw me so much that I felt sick.

In the midst of everything, one clear thought ran through my cracked mind. I had a *crush* on my *best friend*. This pain that I felt? *Jealousy.*

Before I stepped away from the glare of the car headlights, I thought I heard my name being called to the wind. I didn't turn around.

Mom didn't get home until eight-thirty, finding me at the kitchen table, struggling through my math homework. I couldn't get my brain to focus, to delete the image of Elijah and Savannah embracing each other. I was so distracted that I was surprised that I could even answer two plus two.

"You're not straining your eyes, are you?" Mom asked immediately, her purse and keys clattering as she set them on the countertop. She seemed to melt against it, sagging.

"Yeah, I am," I said, leaning my chin against my fist. The headache hadn't gone away entirely, but after a cool compress and some medicine, the dull pain had lowered to a manageable level. "Straining them so bad. Want to do it for me?"

"Ha-ha," she tried to mock, but it fell flat, her eyes distant. "I've had such a long day. How on earth is it still Monday?"

I smiled a little. "Well, Mom, the days of the week work in a pretty obvious order—"

"Kathleen called me today."

It was all she had to say to stop my train of thought in its tracks and turn the calculus problem in front of me to gibberish. One would think in times of a crisis, people would pull their friends and family closer. But two weeks ago, when Terry's plea deal was being worked over, Mrs. G had done the equivalent of ghosting Mom. Stopped answering her calls, ignored her when they saw each other outside. Much like how she treated me Thursday night, barely aware I was there. "Mrs. Greybeck calling you is a good thing, isn't it?

That means things are going back to normal between you two."

Mom unwound her small ponytail, letting her locks fall around her shoulders in a bumpy, wavy mess. "No, she wasn't calling for me. She asked for your father's number. She said she wanted to fact-check what their attorney told them about Terry's case."

"His case?" I asked, my brow furrowing. "What do you mean? I thought everything was decided. He took the deal to lessen his sentencing and all that, right?"

"He did. He got an accomplice charge instead of larceny involvement. Thirteen months in a correctional facility and community service once he gets out. Cut and dried. Pretty good for what he faced originally. But you also know that Kathy, she...isn't taking it well."

Despite the fact that Elijah never went into details about Terry, I knew a handful of information. It was hard not to in a small town like this. Terry and a bunch of his friends had thought it would be a great idea to rob a drug store, and then a gas station, in the middle of the night. Someone made an anonymous phone call, a phone call that ultimately got them caught. One brought along a BB gun and nearly got them all felonies for armed robbery. Geniuses right there.

Terry and another guy were parked in the getaway car and had been able to get a lesser sentence through some legal mumbo jumbo. Dad didn't represent him in trial but had recommended a great lawyer.

I remembered last Thursday, Mrs. Greybeck's fixation on the law firm's webpage. "Did you give her Dad's number?"

"I gave her his office number. I wouldn't give out his cell without his permission."

The house quieted while both of us stewed in our thoughts. If Mrs. Greybeck was still worried about Terry's case, I wondered how Elijah's home life was. Were they still talking about it at dinner every night? Did they even *have* family dinners anymore?

Something seemed to occur to Mom because she lifted her tired gaze to mine. "How did your evening out go?"

I shrugged a shoulder, trying to force my focus back to my homework. "It was all right."

"Did Elijah go?"

Elijah was too busy locking lips with his girlfriend in his driveway. "No."

But Mom hadn't finished prying. "Are you two okay? Have things been strained since everything happened? I haven't seen him around lately."

"I've got homework, Mom," I said, a little snappish, but I didn't want to talk about Elijah or his family anymore; I didn't feel like talking at all.

"Did you get any dinner? I ate while I was out."

"I warmed up leftovers."

"I'm going to get ready for bed, then," she replied quietly, pushing off the counter. "If you need anything, you know where I'm at." She stopped halfway down the hall. "I love you, sweetheart."

My lips felt tight when I spoke. "Love you."

There were three unanswered questions on my math worksheet, but I closed the book and covered the numbers, kneading the heel of my hand into my forehead. So many things ran through that stupid brain of mine in a way that only added to the pounding. I could account for three names in the cacophony of pain: Jeremy, Mrs. Keller, Elijah. Three names that caused my brain to work overtime. Three seemed to be the magic number of the night. Three math problems, three names, three reasons my life was stressing me out to the max. Perfect.

I hardcore avoided Elijah the next morning, and it went well —until school actually started and we were in homeroom together. American History. And of course, we sat by each other. His pestering proved unavoidable.

"How did it go?" he whispered, leaning in slightly to avoid suspicion. We were watching a documentary about World War II, and the dimmed lights and film noises covered up his attempt at conversation. "You never texted me."

He was right; I hadn't texted him back for a lot of reasons. Many included the fact that I hated myself and those stupid butterflies I got whenever I thought about him. Because now, with him so close, those butterflies were impossible to ignore.

"It was fine."

"*Fine?* No sparks, no fireworks?" A pause. "Did you kiss him?"

"Nosy much?"

A cough rendered both of us silent, and we pretended to be engrossed in the film as several seconds ticked by.

Elijah glanced over, folding his hands on the top of his desk. "Are you going out again?"

"Probably," I whispered back. "I thought we were going to double date one day this week."

"I didn't know if you'd want to. I wanted to check with you before I asked Sav."

I didn't know how to respond so I kept quiet, rubbing the pad of my thumb over the tops of my fingernails. Did I want to double date with him and Savannah? After last night, I really wasn't sure. Seeing them together, thinking about them together...it made knots form in my stomach. Tight knots. Could I really survive a double date with them?

I rubbed the edge of my nail, trying to screen my thoughts. I really needed to get my nails painted. It'd been a while since I'd gotten a proper manicure, and the hangnail on my thumb was starting to bother me. *If I keep focusing on my nails, maybe I'll stop thinking about everything else.* I hated that he knew me so well, that he had a free pass to speak to me when I tried to ignore him.

Every small part of me, every thought and nerve and cell, short-circuited when Elijah laid his hand on mine, stopping my movements. The edge of his thumb felt worn down from sculpting, nails short. I jerked, but he held fast.

"Are you okay?" he whispered, and I didn't realize he was leaning close enough for me to be able to feel his breath against my neck. "You're acting weird."

Weird, huh? Nothing weird at all about the fact that my armpits are starting to sweat like it's the middle of summer just by you touching my hand, right? No. Not weird at all.

"Is this because I talked to Jeremy yesterday?" he went on in the same tone, fingers ever so gentle against mine. "I just wanted to set him straight, that's all. Make sure he treated you right. No funny business and—"

"Mr. Greybeck and Ms. Beaufort," a voice snapped from the back of the classroom, and Elijah immediately jerked his hand away, pushing it through his hair. It was a quick movement, too quick for anyone's darting eyes to notice. But I caught the rigid pose of his spine, the stiffness to his shoulders. "Quiet."

We were both silent as we watched the film, though I didn't really take in any of it. I pulled my hand into my lap, running my fingertips across where Elijah's had rested, the pressure still tingling my skin.

Before, I'd thought that it would be impossible to hate Elijah, but in that moment, I felt a rush of anger. The kind that made my body tense, the acrid taste lingering in the back of my throat. Anger with Elijah was about unheard of, one of the rarest things on earth, and yet there it was, potent and piping hot. It was Elijah's fault that all of this was happening. For putting these thoughts in my head, for our stupid closet kissing, for my stupid concussion. All his stupid fault.

I should've shoved the feeling down, forced it away, but I latched onto the emotion, almost choking on it.

"Remi," Elijah whispered again.

"Shut up," I hissed, settling back in my seat and all but glaring ahead. I tucked my hands underneath my armpits, folded and stern. It didn't stop the tingling. "You're going to get us in trouble."

For the rest of the hour, Elijah didn't utter another word, sitting beside me in my stiff silence. I had no hope of focusing on the documentary, not when I could hardly sit still.

When the bell rang to switch classes, I practically bolted from the room.

Eloise popped her gum loudly beside my locker, waiting for me to grab my things. In addition to her noisy gum-popping, she shook her car keys back and forth, the chittering sound loud against my skull. "Are you nervous or something?" I asked her, pulling out a book for English. "Why are you fidgeting?"

The popping and shaking stopped. "I'm not."

"You definitely are."

She gave a falsely bright smile. "There's a quiz tomorrow in world history. I'm...thinking about it. Running through the glossary terms in my head. That's all."

Eloise was a junior, a year under me, so we didn't share any classes. Even so, I had a strong feeling that there wasn't a quiz in world history tomorrow.

"Incoming."

I looked up to see Savannah a few paces down the hallway, walking with another girl. We locked eyes, but Elijah wasn't with her, and I didn't expect her to stop. There was no time to hide my surprise when she did.

"Hey, Remi," she said, slowing down to pull up beside me. Her blonde hair hung loose in her face, her curls perfect, of course. A girl from our class stood beside her, eyeing me. "How are you feeling today? Any headaches?"

I remembered to grab my jacket this time, winding my arms through the sleeves. "I'm okay, Sav. Better and better every day."

"That's great. You know, I just told Elijah that your head's as hard as a rock. Nothing too bad will happen to you."

"Hard as a rock?" Eloise interjected, frowning. "Was that supposed to be offensive?"

The shock that fluttered over her expression seemed genuine. "No! I just meant that you can come back from anything."

I forced my features into a pleasant expression. Whatever would rush this conversation along. "Thanks for being positive, Savannah."

Her dark eyes leveled with mine. "You're welcome. I mean, head injuries just suck, don't they? I hit my head at Jer's party too, but I bounced back quick. Hopefully you do too."

Just from watching her, I couldn't decipher whether or not she knew the truth. Her face seemed relaxed, her lips formed into a loose smile; if she knew or suspected, she wasn't letting on. But the thing was that it *wasn't* her in the closet. It was me. So why was she lying?

"Yeah," I said instead of asking that question aloud, feeling like I was caught in a web with no way out. "Hopefully."

"Well, I'll see you tomorrow," she said, lifting her hand in farewell before moving off.

"I can't get a read on her," Eloise said from my side, watching her go. "She *seems* nice, but I can't tell if it's genuine or not."

"I don't know." I frowned a little, turning back to my locker. "I had a date with Jeremy last night."

"*What?*" she all but shrieked, causing several people to

look in our direction. Eloise smacked my shoulder. "And you're just now telling me? How was it?"

I flinched, torn from my train of thought. "How was *what*? You slapping me?"

"The date, idiot. I can't believe you're just mentioning it now. You should've called me."

"In my defense, I had a headache and homework." Yeah, both excuses were lame. "I'm a bad friend, I know. We went out for dinner. He talked...a lot."

"Is that a bad thing?"

Maybe not. It was just that I was so used to doing all the talking. Elijah wasn't much of a talker, but he listened. More than anyone else I knew, he listened, and he enjoyed listening. At least, I thought so. I shook my head to clear it because I so didn't need to be thinking of a certain someone. "It didn't seem like he listened to me much, either."

Eloise watched as I wrapped my scarf around my neck, folding her arms over her chest. "He was probably just nervous. I mean, you probably looked all cute and mysterious, sitting across from him. Giving him your flirty eyes."

"My *what*? I don't have flirty eyes." For some stupid reason, my thoughts backtracked to Elijah. His face just appeared behind my lids and I couldn't shake it. *What the heck?* "We're going out again. Maybe it'll be better."

Eloise wrapped her arm around my shoulders and pulled me close. "It definitely will be. First dates are always awkward. Now come on, I'm definitely driving you home so you can give me the rundown of everything he said."

"Fine," I said with a sigh. "But it's going to be a lot."

coerced Eloise into stopping by the craft store on the way home so I could finally begin the snowflakes for the dance. Though a part of me wanted to put the snowflakes off and ignore them until they became a big deal, that was the kind of mentality that had gotten me into this predicament in the first place. This time around, I needed to be smarter. More responsible.

Yuck.

By nine o'clock that night, and after I'd finished all my other homework, I'd gotten seven snowflakes into 150, and my fingers were cramping something fierce. Not to mention that I had glitter *everywhere*. On my clothes, underneath my fingernails, in my eyes—heck, I probably even ingested some at one point. Mrs. Keller hadn't said anything about how glitter really was the devil's dandruff, evil and gross.

She also didn't mention that the coupons she gave me didn't actually cover the entire price, only discounted it. I ended up having to pull out my wallet. Yeah, she probably didn't plan on reimbursing me for that either.

Since the snowflakes had to be twelve by twelve, it took quite a bit of intricate cutting to match the template Mrs. K had given me. Each snowflake took about fifteen minutes to complete, and that didn't include the dry time for the glue. At this rate, I was never going to graduate.

I clipped the scissors around the light blue paper, making sure to keep my cuts small and precise to match the template. They needed to be as close to perfect as God would allow. Even though Mrs. Keller was supposed to teach about expression, I had a feeling me half-doing this project wouldn't go over her head.

Mom drifted through the kitchen with an empty cup in her hand, walking over to the tap. "Do you want any help before I go to bed, sweetheart?"

"That's okay," I said, sticking my tongue out a bit in concentration, trying to get the final corner. "I don't think I'll be at this much longer. My thumbs are about to fall off."

Mom smoothed her hand down the back of my head and pressed a kiss against my skull. "Love you, darling."

I hadn't told Mom exactly why I was doing this little art project. I imagined that she just thought it was an assignment for class. No way I'd tell her how close I was to failing. She could find out after the fact, when report cards were sent out. She'd see for herself that I had a sixty percent. Yeah, that wasn't going to be pretty.

A knock on the front door startled me enough that my final cut came too close to the other lines, merging the white spaces together, effectively ruining the pattern. Tape could fix that, right? *Ugh.*

I all but slammed the scissors down on the tabletop, pushing away and padding to the front door. Whoever interrupted my snowflake time was going to get an earful. Especially since they forced me to ruin one. The porch light made the steps glow, and I peeked out the window to see who stood over the threshold.

"I come bearing gifts," Elijah called through the door. "A white flag of surrender and Thai takeout."

I flipped the deadbolt over and tugged on the handle. "This stupid door," I muttered.

"I think all the damp is rotting the frame, causing the door to stick," Elijah said from the other side. "It's an old frame, anyway; it's starting to rot in the corners and by the threshold. I hate to say it because it's a crummy time to do this, but it probably needs replacing."

"Then you need to fix it."

"If I'm by the hardware store, I'll drop by and see if I can get some supplies." Elijah kicked the corner of the door from the other side, and it about knocked me in the forehead as it swung inward.

I moved in front of the doorway immediately, not letting him through, taking in the sight of him. He wore his denim jacket, his hair rucked up from the wind, and from his fingertips dangled a white plastic bag with a yellow smiley face on the front.

"It's nine o'clock at night," I informed him.

His face remained determined, eyebrows aloft and

hopeful smile in place. "I'm pretty sure there's no law against eating Thai after nine."

"I just finished washing tonight's dishes an hour ago."

"Then it'll be great leftovers, yeah? Let me in." When I didn't move, he sighed. "Let me in so I can properly apologize for butting into your love life."

"Oh, if you're going to apologize, then..." I stepped out of the way so he could pass, a breeze of cool air sneaking in behind him. He immediately slipped off his sneakers and placed them on the shoe rack, handing me the bag so he could take off his jacket. "So this is bribery Thai?"

"More like guilt Thai. I was coming home from Sav's and thought it would be a good apology present."

I felt my good spirits wither away in an instant, along with the generosity I had been feeling toward him.

Elijah noticed the change in expression immediately, even though I turned away to try and hide it. "Did something happen with you and Savannah?" he asked, trailing after me as I made my way into the kitchen. "You two were strange in the car yesterday morning. And last night—I saw you, you know. Outside in the snow. Is everything okay?"

I set the bag down on the countertop, bracing myself against the granite. Having my back turned to him was better because I couldn't see what expression graced his features, whether his face was pulled into a taut frown or open like a book. When I had my back to him, it felt easy to stay like this, trapped in a frozen state of discomfort. Annoyance. Bitterness. Better than the butterflies. "What is this, twenty questions? I'm fine, Eli."

"You know I'm your best friend, right? I've seen you throw up pizza, eat worms, and bawl your eyes out over cartoons. If I can't tell when you're lying, I think you'd have to fire me." Elijah came up close behind me, something I could feel rather than see. I knew it a moment before he placed his hand on my shoulder, encouraging me to turn around. It was a sixth sense. "Talk to me, Beanie. What's going on with you?"

My back pressed up against the edge of the counter, my body trapped between it and Elijah, only a handful of inches separating us. I could feel the body heat seeping from him, spreading to me and nearly making me shiver. And his eyes—those dark eyes—seemed even deeper in the low lighting, staring into mine.

"Why does it have to be something with me?" I demanded, glad that my voice sounded neutral. "Why don't you assume that you're the one who's being weird?"

"I'm never the weird one," he objected lightly, tucking a strand of hair behind my ear, fingers grazing my skin as he did so. A gesture so affectionate, so like what he'd done in the closet, that I jerked away from the touch as if it burned. He raised an eyebrow in response. "See, definitely not me. Did something happen that you're not telling me? Did Jeremy do something?"

"Jeremy?" I scoffed, shaking my shoulders in hopes of shrugging off the heavy feeling. "Jeez, no. Well, except maybe act totally and completely unlike himself yesterday because *somebody* freaked him out. Seriously, couldn't you have minded your own business?"

Elijah held out his palms. "Hey, don't yell at me. I was

just trying to look out for you. I did the big-brother talk thing."

"You've never done it before."

He rolled his eyes. "I do it for every guy, Beanie. The whole 'be on your best behavior, treat her like a princess because she is' spiel. Jeremy's no different."

I stared up at him, scanning his expression for a hint of deception, but found none. Honestly, it wasn't that surprising. It was such an Elijah thing to do. Give boys a talking-to, taking over that brother role. But that wasn't the part I wanted him to play. "'Treat her like a princess'? Like you said before, I ate worms as a kid. Definitely not a princess."

Elijah smiled a little as he stepped back, allowing more oxygen to pass between us, making my heart fall in response. *No, oxygen is a good thing. Space is a good thing.* "Princess of Worms. Fitting. Hey, what's this all over the table?" He moved over to where I'd left my chair pushed out and picked up a shaker of blue glitter, rattling it slightly. "Are you redecorating your bedroom? Maybe you should be the Ice Princess or something edgy."

I rubbed my arm, still trying to fight for mind over matter. "Ha-ha. No, these are for Mrs. Keller. For the dance."

"Why are you decorating for the dance? Even I'm not that lame. For the extra credit?"

I tried to school my features. "Why would I need extra credit?"

Elijah sat down in my seat, brushing his fingers along my finished snowflakes, careful not to upset the drying glue. "I had to do your papier-mâché project for you. I'm going to say it's no secret that you're not doing the best in art."

Yeah, I guess that was kind of obvious. And I could've told him how bad things were for me, how close to failing my grade was, but I just couldn't. I sat down in the chair next to him, sighing. "This will boost my grade before the end of the semester, so that's good. I have to do 150 of these things."

"Well, where are the rest?"

"You're looking at them," I said, gesturing at my finished pile. "All seven of them."

His eyes widened with something that looked like alarm. "And you have to get these done by next Saturday? You only have *seven* done?"

"Judgey much?"

Elijah scooted the chair closer to the edge of the table, pushing up the sleeves of his shirt. "Break out the Thai, Beanie. We've got some work to do."

"Um, no. You can't help me." I snatched the scissors off the table as he made a grab for them, holding them hostage against my chest. "Mrs. Keller said no enlisting help." Or, you know, something like that.

"You're not enlisting. I'm offering." Elijah saw that I didn't plan on releasing my grip on the scissors. "C'mon, Remi. You need my help. No way you're going to get all these finished by then. Not with your other homework and stuff. Let me help." When I still didn't relinquish the scissors, he added, "Let me help you, because I'd bet money on the fact that you haven't started the sculpture assignment yet."

I felt the blood drain from my face. Of course he was right. The sculpture assignment. Why couldn't Mrs. K let me just work on these stupid snowflakes instead of having to do both? Was she trying to get me to hate art? Trying to make me fail?

Her voice echoed in my ears, threatening me. *Without cheating.* But what counted as cheating, exactly? Elijah offering help was different than enlisting him, right? And he was right: if he helped, that'd give me more time in class to work on that other project.

"Just a few," I said warningly, my fingers beginning to uncurl. Along with the fingers wrapped around my heart. "I mean it. And make them subpar."

Elijah took the scissors from me, curling the edge of his paper and aligning it with the template. "Don't worry. Glitter makes everything subpar."

We spent the next hour working on the snowflakes, and in the time I would have been able to finish four, we were able to get nine done. I had sixteen snowflakes, glitter-fied and all. Empty Thai containers littered around the tabletop, chopsticks sticking out, as well as a couple of forks. While I liked to at least attempt chopsticks, Elijah started off with silverware.

Elijah scrubbed at the glitter trapped against his nails, frowning. "Ugh, this isn't coming off anytime soon, is it?"

I leaned my elbow on the kitchen table, watching him while he was distracted. The memory of us going shopping surfaced, and I remembered him saying he couldn't imagine me naked. I couldn't ask for a clearer indication that he had zero feelings for me. But then again, at the time of that conversation, neither had I. Could one kiss really change someone's feelings like this?

If I kissed him now, right here under the strain of the LED pendant lights, would it be the same? Would I *feel* the same?

Elijah happened to glance over during my mental struggle, but when his eyes caught mine, he didn't speak. The crooked dip to his nose caught my eye, slightly off-center on his face, and I couldn't stop looking at the actual curvature of it. That, and all the other little things that suddenly seemed new to me. Like the fact that one eye had probably a handful more lashes than the other, or one corner of his mouth pointed a bit sharper than the other, or how there was a freckle just underneath one eyebrow.

But those were just his looks, and I couldn't help thinking about the deeper things, too. The way he touched his lips when he was nervous, or how if he laughed too loudly, he covered his mouth. Or when he was sculpting something with clay, entirely in the zone, he'd start to subconsciously smile, like he couldn't help it.

Those were the kind of things that girlfriends noticed because they were close enough to. Not best friends. It felt strange, noticing these things now, and all I wanted to do was find more little things about him, to know every freckle and mark on his body personally.

Elijah's lips spread into a wide grin as he sat back in his chair, and for a sharp, fearful moment, I thought I had spoken aloud. "Ha, you blinked. I win."

"Congratulations," I said, leaning back into my seat while

swiping my shaking fingers over my eyes. "Thanks for helping me. I've got a good leg up."

"Anytime, Bean. How's Harmony?"

I peeked at him. "Harmony?"

"Your baby sister?" He chuckled. "Is she walking yet? I haven't seen her in so long—I can't even imagine those chubby legs holding her up."

I shook my head, unable to keep the small smile off my face as I thought about her. "Not yet, but they hope soon. I want to be able to see it."

"Well, if you need someone to drive you to Biscayne Park on short notice, just text me. We'll see those first steps if it's the last thing we do." Elijah was still picking at his fingernails, trying to scrub away the last speck of glitter. It was good that he wasn't looking at me—he didn't notice my staring. "You know, Sav agreed to do the double date thing. I texted Jer and he was thinking tomorrow could be a good day. We could all just come over and do some arts and crafts together."

I was a bottle of mixed emotions; every time someone shook me, a new one surfaced. "This is news to me."

"I thought Jeremy would've called you."

A part of me really, really wanted to start gushing about Jeremy, but for the wrong reasons. But making Elijah jealous would be impossible. And my soul felt too weary to even try. "I'm sure he'll mention it tomorrow."

"Do I have to say again the part where we don't keep secrets from each other?" Elijah asked, nudging his knee against mine underneath the table.

"We keep secrets," I corrected him this time, laying my head against my folded arms. I could smell the cleaner Mom used on the wooden surface with my nose so close, and also the lingering smell of glue. "You have yours and I have mine and we don't talk about them."

Elijah didn't answer, at least not right away. From the corner of my vision, through the little sliver open near the crook of my elbow, I saw him pull his chair closer to me. Our knees connected again, but this time he didn't move his away, allowing it to rest against mine. I felt his fingers walk their way up my skin, a tickle of a touch, barely there.

"You can tell me your secrets if you want to," he said quietly, his voice soothing and soft near my ear. "I'll always want to keep them."

And then Elijah pressed his lips against the back of my head, unwittingly kissing the spot where I'd hit the shelf.

"I should get home," he said finally, pulling away from me and scooting his chair back. The pressure of his knee disappeared. "I've got to work on my sculpture for the contest. Do you want me to drive you in the morning?"

"No," I said into my arms, hoping that my muffled voice would hide the sound of tears. "I'll see you in homeroom."

Before, I'd been holding onto the anger, but now the feeling deflated. I knew the anger wasn't going to last long, and now that the strength of that emotion had fled, I felt empty. There were times between us that felt totally normal —like, almost the entire time we'd been cutting out snowflakes, things had felt *normal*. I hadn't been staring at his mouth or imagining his body heat enveloping me into a hug. We joked like normal, laughed like normal. But the quiet moments between us had my heart aching, wanting.

"See you tomorrow," Elijah said, and I saw from the

corner of my eye the shadow of him rising to his feet. He pressed his hand once against the spot between my shoulder blades before walking off, his socks silent on the wooden floors. I counted each of my breaths as I waited for the sound of the door to open. It took seven slow inhales and exhales and then Elijah was gone, leaving me with a torrent of thoughts and a hurting heart.

twelve

On my way out the door Wednesday morning, I saw Mr. Greybeck backing out of his driveway, tires slipping on the slush near the storm drain. Elijah must've already left to pick up Savannah, because his truck was gone.

I lifted my hand as Mr. Greybeck put the car into drive, but instead of continuing past me, his sedan slowed, and he rolled his window down. "Good morning, Remi," he said tiredly, blinking sleep out of his brown eyes. "A bit chilly to be walking, isn't it?"

"I take the bus," I told him, gesturing with a gloved hand. "The stop is over on Custard Street."

"Custard Street," he echoed. "Well, why don't you hop in and I'll drive you? Koski's just down the road from the school."

Mr. Greybeck worked at a place called Koski Printing and Shipping Company, packaging items and doing other kinds of factory work. Mom used to work there too, before she went back to school for interior design.

"Are you sure? I don't mind riding the bus." Okay, that was kind of a lie, but I felt bad taking him up on his offer.

His lips twitched. "Please, I know a fib when I see one. I raised two teenagers, you know. Hop in—I even have heated seats."

"Okay, fine, if you insist," I relented, hearing the locks disengage as I rounded the car.

Mr. Greybeck handled things much, much differently than Mrs. Greybeck, at least from my outsider's perspective. Though I hadn't seen either of them all that much, Mr. Greybeck still tried to carry on a semblance of normal life. Picking up extra shifts, shoveling his driveway, all sorts of things he did before everything happened. The bags underneath his eyes were dark and bruise-like, but behind them was a person, a light. His son's arrest didn't end his world, but merely rocked it. And I couldn't blame him. But after everything, he was still in there. I didn't know if I could say the same thing about Mrs. Greybeck.

As I clicked my seatbelt into place, Mr. Greybeck started down the street, a soft sort of silence hanging in the front seat. A quiet jazz song filtered out of the stereo speakers and the smell of cloves tickled my nose. "Thank you for this, Mr. G."

"How come Elijah doesn't drive you? With him using Terrence's truck, it makes sense that he would."

"He picks up Savannah," I said, glad that my voice remained neutral. The backpack in my lap was heavy, and I shifted it to my knees.

"And you don't like her?"

I turned to squint at him. "Why would you say that?"

"I raised two teenagers," he repeated, as if that answered everything.

My seat started to heat up, and with the warm air puffing in my face, I found myself needing to take my gloves off. "Savannah's nice. I think. I just don't know her very well, so I give them space." Hopefully that was enough, because no way was I going to go into detail in this conversation with him.

Mr. Greybeck made a noise in his throat, a *mmm* sound. I could see the school's roof come into view over the wintery tree line. "She's threatened by you."

Me, a threat to Savannah? I could've laughed at the idea. But the more I thought about it, the more I realized how much I wished I were. A threat. If I were a threat, that would've meant I had a chance of winning over Elijah, of having him to myself.

"She's not threatened," I said. "We just don't know each other very well."

"Have you tried getting to know her better?"

Despite his prying, it actually felt kind of nice to talk about this with him. Maybe it was the steady timbre to his voice, slow and rich, like an audiobook. "No," I said as he turned his sedan into the parking lot of the school, gripping my backpack strap. "I haven't tried. But maybe I should."

Elijah's dad pulled right next to the curb of the school and pressed the unlock button. "I'll try to persuade my son to drive you more often, though I'm not sure how effective that will be. He doesn't listen to me much these days."

"Really?" That seemed a little strange to me. Elijah was a goody two-shoes.

"I think it's the stress of Terry getting to him," he confessed, rubbing his hand over his peppery beard. "I try, you know. To talk to him, to live life the way we used to. But things are...different now. His mother hasn't been able to get over it either, not really. They're both convinced if they don't talk about it, things will be fine. And it hit Elijah the hardest. He really looked up to Terry, you know. Elijah was Terry's wingman for almost everything, and I worry about him."

Again, the mention of Elijah's brother made me feel tense, especially since it was coming from Mr. Greybeck. I couldn't think of a good response, so I just sat there, watching his face shine blue in the dashboard lights.

"Although," Mr. Greybeck went on, "it's a good thing Elijah wasn't his wingman for everything. Don't you think?"

An image raced across my vision, nearly making me dizzy. Elijah with a ski mask on, fake gun in hand. Elijah in an orange jumpsuit, handcuffs. The idea left me feeling off-kilter. "Yeah," I responded, sounding dazed. "Definitely."

I had been right last night: Jeremy broached the topic of a double date when he ambushed me at lunch.

A foot kicked my shin underneath the lunch table, effectively tearing me from the stew-and-brew glare I'd been shooting at my mashed potato casserole. "Ow," I said immediately, locking eyes with Eloise, who sat across the table, on the other side of Elijah.

She was presumably the culprit, given how bug-eyed she looked. "Hottie incoming."

It was dumb, so dumb and so obvious, but I couldn't help

it; my eyes lifted involuntarily to Elijah's. My insides jolted in surprise to find him already watching me, expressionless. I knew this was hard for him, being in the lunchroom. Since everything that happened with Terry, I knew he liked to keep his head down, and being in the center of the lunchroom was so not inconspicuous. More than anything, I wanted to ask him if he was okay, if he wanted to go to the library to eat or something, but I didn't open my mouth. Instead, I pulled away to figure out who exactly Eloise was talking about, and came face-to-face with a smiling Jeremy Rivera.

"Hey, sweet thang," he said, leaning close to me and pressing both of his palms against the table. Jeremy bent his head down and pressed his soft lips to my cheek, quick enough for the cafeteria monitor to miss it, quick enough that I didn't have time to dodge it. "I realized last night when I was thinking about you that I don't have your cell number."

I could practically feel everyone's eyes on me, probably enjoying the mortification that was no doubt evident on my face. Was that line supposed to be smooth? I had to quickly shrug on my flirting persona, but I struggled. Mindlessly flirting with Jeremy felt like a chore right now, one that felt wrong, wrong, wrong with Elijah sitting across from me.

"You know, I thought the same thing," I told him, looking into his eyes. "We should fix that, yeah?"

"Give me your cell and I'll plug me in. Did Elijah tell you about our double tonight?"

My gaze once again cut toward Elijah, but he wasn't looking at me anymore; instead, he eyed Jeremy, tightly gripping his fork. "Yeah, he said something about it." I passed Jeremy my phone, and I looked over at Savannah, on Elijah's other side. She *was* watching me, eyebrows drawn. "Where were we thinking of going? Somewhere fun?"

"It's rude to talk about plans in front of someone who's not invited, you know," Eloise said, glancing between all of us.

"You can come," I told her, almost desperate to hear her say yes. I couldn't imagine being alone with the three of them, seeing Elijah and Savannah cuddle up right in front of me. "You should come, Eloise. Totally."

Elijah nodded beside her. "The more the merrier."

Jeremy and Savannah, I noticed, kept silent.

"Ah, I'm just being bratty on purpose," Eloise said, waving a hand. "Mom and I already have plans to see a movie tonight."

"Too bad." Jeremy's voice came quick, eyes flicking to me. "So what do you want to do?"

"We should get ice cream," Elijah offered, voice sounding...off. No one else at the table seemed to notice it, but maybe that was because they didn't know him like I did. I caught the slight dip in pitch, and I also noticed the way he refused to look at me, dragging his fork through his own mashed potato casserole. "I'm really craving it."

Savannah rolled her eyes. "Are you joking? It's freezing out."

"I wouldn't mind ice cream," I said in his defense, but that wasn't the best thing to do. Immediately, Sav's eyes slid to mine, making me wish I'd bit my tongue. Her gaze wasn't negative, just blank, all emotion concealed. She could've been looking at me indifferently or silently plotting my death. I'd never know. "I mean, I could do whatever."

"You two are strange." Jeremy laughed, pulling one hand back to run across the skin of my cheek. His fingers lingered a little behind my ear. "But I'm good with ice cream if you are, Rems."

Come on, body, react to his touch. Just a little flutter or blood rush, that's all. "After school?"

"Basketball practice," he said on a sigh. "But how about six?"

"Sounds good to me. Are you going to pick me up?"

This seemed to surprise Jeremy, and he pulled away from me completely. "You can ride with Elijah, right? I mean, he *is* right across the street. I can pick up Savannah, though. She lives close."

Elijah nudged my foot underneath the table, much gentler than Savannah, the toe of his shoe practically caressing my calf. A tingle of heat prickled up my leg, and I stilled under his gaze. "I don't mind, Beanie."

Jeremy was right; it made no sense for him to drive all the way to my house to backtrack for ice cream. I found myself nodding in agreement, almost too eagerly. "See you there, then."

"Wear something nice," he teased, squeezing my shoulder. "See you later, guys."

After he'd released his grip and walked away, I could still feel the pressure on my skin through the cotton of my t-shirt. Eloise reached over and nudged my arm. "You know, Remi," she said, winking, "if your concussion gives you a headache or anything, I so wouldn't mind being your understudy for tonight."

"Eloise." Savannah gave a slight chuckle. "He's obviously into Remi. I mean, he *kissed* her."

I wanted to point out that it'd just been a kiss on the cheek, but Elijah spoke. "Over-the-moon into you," he agreed, smirking at me. All traces of weirdness were gone now, and I convinced myself that I'd imagined it. He waved his fork at me. "What does it feel like, having all your dreams come true, sweet *thang?*"

I threw a piece of creamed corn at him, which narrowly missed his ear. "You're just jealous that his hair is prettier than yours."

"His hair is not prettier than mine, thank you very much."

"If you say so."

Savannah leaned her head against Elijah's shoulder, her wheat-colored braids falling over his shirt. "Ignore him and Eloise, Remi," she said, patting Elijah's bare forearm. Her smile was soft. "I think you two are perfect for each other."

Perfect for each other. More or less the same thing that Elijah had said on Monday.

I looked down to where my cell sat in the palm of my hand, scrolling through the contacts until I found the newest addition. He'd labeled his contact Hot Stuff ;). I slipped my cell into the pocket of my cardigan, returning to glaring at my casserole as the conversation continued around me.

Mom came home early from work that day and invited me to go grocery shopping with her. It had been a while since we'd last gone, and she needed help getting everything on her list. I didn't mind. Though I had snowflakes to cut, I also wanted to make sure she got the right kind of cereal this time.

"No, not frosted puffs, just normal puffs," I said, placing the box in our full cart.

Mom made a face. "Why would you want normal puffs? They're tasteless."

"They're healthier for you."

Our cart creaked as we rolled down the aisle, a constant noise that ratcheted up my annoyance. Why did all the carts seem to squeak? Didn't anyone maintain ever them? I mean, almost every time we came here, we got a cart that sounded like a wheel was about to pop off. What was—

Someone's cart turned the corner of the aisle quickly, its front ramming into ours and rattling our contents. "Excuse me," Mom said politely, drawing the handle back. "I wasn't watching—Kathleen?"

After everything that'd happened in the Greybeck household, I half-expected Mrs. Greybeck to look rundown. Lines around her mouth, circles under her eyes. Hair undone, tangled. But looking at her now, one would think nothing had happened. I'd never have guessed that her son sat in prison.

"Hello," she said, her voice sounding the same as it always had. Still light, still soft. "Sorry, I'm in a bit of a rush."

"Everything okay?" Mom asked, and I could hear the undercurrent of concern in her voice. "I haven't heard from you in a couple weeks."

"Oh, no, everything's fine. Just a million things to do, not enough time to do them." Mrs. Greybeck looked between us as she angled her cart away, offering a farewell smile. "Grab some great deals, you two."

And with that, she hurried and wheeled away.

It took Mom a moment to recover from the encounter, and I suspected it bothered her more than she let on. "Let's keep going. What's next on the list?"

I felt bad for her, watching her try to feign nonchalance. Mrs. Greybeck had been Mom's best friend; they had done everything together. Now that she was gone and Dad was gone, she only had me. Which sucked on my end of things, because I was the one always getting babied.

I looked at the piece of paper in my hands. "Cottage cheese."

Jeremy's request that I "wear something nice" wasn't going to singlehandedly influence my outfit, but I did want to look at least somewhat put-together for tonight. Maybe if I looked pretty enough, Elijah would open his eyes and see what he was missing.

Hey, a girl could dream.

Mom poked her head through the crack in my bedroom door mid-way through me getting ready. "What are you getting dolled up for?"

"I've got a date," I said, glancing over my makeup supplies. "Sorry, I should've told you earlier. Elijah's picking me up soon."

"Elijah?" she demanded with wide eyes, coming into my room to sit on my bed. I sat at my desk, using a compact mirror to apply a wave of eyeshadow. "I—you—you're going on a date with Elijah?"

"Uh-huh," I mumbled, contorting my features to make my skin taut. "We're going to get ice cream."

She didn't say anything for a moment. "I guess I didn't realize you liked him like that, sweetie. Why didn't you tell me?"

I jerked in my seat, my eyeshadow brush slipping and dotting bronze near my temple. "Mom! We're not *together*. We're going on a *double date* together. Like, we each have dates."

But man, wasn't that a thought? Elijah and me sharing a booth, my head tipping onto his shoulder, his laughter shivering its way down the length of my spine. His hand finding my knee underneath the table, giving it a reassuring squeeze.

"Oh, darling, that makes so much more sense." Mom laughed from where she sat. "I couldn't even comprehend the idea."

I reached for a makeup remover wipe but hesitated before lifting it, turning in my seat to face her. "Would it be so bad? Elijah and me...together?"

Stupid, stupid, stupid. Why would I even say something like that? It was like I held a giant neon sign that read, I LOVE MY BEST FRIEND. I'M READY FOR AN AWKWARD TALK, MOM. Because no doubt she'd say, "it's not bad if it's what your heart truly desires" or something sappy like that. Or maybe she'd discourage me, tell me some friendships were meant to stay platonic.

I thought about her and Dad, how they would've been better off staying just friends. They wouldn't have had me, of course, but they wouldn't have had to go through the whole separation. For them, getting together had been the beginning of their end.

"It's hard to think about, isn't it?" Mom said, pulling me from my thoughts. Her expression was more thoughtful than negative, as if she were really trying to picture it. "Things would really be different. I wouldn't have to worry about you finding someone who puts you first. But I think that family's got a lot of baggage."

"Baggage? You mean Terry." I tried not to sound too defensive. "It was a crappy thing that happened, but that's on Terry. Elijah's handling it well."

"Is he?"

I turned back to the mirror to wipe off the eyeshadow, swiping at my skin irritably. "What's that supposed to mean?"

"Sometimes it's hard to come to terms with someone you love making a bad choice," she said slowly. "I'm not sure if he's done that yet. Come to terms with it."

"Okay, Mom," I said, wishing she'd stop talking about Elijah and Terry. "You majored in interior design, remember? Not psychology."

She laughed a little, and I heard my bed creak as she rose to her feet. "You're right, you're right. You know, I'm glad you're going with Elijah. He'll keep whoever this boy is in check." Mom's hands came down on the tops of my shoulders and squeezed. "I'm glad you have him."

"Yeah." I put the wipe down and started to redo my eyeshadow, that sickly feeling in my stomach only growing larger. "Me too."

lijah angled his truck in front of my house at five-fifty, honking his horn. I hurried out across the snow-covered lawn, careful not to slip on the cobblestone walkway. I couldn't bring myself to look up and meet his gaze, the conversation with Mom still fresh in my head. I rounded the front of the truck to the passenger side without glancing up, telling myself to try to be cool.

A second before I reached for the door handle, I realized someone already sat in the seat, staring at me through the glass. *Savannah.* Wasn't she supposed to be riding with Jeremy?

Awkwardly, I pulled open the backseat door. "Thanks for picking me up," I said in an uncomfortable greeting, closing the door behind me. "It would've been a long walk."

Elijah didn't say anything, just nodded as he drove away from the curb. I watched the back of his head, waiting for him to speak or turn, but he did neither.

Savannah turned, though. "I hope it's okay that I took

shotgun," she said pleasantly, tucking a piece of hair behind her ear. "I just figured since you had it last time—"

"It's not a big deal," I interrupted. "Besides, the girlfriend should always get shotgun."

"I completely agree," she said at once, gaze tightening as she grinned. Then she tipped her chin toward Elijah. "Don't you think so?"

Elijah passed her a look as he slowed for a stop sign, but didn't answer.

O-kayyy. I'd definitely missed something. Awkward. "I'll text Jer and tell him that we're on our way," I said to no one in particular, pulling my cell from my pocket. There was a picture message from Dad. A selfie, horrifyingly enough, but baby Harmony was also in the frame. He had her tucked against his side, her wide eyes gazing at the phone screen. He'd added the text, She has your eyes.

Me: Don't put her down until Saturday. If I miss those first steps, I'm going to be livid.

Dad: Won't be hard. Girl likes her cuddle time. See you Sat.

And then he quickly typed back, Love you.

After that, I shot a quick text to Jeremy. We enjoyed the rest of the car ride in silence, with tension so thick that I almost had the desire to roll down my window. Were they fighting? Was that why there was a cold silence? Or was it me?

I pulled my jacket sleeves over my fingertips, playing with the seam as Elijah angled the truck into Freezing Fred's parking lot. It felt strange to think that Elijah and I had been here only a week ago, sitting in a cracked booth of our own, talking and joking like normal. Only a week ago that we'd kissed.

Sav opened her door, allowing the winter air to sweep in. "This feels wrong," she said, voice carrying as I slipped out. "Ice cream in January. It should be illegal."

"That's what I said at first," I told her, reaching my hand back to readjust my bun. "But it comes in handy when you're craving a blue goo ice cream cone around Valentine's Day."

From the other side of Savannah, Elijah said, "Yeah, that's right. Appreciate my quirks."

"Your strange quirks," Savannah scoffed. "First pottery, now ice cream in January. What's next?"

It was quick, so quick that I wouldn't have noticed it if I hadn't known him inside and out, but I watched as Elijah's features shifted. I knew immediately why—pottery wasn't a quirk of his. It was basically *who* he was. It made me look at Savannah differently, unsure.

Standing next to her, I realized yet again just how similar we looked. Blonde hair, dark eyes, almost the same height. She was thinner than I was, more definition to her cheekbones and jawline, but the similarities were still there. An outsider probably could've guessed we were sisters.

You shouldn't be comparing in the first place, idiot. You're literally walking into a date.

Gosh, I hated when my thoughts were right.

"I don't see his car," Savannah said as Elijah grabbed the parlor's door, already reaching for the zipper on her coat. "You should text him that we're here."

A part of me stiffened as I walked past Elijah, mostly because if this were like old times, he would've taken the opportunity to poke or tickle me. Or maybe I would've reached out to pinch him. But now we both kept our hands to ourselves. Instead of reaching for him, I reached for my cell.

Me: We're here. No rush.

Jeremy (yeah, I definitely changed that contact name as quickly as I could): K. Almost there.

"He says he's on his way," I told them, shaking off my own coat. The inside of the ice cream shop was the perfect temperature, almost like I could close my eyes and imagine it being summer outside. "We could probably order without him, right?"

Savannah's eyes were narrowed on me. "Um, isn't that rude?"

"I bet he wouldn't care," Elijah said, stuffing his hands into his own jacket pockets, already heading toward the counter. "You girls do what you want, but I want ice cream."

We watched as he walked away from us, not even glancing back to see if we were following. "Is everything okay?" I asked her quietly.

Savannah lifted her chin, not meeting my eyes. "Of course. I'm going to go pick out a flavor. Maybe you should wait for Jeremy, since *he* is your date and all."

She walked away from me with her hips swinging, leaving me wondering why she'd emphasized *he*. But I did take her hint. I made my way to where Elijah and I normally sat when we came here and slid into the booth, making sure to give Elijah and Savannah the cracked one. Perfectly split down the center, forcing a space to separate them.

I fluffed my bangs a bit, readjusting my posture. Jeremy would be here any minute, but I wanted to seem as nonchalant as possible. As if I weren't watching Elijah and Savannah standing in line for ice cream.

We weren't the only people in here, surprisingly enough, so Elijah and Savannah were waiting in line, not speaking. She had looped her arm through his, his hand firmly in his pocket, but he seemed stiff. Like his bones had been replaced with lead.

Or he seemed stiff until he removed his hand from his pocket and wrapped it around Savannah's shoulders.

I looked down at the tabletop, tapping my fingernails along the surface, trying to distract myself.

The door chimed as it opened, and Jeremy sauntered through, his varsity jacket a loud shock of blue and yellow covering his torso. He scanned the place, the broken booths and the mismatched floor tiles. "Interesting," he said with a frown. "Not as impressive as Dizzy's."

"But unlike Dizzy's, Fred's is open all year," Elijah said from where he stood in line. "And without the chalky freezer burn taste."

Jeremy's eyes flitted right past him to find me alone at the booth, and he gave a half-tipped smile. "Your hair looks pretty pulled back like that," he said in greeting, coming close enough to run his fingers over my bangs, ruffling them up. "I like it."

"Thanks. Should we get in line?"

Jeremy stepped away from the mouth of the booth and allowed me to pass. "How's your head?"

"Better. Way better. The headaches are pretty much gone, except for when I wake up." Which was really great, though I wondered when everything would stop completely.

"I'm really sorry about my evil porch," he said, rubbing a hand down the edge of his bicep. "Guess you were falling for me a little early, huh?"

Did he seriously just say that? Trying hard not to outwardly cringe, I glanced at the menu that hung over the display of hand-dipped ice creams. Elijah ordered his usual—soft-serve chocolate on a cone—and the girl behind the counter was in the process of getting whatever Savannah had ordered.

"What sounds good?" I asked Jeremy.

"I'm thinking a slushy or something like that. How about you?"

"I usually order a vanilla raspberry swirl in a cup."

Jeremy fished his wallet from his pocket. "I'm not much of an ice cream guy. Slushies are really good, though."

The girl handed Savannah her cone stuck in a plastic cup and turned to Jeremy and me. He ordered for me, a small when I usually got a large, pulling out a ten. "You can keep the change," he said to the girl, winking as she took the bill from him. Her cheeks pinked, and she went to work getting our orders together. I didn't miss that she made his first.

"So." He drew the word out, wavering on his feet as we waited. "Are you excited that this semester is almost over?"

"Yeah." *Aaand we're talking about school. Probably not a great sign.* "Only one semester left before graduation." You know, hopefully.

"Here you go." The girl offered the slushy to Jeremy before turning to me. "What did you order again?"

Jeremy slipped the straw between his lips. "I'll meet you at the booth," he said around the plastic.

He walked off toward where Elijah and Savannah were already seated, and I watched as the girl began to dispense my ice cream. *You can do this, Remi. Really. You can. Your flight sense is only reacting because this is out of your comfort zone. You can do this.* I shook out the tension in my fingers, popping my knuckles. If Elijah had heard it, he would've swatted at me, hating the sound.

After getting my order, I went back to where they sat and slid into the booth beside Jeremy, his arm almost immediately snaking around my neck and pulling me closer to him. Savannah glanced at my cup with disdain. "Is that stuff any good? Always seems so syrupy to me."

"It's good." I dragged my spoon through the edge of one of the swirls, using the moment of silence to take a nice big spoonful. The rush of coolness crashed through my senses, creeping into my brain. "Maybe I just like a lot of syrup."

"Twins," Jeremy said as he knocked his large slushy against mine. "Elijah, you seem to be the only boring one. Plain ol' chocolate?"

Elijah looked really interested in his ice cream cone. "Classic, I think you mean."

"Jeremy, how's the basketball season going?" Savannah asked, stabbing at her own ice cream with a spoon. "I haven't been able to get to many games this year. Not with student council eating up my time."

"Oh, it's going great. At least my season is. The team's, eh...we've been close in most of our games, but the other players let it slip through their fingers during the last half." His eyes slipped to mine. "How come you never played sports, Remi?"

Uh, had he forgotten that past conversation? I made a face as I took in a giant spoonful of ice cream and spoke around it. "Never liked them."

"That's gross, Remi." Savannah's features screwed up. "Don't talk with your mouth full."

I had the biggest urge to just open my mouth to let her see the ice cream melting on my tongue, but amazingly, I resisted. And swallowed. "Sorry. But sports weren't my thing. I played when I was little, but that's it."

"A bummer," Jeremy said, pulling me closer. "I would've loved watching you."

Elijah snorted at that, biting on the corner of his lip. I tried to meet his eyes to see what he was thinking—if I could just look him in the eye, I'd be able to tell—but he wouldn't glance up. He wouldn't lift his eyes to mine, not even for a millisecond.

"You never played sports either, right, Eli?"

I closed my eyes briefly. Another thing we'd talked about —Elijah's nickname. I'd told him how Elijah didn't like it, only liked it when I said it, but he didn't seem to have listened to that, either.

A plastic-looking smile played at Elijah's mouth. "Nope. My sports career began and ended with Remi breaking my nose."

"What? You broke his nose, Rem?"

I winced at the memory. "Yeah. Gosh, Elijah, do you remember how much blood gushed from your face that day? I thought you were going to die."

His lips twitched as he shook his head. "It was like we

were filming a horror flick. Your mom about had a heart attack."

"Okay," Savannah said quickly, glancing at each of us. "Let's stop. All the blood talk is ruining my appetite."

A silence fell over the table at that, and each of us studied our respective ice creams. Jeremy took a pull from his straw, the clogging noise almost obnoxiously loud. He smacked his lips together. "Did Terry ever break any bones?"

Elijah's gaze lifted as I pulled in a sharp breath. "What?" he asked.

Jeremy leaned forward on the table, dropping his arm and propping it against the top. "Did your brother ever break any bones? I remember he played football, didn't he? Football's a tough sport to play without getting any injuries. Any broken legs or arms or anything?"

I tried to stop him. "Jeremy—"

"No, he didn't break any bones," Elijah replied in a tone I never would've expected. Light and airy, as if he were mentioning the weather or something boring. Not at all the tone he'd used with me when we were shopping. The fact that he was talking to Jeremy so nonchalantly made my stomach drop. "At least, not that I can remember."

Savannah's eyes were wide as she stared down at her ice cream cup, as if afraid to look anywhere else.

"About Terry," Jeremy went on, obviously not reading the room. "Is it true that he robbed two gas stations in one night? At *gunpoint*? Word is they had hostages and everything. Someone put in an anonymous tip, or at least that's the rumor. That's what got them caught."

Only one word could describe Elijah's expression: scary. Scary calm. Scary blank. Jeremy's words conjured an image of Terry in my mind, and I realized I hadn't allowed myself to really think about him. Not really. His hair wasn't blond like Elijah's, but brown, the color of tree bark. They had the same dark eyes, though, but Terry's weren't nearly as luminous. How had he gotten himself into that situation? I remembered him hanging out with a strange crowd, but never in a million years would I have thought he'd be an accomplice to a robbery.

Terry had been a good kid. Kept his head down, helped others out, had great grades. He'd been kind, helpful.

Just like Elijah.

I cleared my throat, realizing that Jeremy still looked across the table and Elijah still looked back, neither one of them speaking. "Jer," I said, jumping on the first thought that came into my mind to defuse the situation. "Switch. You try mine, I'll try yours." I pushed my cup toward him as I grabbed ahold of his blue straw, closing my mouth over it and drinking.

Jeremy lifted my spoon, effectively distracted. "Sounds unsanitary," he muttered, but took a bite of my ice cream.

A golden light hung just over the top of our booth, casting Elijah's face into a shadow when he leaned back into his seat, his free hand running through his hair. Something washed across his expression, something dark and sharp, but it was quickly masked. The only clue that it'd been there was a fine line between his light eyebrows. His eyes focused on my cup of ice cream, and he never answered Jeremy's question.

We talked at the table a little longer, avoiding any and all topics of conversation that could've led back to Terry. Not that Elijah talked much after that. After I'd handed Jeremy back his drink, Elijah fell silent, licking his ice cream slow enough for it to melt down the cone.

When we were all finished, it was determined that Savannah would ride home with Jeremy, since they lived on the same side of town, and I'd catch a ride back with Elijah.

It had started snowing a bit while we were inside Fred's—either that or the wind was just pushing around loose snowflakes. The little crystals were swirling in the air and falling onto the ground, like they were trapped inside a snow globe. I wanted to stick out my tongue and try to catch one, but they weren't falling steadily enough.

Jeremy wrapped an arm around my waist from behind, catching me before I got too close to Elijah's truck. "We didn't get to talk too much tonight," he said with a pouty face, his bottom lip pushed out. "I would've driven you home, but I don't feel like driving all the way to Grisham Street. Especially since it's starting to snow."

The "snow" was just flurries, but I didn't say anything. "Yeah, I understand."

When Jeremy tugged me even closer, I realized that he was about to kiss me. I had a split-second window to either let it happen or pull away. It wouldn't have been a bad thing, kissing Jeremy. I'd been waiting for a long time for this opportunity, to kiss my long-standing crush. But even though all of that was true, I found myself tipping my head at the last second, his lips connecting with the edge of my cheek. When he pulled back, I tried not to see if there was disappointment on his face.

"I'll see you tomorrow, Remi."

I untangled myself from his arms, finding Elijah watching us just a few steps away. Savannah tried to hug him goodbye. "Pick me up tomorrow morning?" she asked him.

Elijah nodded, leaning away from her expectant lips. Despite the horribleness of it, I couldn't help but fantasize what him not kissing her goodbye could've meant. "I'll be there at my normal time."

Savannah joined Jeremy at his car while Elijah and I walked the rest of the way to his truck. He didn't look at me or say anything, and I glanced up at the sky, wishing the snow would fall heavier.

My boots caught on a patch of ice in the parking lot, one foot slipping in front of the other. I put my arms out to try and hold my balance, wavering as I almost face-planted into the frozen asphalt. At the last second, Elijah grabbed ahold of my upper arm, pulling me against him.

"Whoa," I gasped, clutching at the edge of his jacket for support. The denim felt stiff and cold. "Look at me. I'm just determined to crack my head open."

"No kidding," Elijah got out, swallowing, and I looked up to meet his gaze. I'd looked at Elijah for years and years, but never before did a rush of energy zip through me when our gazes locked. A gust of winter wind tangled its fingers through his hair, brushing his golden locks across his eyes. *I could stay here forever in his warm arms, just in this moment.*

On a foreign impulse, I brushed the hair out of his face, his skin warm underneath my fingertips.

A strange look flashed across Elijah's eyes and he released me. Without allowing a word or a second to pass, he started toward his truck, leaving me staring after him. It took me a moment to get my feet moving, and my heart beat much faster. How did those situations just keep happening?

Thankfully, Jeremy's car was already pulling out of the lot. They wouldn't have seen us.

I made it to the door—arms out wide to be extra careful and keep my balance—and settled in as Elijah switched the gear from park to drive. The glass fogged slightly from the air that pumped from the vents, still holding a chill as the engine warmed up.

Elijah lapsed into the same silence he had in the ice cream shop as we drove home, the glare of his headlights catching the falling snow, making it almost seem like we were traveling through time. The drive back to our street lasted less than ten minutes, but I found myself wishing it were longer, even though we weren't speaking. I didn't want the ride to end.

Until Elijah finally opened his mouth. "I know I've never asked, but I would appreciate it if you don't talk to your boyfriends about my brother."

"Wait, what?" My eyebrows slammed together. "Boyfriends? What are you talking about?"

"I know Jeremy loves gossip, but it's none of his business."

"He didn't mean anything," I said, turning in my seat to face him fully. Even in the dim light, I could tell his face was flushed. "And I don't talk to anyone about Terry, Elijah. Ever. I don't even know anything to talk about it."

Elijah grew quiet again, choosing his words. He had his one hand resting on the gear shifter, the other loosely clutching the wheel, but nothing about his posture seemed relaxed. "Just forget it."

The anger in the cab was so palpable that I could hardly breathe around it, the pinching in my chest almost painful. Gone was the beautiful feeling from a moment ago, when I'd been in Elijah's arms, staring into his eyes. Long gone. "You know, Terry isn't dead, Elijah."

"Do you seriously think I don't know that?"

I winced at his sharp tone, surprised it had come from him. "He made a mistake. It's okay to talk about him like he's a person who screwed up because he *is* a person who screwed up."

A muscle in his jaw ticked. "You don't know anything, Remi."

"You're right. I don't, because *you* don't talk to me about him. You say we don't keep secrets? Well, then tell me!" My voice shook as it rose. I wanted him to just break open and spill out all his emotions and feelings, but Elijah didn't do that. He shoved things down, pushed things away, didn't deal with them. He was like me. And Mom had been right—he really should be talking, because it was only a matter of time before it spewed out. "I'm not Savannah, Elijah. I'm not going to judge you or pretend to listen, or—"

"This isn't about Savannah." Elijah cut me off, taking a sharp turn onto our street. "This is about us. No, it's about you. You're a—a bad influence on me."

I blinked at him, brows drawing together. "Uh, what?"

"You heard me," he said, voice growing with strength and heat. "A bad influence. Let's take last Thursday, for example. Me shopping with you—did you know that that really bothered Savannah? She didn't like the fact that I went underwear shopping with you."

"We weren't underwear shopping," I protested. "I just wandered over there and you followed—that hardly counts as exclusive panty shopping."

"And asking me to go to that party, to sneak out? Or even that stupid art project. Remi, I cheated for you. I *lied* to my favorite teacher for you. I faked a project to boost your grade and didn't think twice about it. It was just second nature."

I gaped at him, a tickle of pain lancing through me. How could he say those things? I mean, fine, yes, I did persuade him to go out, but I never asked him to turn in that project for me. But was he right? Had I influenced him somehow into doing it for me? Was I a bad influence? "Elijah—"

But he wasn't finished. "My brother hung out around the wrong crowd, and look where it got him. That's what happens when you're around the wrong people. You make dumb choices that have severe consequences."

"And you're comparing me to those people your brother hung out with?" I demanded, feeling the burn of tears in the back of my throat. His anger, fully directed at me, was not something I'd dealt with before. Looking at it now, square in the face, made me want to run and hide. "You're comparing me to *criminals*. How could you—how could you even *say* that?"

Elijah stomped on the brake just in front of my house, and the car slid to a stop after a second of hesitation. I jarred in my seat, my seatbelt holding me back. "I'm not in the right frame of mind to keep talking." Elijah leaned across from me and reached out, his hand closing around the door handle, popping it open. Winter air swept in. "I'll see you tomorrow."

"Elijah." He didn't even glance my way, just stared

straight ahead. A clear dismissal. *One last look, please. Just let us work this out, Elijah.*

But he didn't look, and he didn't speak again. After a second of strained silence, I climbed out of the cab of the truck and found my footing on the ground.

Almost immediately after I shut the door, he pulled away from the curb, driving down to round the end of the cul-de-sac. He eased the truck into his driveway and didn't stop for a moment to glance back at me. In a matter of seconds, he was out of his truck and shutting his front door, not seeing me standing in the snow, staring after him.

I slammed the door shut, all but flinging off my boots at the back mat and letting them crash against the wall. My toes caught on one of the three shoe racks by the door and I yelped, kicking it out of my way with a giant clatter.

Mom rushed over with a bowl of salad in her hand, looking at me with a confused expression. "What in the world?"

"Your stupid shoe racks," I said through gritted teeth, hoping the pain would subside in my toes. "You have so much junk in this house, it's ridiculous!"

Mom's eyes widened. "Whoa. Did something happen tonight?"

"I don't want to talk about it."

She set her fork down in her bowl. "Why not, Remi? What happened?"

"Mom—"

"I'm your mother, you know, but I can be your best friend right now. You can tell me anything."

"You're never going to stop. Right?" I demanded in exasperation. "You're never going to stop babying me. I'm almost eighteen and you're still cooing over me straining my eyes or going out with friends. I'm almost an adult, and you treat me like I'm ten."

Mom blinked at me, clearly shocked by my outburst, and I couldn't blame her. Rarely did I raise my voice, and *never* at her. But everything had been bottled up for too long. Her hand hung half outstretched, as if she'd been reaching for me. "That's what a mother does, Remi. And a mother also reminds her children that no matter how bad of a day they've had, they do not have the right to talk to people the way you're talking to me." She took a step closer. "I just want to hear more about your day, Remi. More about *you*."

I threw my hands up. "I need my space! I don't need kisses on my forehead or you coddling me. I don't need you knocking on my door and in my business. Gosh, sometimes I wish I wasn't the only person in your life so I wouldn't be smothered so much!"

Mom's face fell from the guarded, slightly angry expression she'd been wearing to something more...pained, as if I'd stuck a pin in her side. But it only lasted for a second before she quickly composed a bland expression. "An adult, huh?" She let out a harsh breath. "You're right. Maybe I need to find someone else to *coddle*." And she stomped from the room, leaving her half-eaten salad on the table.

I wanted to scream and scream at the top of my lungs.

Did everyone have to be so infuriating at the same time? Why did they all have to choose now to be so selfish?

Just like that, I'd managed to push away two of the most important people in my life. Fantastic.

I arrived at school thirty minutes late and with a body heat of probably negative forty.

Okay, well, not really. But despite the fact that this morning had held the promises of snow/sleet/freezing temperatures, Greenville High still decided to have school, and the stupid school bus had come and gone without taking me with it. That could've been because I had overslept— Mom didn't poke her head in to make sure I woke up like she normally did—and it took an extra fifteen minutes for my sleep-ridden ears to make sense of the alarm blaring at my bedside.

My last hope was Elijah—even though we were fighting, I hoped that whatever happened last night could blow over. But I'd looked out my window to find his truck gone from its driveway.

So now I was frozen *and* pissed. Not a cool combination.

My teeth chattered as my boots slipped across the school's linoleum floor, my stiff fingers clutching an ugly yellow excuse slip. Technically, it should've been a tardy slip, but I told the secretary that I'd had an early doctor's appointment and forgot my doctor's note in my mom's car. The lie came out so smoothly that it startled me, but she didn't bat an eye.

There weren't many people wandering the halls since first period was still in session, though it was almost over. I took my time getting to my locker, stewing with each step. My frozen fingers were starting to thaw with the temperature of my frustration, and I could even feel my features screw up. Once in front of the metal locker, I tugged my scarf from my neck, shoving it inside.

"Whoa, what's got your panties in a twist?" Eloise came alongside the open door of my locker, peering at me around it. She'd pulled her hair into two buns on top of her head with sparkly ties keeping them in place. "It's rare that I see you this angry, except when they run out of those good cookies in the vending machine."

"Don't ask," I said through gritted teeth, hooking up my coat, "because I am so not in the mood. What are you doing out of class, anyway?"

Eloise lifted a wooden square with a piece of red ribbon slipped through a notch at the top, the letters *BP* engraved on the surface. She waved it back and forth. "Bathroom pass. I saw you walk past Mrs. Galvery's door with your coat on. I thought you were more interesting than sonnets."

"I overslept." *My mom didn't wake me because I'm apparently a horrible daughter; Elijah hates me because I'm apparently a horrible friend.* "I had to walk. In the freaking snow."

"*That's* why your nose is so red. I wondered why you were going for a weird Rudolph look." I turned my eyes to her, and she took a large step back, raising her palms. "Sorry."

"Have you seen Elijah this morning?"

Honestly, I didn't know why I asked. Maybe because I hoped he looked miserable this morning, his outsides matching my insides.

"I haven't looked. How did your date go last night?"

It was a perfectly reasonable question, but it only intensified my annoyance. "What are you doing after school today? Let's go shopping and I'll tell you then."

Eloise tapped her nails against the bathroom pass. "You know, I did need to get some new bras. My sister keeps stealing mine, even though we are *so* not the same size." She shoved her chest out. "I should get back before Mrs. Galvery decides to come find me, though."

"I've got to get to history before the ladies in the office call down," I said as she backed away, and shut my locker door. A part of me didn't even want to go to the last bit of first hour because I knew Elijah would be there. I'd have to sit right next to him. At least we were still working through our documentary, so it gave us a reason to be quiet.

As I made my way to my class, I tried to school my features into a mask of blankness, along with an icy touch of indifference. Whether the mask would stay in place once I saw him, though, was a whole other story. Drawing in a deep breath, I cracked the door open, entering the dark room.

It took my eyes a minute to adjust, but when I saw our assigned seats, I found two empty spaces, both mine and his.

Elijah never showed to homeroom, leaving me fuming the rest of the time. He didn't have the audacity to call in sick, either, because when I asked Mrs. Maples if there were any notes I could drop off to Elijah, she told me, "Oh, he was down in the art room this period, not home sick."

How exactly he'd gotten out of history to go to art was beyond me—did all the teachers seriously have a sweet spot for him?—but it only made me angrier. However he'd done it, he'd skipped history so he wouldn't have to see me.

By lunch, I was out for blood.

In my rush to get to school, I'd had no time to pack my lunch, so I made my way to the lunch line. The lunch trays were set out just before the line started, and I swiped one up as I passed.

"Hey."

I looked up at the figure behind me and met a set of hazel eyes. "Hey, yourself."

Jeremy grabbed a lunch tray and twirled it between his fingers, nudging me with his elbow. "You didn't text me last night."

I opened my mouth before I found out a good defense but realized there really wasn't one. "You're right, I didn't." Not like he texted me either.

"I'm sorry I brought up Terry," he said under his breath, glancing at the kids who were standing in front of us. At least he was trying to be discreet now. "That was kind of messed up to do."

"You don't need to apologize to me," I said, catching his eye. "Elijah, though, would probably appreciate it." *And maybe that would fix whatever happened between us last night.* Although even I knew that an apology from Jeremy wasn't going to erase what had been said. Was Elijah right? I mean, sure, I asked him to go shopping with me and encouraged him to go to the party with me, but wasn't that what friends did? Live life together?

The idea of us fighting had my insides bound in a knot so tight that I could hardly stand upright. We never fought, at least not over things as serious as this. It left me feeling off-kilter. Lately, things between us were not what they should've been. I couldn't stop thinking about him; he was angry with me. Everything felt like it was unraveling.

Jeremy shrugged. "I tried to, but he didn't seem to buy into it. He said some stuff, actually."

I stepped forward in the moving lunch line. "You talked to him? What did he say?"

"He said that you weren't into me, that last night showed you that. It doesn't matter." He shook his head. "That's why I wanted to apologize and talk to you. I didn't know where you stood. Where *we* stood."

The line moved forward again, but I didn't; I stared at Jeremy, my thoughts whirring at a fast pace. He was still talking, his mouth moving, but my brain couldn't process all the words. "What do you think?" he finished, and I nodded fast.

"Good, yeah. Excuse me." I pressed my tray into Jeremy's chest and moved out of line, heading straight for our usual table. I heard him call after me, but I didn't stop. Apparently, things *hadn't* cooled off after last night, but I wasn't going to let it fester any further. "Never minds" and "forget its" weren't going to fly. We were going to talk this out. Right now.

I found the lunch table, but Elijah was missing from it.

Savannah and Eloise were there, but no green backpack and no blond boy.

"Where is he?" I demanded as I got close, interrupting the silence of the table, trying to keep my voice even and low. Both of their heads swiveled toward me, along with some from nearby tables. "Where's Elijah?"

"I'm not supposed to tell you," Savannah said, nose upturned, the words spoken to her packed lunchbox. "I don't know what happened between you two yesterday, but he told me not to ask."

"Screw that," I said, wanting to throttle her, to evoke some sort of emotion from her. It seemed like she was more concerned with not stepping on anyone's toes, and right now, that was the only thing I wanted to do. "Where is he?"

"When third period ended," Eloise said, a little wide-eyed from the severity of my tone, "he didn't pack his stuff or clean up his station."

She'd barely gotten her words out before I turned on my heel and stalked toward the doors of the cafeteria, pushing them wide and slipping out into the hall. Our cafeteria monitor called after me, but I didn't stop or slow. I knew Elijah's class schedule by heart, and I knew exactly where to find him.

He wasn't at the pottery wheel when I got to the art room but washing his hands at the sink. The sound of running water threatened to soothe my mood, but I clenched my fists tightly, giving over to my anger.

"What is your problem?" I demanded as I stepped over the threshold, striding up to him. I forced all those feelings of affection down, channeling the anger needed for confrontation. "You can be pissed at me all you want, but don't take it out on Jeremy."

"Don't take it out on Jeremy," he muttered to himself, and then louder, "because Jeremy is so undeserving of what I said."

"He told me that you said I didn't like him."

"You don't."

I flinched. "What?"

Elijah grabbed a paper towel from the dispenser and mopped off the water before heading to where his backpack lay on one of the tables. "You don't like him. Don't give me angry eyes, because I'm right."

"Y-You're *not* right!" I sputtered after him, my cheeks heating up. "I do like him. A lot, in fact."

He didn't look at me as he started to pack his bag. "Is that why you dodged his kiss last night as if his lips were on fire?" he asked, voice condescending. "And yesterday, at the lunch table?"

"I was unprepared for it!" I drew in a shaky breath. "You know what, you have no right. No right to yell at me and then stick your nose in my business."

Elijah didn't say anything to that, but it wasn't because he lacked words. The bored expression on his face was a sure sign of his annoyance.

Elijah moved to brush past me, pulling his backpack up over his shoulder. I shot my hand out and grabbed his upper arm, dragging him to a halt.

"What is your problem?" I asked again, staring into his eyes as if my gaze alone would break the wall he'd built between us. "Is this seriously all about Jeremy asking about Terry last night?"

"Jeremy's not good enough for you," he said, glaring past me.

Okay, *not* what I'd been expecting him to say. "Are you doubting your matchmaking abilities?"

Elijah's gaze grew stonier. "Move, Remi."

Remi. Not Beanie. That was how I knew something truly was up. "Make me." I scanned his eyes again. "Answer me. Is this about Terry?"

"Just forget it."

I'm going to smack him. "How can I forget that you said I was a bad influence?"

I hadn't spoken with savagery, but my words made him wince, and whatever satisfaction I thought I'd feel at seeing him hurt was absent. The darkness in his eyes seemed to grow exponentially. "I shouldn't have said that."

"Yeah, no kidding. I never made you do anything, Eli. I would never make you do anything. Those were your choices." I squeezed his arm, pressing closer. I could feel his body heat, and wondered if he could feel mine; our breath mixed. "What did I do that made you so angry? You skipped first hour to avoid me, didn't you?"

"Mrs. Keller asked me to help her class of freshmen with their sculpting technique." He still wouldn't look at me.

Yeah, I sincerely doubted that Mrs. Keller had asked him; he probably jumped to volunteer. "Tell me what's going on between us so I can fix it," I told him, my voice dropping to a whisper. "It's me. It's just me. You can talk to me."

I had never wanted so badly to go back to the way things

were before our kiss. Sure, he hadn't realized it was me, but he still felt its effects. Everything jumbled now. Before the kiss, Elijah and I had never fought, never even dreamed of it. Our communication had been near flawless. But now here we were, fighting, neither of us able to read the other's mind.

Something between us cracked at that moment, like a window taking one too many stones, a fine fissure spreading from the bottom to the top. It didn't shatter, but it was close. Elijah's chest moved up and down, his sweater pressed against my hoodie, and those brown eyes just locked to mine as if compelled.

Neither of us moved for what felt like forever, and my heart started to realize that the distance between us was minimal. A haze blanketed my thoughts, and I couldn't do anything but stare.

And then— "That's just it," he said with a soft sigh, a resigned sound. "It's *you*."

Elijah pulled his arm from mine, not rough enough to be jarring but firmly enough that I released him.

"What's that supposed to mean?" I demanded as he strode past. My anger rose to a crescendo with a brilliant, vicious clang. "Elijah!"

But he didn't answer, and he didn't turn around.

I moved to storm after him into the hallway, ready to dig my demon claws into his back and keep him from walking away.

Just as I exited the art room, someone stepped in front of me, blocking my path. Taking a startled step back, I looked up, locking eyes with Principal Martinez. The glare she gave me was sharp and piercing.

At first, I didn't realize why she'd be glaring at me—was she just mad that I was yelling in the halls?—until I saw the secretary I'd signed in with this morning at her side. And she didn't look happy either.

Crap.

etention.

Two weeks' worth. Turned out Mrs. Secretary hadn't signed my excused pass as blindly as I'd thought. She called Mom after I left the office, who told her that I did not, in fact, have a doctor's appointment that morning. Lying and receiving my fifth tardy equaled two weeks' worth of detention.

It wasn't as horrible as it sounded. Two weeks of detention was only four days—two Tuesdays and two Thursdays—but still enough to be a drag. I had to sit through an hour of it before I could meet up with Eloise and go shopping.

Eloise now watched me over the rack of clothing, her dark eyes tracking mine. She hadn't said much since we got to the mall, her attention divided between the clothes and her shoes. She only watched me when she thought I wasn't looking. But I noticed. And it was hard to ignore. "What?" I asked.

"Nothing."

"You're staring."

"I'm not."

I narrowed my eyes. "Eloise."

"You never mentioned how your date went," she said, sifting through the hangers on the clearance rack. She kept moving the pieces aside, but she didn't look at the clothing, not really. "You doubled with Elijah, right?"

I fought the urge to roll my eyes, the mere mention of it all setting me on edge. "It sucked. Seriously. I got in a huge fight for Eli." I angrily pushed a white sweater aside to reveal a lime green t-shirt. It was the same color as Elijah's backpack. *Ugh.* "I don't know what his problem is. He called me a bad influence, Eloise. Me! A bad influence on *him*. As if he's three and can't make choices for himself. I never *made* him do anything. And really? Me taking him shopping and to parties isn't that big of a deal." I rounded another rack of clothing, delving deeper into the store, closer to the underwear section. "I mean, if it's about Terry, I don't get why he won't just tell me, you know? Talk to me. I'm his best friend. Why can't we talk to each other anymore?"

Eloise trailed after me. "What about Jeremy?"

"Jeremy was the one who set this all into motion!" My frown intensified. "At least, I think. No, Eli was weird even before that. When they picked me up, he seemed...off."

"I mean, was the date bad because of Jeremy?"

A tangled noise came from my throat, my frustration reaching its peak. "Gosh, Eloise, *no*. It wasn't bad because Jeremy—I don't care about Jeremy. I care about Elijah."

Eloise's eyes widened as she looked at me. I hadn't meant to snap at her—everything just boiled over. Could that have been how it was for Elijah last night—everything had reached a tipping point, and I was just there to take the fire?

It only took a few more beats of Eloise's silence for me to realize what I'd said. I briefly shut my eyes, blindly picking up a pair of underwear from the tier of cloth. "I mean, I do care about Jeremy. I didn't mean it like that."

Gosh, everything was so freaking screwed up. I'd gotten detention again, and Mom was going to kill me. That is, if she would speak to me. I was sure she'd been brewing and stewing all afternoon since the secretary's call about my doctor's appointment. Just waiting for me to get home so she could yell at me. "You don't want me to coddle you?" she'd demand. "Well, fine! You're grounded! Give me your phone."

And that was why I was here, stressing out and draining my bank account.

I looked down at the cloth in my hand, rubbing it between my fingers. It was an ugly print—pineapples and donuts dotted on a yellow background—but as I stared, my mind took me back to a different time in this same store. If Elijah were here now, would I still feel so nonchalant about buying underwear with him? Or would I hold the garments close to my chest, embarrassed?

"I have to tell you something," Eloise said suddenly.

"What?"

A beat of silence passed, and I wondered if she was going to keep her silence after all. And then, in a rush: "I know it wasn't Jeremy you kissed at the party."

The pair of panties slipped from my fingers, falling back on the tier without a sound. Eloise's eyes were still wide, their dark centers edged by white as she focused on me. Her words rang back and forth between my ears, pinging off the sides of my skull. My brain felt like it was sucked back to the night in the closet—Elijah's mouth against mine, a shiver running down my spine, my fingers on his waist, his hands on my skin—

I swallowed, hard. "What did you say?"

"I know you didn't kiss Jeremy at the party," she repeated, dropping her voice. "I know it was—"

"Don't say it. Don't...just don't." *Don't say it aloud, Eloise. You can't say it aloud.* My fast-beating heart felt like it was running a marathon in my chest, crashing into my ribcage. "What did you do?"

"Nothing!" she said immediately. "I swear!"

"Then how do you know?"

"I took you to the room and left you there. I'd planned to come back in a few minutes—you know, like I said—so I just went to get a quick refill." She drew in a sharp breath, and I could tell she wasn't sure she wanted to finish her explanation. "I saw Jeremy come out of a different room a few minutes later. Not the room I'd left you in. I ran to find you, but when I opened up the closet door, you were gone..."

Don't say it, don't say it.

"...and *he* was in there."

He. Elijah. Elijah.

"We both just stared at each other for a second. He seemed more dazed than anything. I told him I was looking for you and quickly shut the door. Then I found you coming out of the bathroom and I took you home."

More dazed than anything. Dazed how? With wide eyes, swollen lips, fog-ridden thoughts? Unable to clear them, unable to think straight. Mouth tingling. Blood humming. Was that how he looked? How he felt?

I leveled my gaze to Eloise's, two feet of space between us. "That's why you never asked about the kiss."

I'd never thought much about why she didn't ask me how the kiss with Jeremy had gone. But now it seemed obvious. She'd known all along I hadn't been kissing him.

"I didn't mention it at first because I thought maybe you two just talked in there," Eloise said. "You know, like, 'oh, hey, you're not the guy I'm supposed to be meeting, how are you doing?' kind of thing. But I saw your face when he came over last Saturday, Rem. That wasn't what happened between you two, was it?"

Deliberately, I closed my eyes, blocking out the image of her tentative expression, trying to force away the memory of Elijah. Remembering now did no one any good. When I spoke, I was surprised my voice sounded remotely even. "It was a mistake," I said. "An accident. But he doesn't know it was me, and we need to keep it that way."

"He doesn't know? What, did he think you were Savannah?"

I drew in a breath, held it for a few seconds, and released it.

Eloise's hand grabbing my own made me jerk, my eyes springing open. "You have to tell him the truth," she said, voice and gaze holding twin amounts of seriousness. "He thinks he kissed Savannah that night, but he kissed you. *Elijah* kissed *you*."

Gosh, just hearing those words aloud... "I know he did." *I was there.*

"Then why don't you tell him the truth?"

"Because I *can't*," I said, tearing my hand back. I walked around the side of the underwear tier to give us some distance, knowing that if she reached out again, I'd probably cave and listen to her. "He's got a girlfriend, Eloise. A really smart, really pretty girlfriend."

She made a face at me. "Who happens to look an awful lot like someone, huh?"

I ignored that. "His brother's in jail. His home life is a mess. He doesn't need his best friend throwing a 'hey, I kissed you, and it totally changed my life in a great way' truth bomb at him."

One of her thin dark brows rose. "It changed your life?"

"Eloise."

"Remi." We held each other's gaze, trying to judge the other from our distance. I stood firm, holding my ground. Eloise was the one who finally wavered, her posture slackened into something of a defeated curve. "You're really not going to tell him?"

"No, I'm not," I said, moving to the next rack. My fingers shook, but I curled them into fists, hoping she wouldn't notice. "Because I'm mad at him."

When I got home from shopping with Eloise, the warm, welcoming arms of grounding greeted me. I wasn't surprised.

Mom took my phone, kidnapped my computer, and I nearly had to laugh at how ironic all this was. Hadn't I said that Mom would never enforce such a bogus rule? But here she was, even going to the extent of locking her office, not putting it past me to use her personal computer. That could've been because of her residual anger, too, since she was still giving me the cold shoulder.

It seemed that everyone was against me. Even the freaking universe.

Detention had one perk, though: I was able to dedicate time to working on snowflakes.

During the detention period on Thursday, while I sat in silence, I clipped away at my extra credit. In that hour, I managed to get seven more done—they weren't the prettiest, but maybe I could hang them in a darker corner—bringing me to twenty-five snowflakes total.

Which meant I had eight days to finish 125 more snowflakes.

Friday after school, I buckled down and got to work. I didn't have my cell phone to play music, so I had to resort to—gasp with me—an old-fashioned CD player. The only CDs I could find were Christmas ones since the season had just passed, but they were better than nothing.

Mom and I still hadn't talked since I snapped at her, but she was pulling long days on-site, designing someone's bathroom or something. I pushed my guilt aside so I could focus on my frustration with Elijah and these stupid snowflakes. There was no time to feel guilty.

I shook the blue and silver glitter onto a patterned snowflake, careful to get as little as possible on the table. Once the snowflake was fully covered, I set it aside and reached for my scissors, cutting into the next pattern.

Stupid Elijah. Why did he have to be so dumb? It made me feel better about whatever idiotic feelings I thought I'd had for him. How could I like a boy who was so stupid, so selfish? Kiss or no kiss. And that had to be the only reason I thought I liked him in the first place—he was just a great kisser. Didn't make him a great boyfriend. Mom had been right—*emotionally unavailable.*

What gave him the right to talk to me like that? Eloise had asked me what had my panties in a twist, but seriously, what twisted his? Family stuff? What right did that give him to be so horrible to me? Calling me a bad influence. Saying he was "done talking" before walking away. How had our friendship devolved that much in such a short time? Tuesday night, we were fine. Better than fine. He'd kissed the back of my head! How had we gotten to this point of me yelling at him and him ignoring me?

My scissors cut into the top of my finger with a sharp, slicing pain. I let out a yelp and dropped the piece of paper. I put my finger in my mouth, wincing.

I hated this internal back and forth, which only gifted me the present of more anxiety. Every time I was determined to speak up, to tell Elijah the truth, I remembered all the reasons I shouldn't. *He's got a girlfriend, it'd ruin your friendship, he doesn't like you like that, maybe he was drunk, you were a little buzzed, it was just one kiss.*

But man, I really wanted to tell him. Even if to just get it off my chest.

A soft sound came from the front door, and I didn't realize it was a knock until it came again, a persistent *thwamp, thwamp, thwamp.*

With my finger in my mouth, I padded my way to the door, trying to peer out the fogged-over glass. Even with the porch light on, I couldn't see who stood over the threshold. "Hello?"

"It's me," came a muffled reply.

I grabbed ahold of the doorknob and pulled. The hinges groaned in response, the jamb rocking against the weight behind my pull. I so wasn't in the mood for this.

After a second of trying and prying, the door swung inward with a loud crack, forcing me off-balance. Jeremy's wide eyes and loose posture greeted me. He stood in the snow with his hands in his pockets, one corner of his mouth curved up. "Whoa there. Looks like you need to get that door fixed."

Normally I would've fluffed my hair or at least attempted to make this loose shirt fit in a more flattering manner, but flirting was the farthest thing from my mind. In fact, I tried to hide my annoyance. "Hey. Uh, were we hanging out?"

His smirk grew wider. "Yeah, remember? Yesterday at lunch, I asked if you wanted to go to the movies tonight. You said yeah." He gestured over his shoulder to where his car was parked on the side of the street, headlights on. "I texted you."

Didn't I tell him that Mom took my cell? I glanced behind him, trying to think of a response. Was it bad that I hesitated? "That's...sweet, Jer, really. I'm actually going to my dad's tonight, though—when my mom gets home from work, I have to go."

"It's only six," Jeremy said eagerly, stepping closer to the threshold. His expensive tennis shoes were caked in snow; my mother would've freaked. "The movie is only a little over an hour and a half. Plenty of time to squeeze it in, don't you think?"

Guilt fluttered over my skin as I looked at him. I knew what he was talking about. The lunch line. After he told me about Elijah, he'd kept talking, but my brain had stopped listening. And here he was, on my porch, looking nice and handsome, waiting for me. How jerky would it be if I canceled?

"I'm grounded," I settled on. "I made those plans before I got grounded."

"What if I dropped you off at your dad's afterward? You're still grounded, just heading out a little early and, well, making a pit stop." He leaned against the jamb of the door and tipped his dark head against it, eyes glittering. "We didn't get to really hang out Wednesday. I want to make it up to you."

Something like that should've made my stomach flutter with butterflies, but my body couldn't summon the excitement. All things considered, it wasn't a *bad* idea. I wouldn't have to spend the hour in the car with Mom and her passive-aggressive silence. And hey, maybe it wouldn't be so bad. Sure, he had talked a lot on our first date, but this would be our first *real* second date, without Elijah or Savannah to distract us. Maybe some more alone time with him was exactly what I needed.

"Let me pack up my stuff real quick. I'll meet you in the car?"

"Sure, sure."

I shut the door in his face. My teeth bit into my bottom lip as I moved into the kitchen and tightened the caps on the glitter bottles, the nick on my finger stinging. The thought of Mom coming home and running into him made me hurry faster. How would I even introduce him? A shock of panic darted through me. Definitely *not* as my boyfriend.

I packed my stuff as quickly as I could, grabbing my overnight bag from my room and doing a quick outfit change. Nothing fancy, just leggings and a t-shirt, and I slipped on a jacket. At the last minute, I spritzed on the perfume I'd worn to the party, the one that Jeremy said he'd liked. I hadn't worn it since, but maybe it would get me back into my old flirty mindset. Even though I could hardly stand it.

Using a scrap of construction paper, I crafted a note to Mom. ***A friend is taking me to Dad's. See you Sunday. -Remi***

Snow fell at a light pace, flecking on my face as I hurried outside to Jeremy's car. Without being able to stop myself, I peeked across the street, but Elijah's truck was missing from the driveway.

"I'm sorry I forgot about our date," I said as I settled into Jeremy's car. "That's...super rude and totally unlike me. I've just had a lot going on lately."

With gentle movements, he eased the car back down the driveway, nodding. "Ah, it's okay. Fighting with Elijah takes a lot of energy."

I frowned. "How did you know I'm—"

"Savannah mentioned it the other day in class."

I looked at my bags, which were stuffed down by my feet. How many people knew that Elijah and I were fighting? Was Savannah going around telling everyone, or just Jeremy? "I've just been so swamped with schoolwork. I'm doing some decorations for the Snowflake Dance, did I tell you that?"

He made a noncommittal noise as he took the road that

led out of town. "Elijah reminds me a lot of his brother. I remember him, don't you? He was a senior when we were sophomores."

"Yeah, I remember him." How could I not? Almost every time I went to Elijah's house, he was there, in his room, in the living room, in the kitchen, a lingering presence. With his charisma and personality, there was no missing Terry. Everyone loved him, looked up to him. They always said he'd go on and do great things.

And now he sat in a jail cell.

"Crazy how people can be so different from what they seem," Jeremy said, almost as if reading my mind. "Makes you wonder who's going to turn out that different in our grade. Sometimes I wonder about Eli. He was really close with his brother, wasn't he?"

Now I couldn't keep my mouth shut. My tone spiked in acidity. "Elijah is *nothing* like Terry. Why would you say that?"

"Whoa, hey, I'm just running my mouth. I do that well. You know how it is." Jeremy squeezed my knee, and I could feel each of his fingers through the thin material of my leggings. "Let's talk about something else, yeah?"

I slumped low in my seat, fighting for peace and calmness even though they felt pretty elusive.

The movie wasn't as bad as I'd been expecting. Though I vastly preferred rom-coms to action flicks, it wasn't horrible. Jeremy had shared his popcorn with me, though it was over-buttered and under-salted. It wasn't a horrible time. But there was something missing about it, something...lacking. Like when you woke up in the morning and the sun was absent from the sky. It was okay, but not *right*.

Talking with Jeremy felt like that. It was okay, but it didn't feel *right*.

But it was easy to talk with him about silly, meaningless things, and after the week I'd had, meaningless things felt nice and mind-numbing.

"That's such a terrible thing to say. Mrs. Cassidy isn't *faking* being married."

"Hey, I'm just saying, that ring looks like it could've been bought at the dollar store." Jeremy laughed, shaking his head.

"Plus, she has a picture of her and her dog on her desk, not her husband. That's a little fishy, isn't it?"

"Maybe she and Mr. Valdez have something going on," I suggested. "I mean, I'm sure no woman could resist that mustache."

Jeremy lifted his hand from the wheel and placed his finger across his upper lip. "You dig a guy in a mustache?"

"Oh, definitely," I said, rolling my eyes. "I'm sure Mrs. Cassidy thinks the same."

Without warning, Jeremy eased the car over to the side of the road, letting it slide to a gentle stop as he flipped the hazards button on. We were on an empty road, though, so I was sure that no cars would be driving by.

He turned in his seat to face me. "I have to tell you something, Remi."

"You're pregnant?" I teased, trying to hold onto the humor from before, blinking at how fast his mood had changed. From jovial to serious in a snap. I glanced over at the side of the road, the snow shining like glitter in the moonlight. "Congratulations. Though I'm curious who the baby daddy is."

"I like you."

Yeah, that jovialness *totally* went out the window. "What?"

"Come on, isn't it obvious? I took you to the movies. I'm driving you an hour out of the way to your dad's house. Why else would I do that?"

I thought about all the times Elijah had driven me to Dad's, even stayed and played with Harmony for a little while. "Well, I mean—"

"Do you want to go to the Snowflake Dance with me?" he asked, grabbing my hand from where it rested on my leg, squeezing my fingers. "I needed to ask somebody, and I want it to be you. I'm throwing a party after too, so you can just tag along with me."

Nothing about his words made me feel like I stood on top of the world, and staring into his eyes didn't make me feel like I was falling. I searched and searched, but there was nothing in his gaze that made me feel like a flower leaning toward the sun. A snowflake falling to the ground. Why? I could've screamed the question at that moment because I desperately couldn't figure it out. Why couldn't I just force my body to react to him? Force the endorphins or whatever to come out and do what they were supposed to when he smiled?

I was so, so lost in my thoughts that when Jeremy leaned forward across the console, I had no time to react.

He pressed his mouth to mine, nearly knocking our teeth together. His lips aligned with mine in a way that made my mouth feel...small. Maybe it was the fact that his mouth opened almost immediately over mine, fighting for control.

His mouth tasted like popcorn and moved quickly. He reached to cup the back of my head with his free hand, fingers pressing against the spot where I'd hit the shelf. The pain there had long since stopped aching, but with direct contact like this, a ghost hurt flared up.

Though the thought was horrible, I couldn't stop myself from imagining it. *I wish this were Elijah.*

I didn't realize that I had my eyes open until the glare of the dashboard lights burned into my retinas.

Things became crystal clear to me at that moment—even

though I was thoroughly ticked at Elijah, I couldn't fool myself into thinking that any of the affection I felt was directed at Jeremy. Him saying those things and showing up unannounced didn't give me butterflies or cute little thoughts. I just felt...bad. Like I was leading him on. And at this moment, with his mouth on mine, I totally was.

I pulled away, disentangling his lips from mine with a wet *smack*. My head felt clear, not clouded and foggy as it had been the first time with Elijah, and my heart beat steadily. No matter what I'd been trying to convince myself regarding Jeremy, there was nothing between us that I could coax out. I couldn't force what we didn't have.

"Jeremy," I whispered, closing my eyes to avoid seeing the expression on his face.

"You don't have to say it. Your face says it all." I heard him sigh across from me, and then readjust in his seat. "So Elijah was right. You don't like me."

Now I blinked my eyes open, surprised at what emotion his face belied. It wasn't pain or sadness, but something akin to confusion, like my response was totally unfamiliar to him. "I do like you, Jeremy. Or...I did. I don't know."

"You flirted with me at the party," he said almost accusingly, frowning at the snow on the shoulder of the road. "Even before the party. What happened between then and now? Is this because of Elijah?"

In an instant, I couldn't breathe. "What?"

"Did he say something that changed your mind? I don't understand, Remi."

"It wasn't anything Elijah said. I'm sorry," I said again, resisting the urge to wipe my lips. "I just—"

"Don't like me like that," he finished, sitting back into his seat. "Figures."

We sat in silence for a moment, and I tried so hard not to feel irritated. This was all my fault. I was messing up literally everything in my life. What was going on?

"I'm sorry," I repeated. "You can just take me home."

"All right," he said on a sigh, putting his car back into drive. "It's fine, Remi. You can't help what you feel. Or don't feel, apparently."

I stared out the window, hating the icky feeling in my stomach, the icky feeling on my lips. Elijah's kiss was no comparison; if I thought about it hard enough, I could almost still taste it.

I had opened my mouth to respond when the sound of snow spinning cut me off, and then the back end of Jeremy's car fishtailed as he tried to veer back onto the road. He'd pulled too close to the edge of the ditch, and with all the snow shoveled to shoulder, it sucked the rear end of his car in.

My forehead struck the window sharply as the car rocked off the side of the road, the windshield full of white.

Seventeen

The ditch wasn't big, maybe three feet lower than the road, but deep enough that Jeremy couldn't reverse out of it. He said something—maybe he swore, or maybe he was talking to me—as I tried to get my bearings, my vision spotty. The spicy scent of my perfume didn't help orient me, seeming to scratch at my nose.

Thankfully, he hadn't crashed hard enough to deploy the airbags. I could hear him say something like "ice patch" and "snowdrift," and I pressed my fingers into my eyes, surprised by the wave of nausea that cramped my stomach.

"Can you call him?" Jeremy was saying, but his voice sounded far away.

I leaned my head back against the seat, letting out a slow breath. "Call who?"

"Elijah. He's got a truck. He can pull us out and I won't have to call my dad. Ugh, he's going to kill me. It'll be okay, baby, it'll be okay." Jeremy caressed his hand down the edge of the dashboard, voice pitching several notes as he spoke to his car. Then he glanced at me. "Can you call him, Remi?"

I blinked at him, trying to remember why I felt inclined to say no. "I—I don't have my cell."

"I think I've got his number," he said after pulling out his own phone, scrolling through the contacts and clicking on one.

I closed my eyes, feeling worse at the thought of him talking to Elijah. Would Elijah even pick up? I hadn't spoken to him at all at school today, and I would be surprised if —"Elijah, hey! My man."

I kept my head against the seat, trying not to listen closely to their conversation, trying not to hang on every word. "Yeah, I know it's Friday night. Sorry to interrupt couple time. Yeah, I get it. It's just...I hit a patch of ice and slid off the road, and I was wondering if you would come pull me out." There was a pause, and Jeremy glanced over at me. "Well, I'm on—what road are we on?"

"Duntley Highway."

"Remi says we're on Duntley. I was taking her to her dad's house." A loud static sound came from his cell phone. "Of course she's fine. And so am I, thanks for asking. It was more of a dip than a ditch. Okay. Yeah, okay. Bye."

"Is he coming?" I asked, wiggling my legs from where they were squished between my bags.

Jeremy nodded. "He's on his way. He was at Savannah's. Probably have to put their clothes on first."

I swallowed hard to force the thought from my mind.

The car had slipped sideways into the divot, with my side slanting close to the ground. Since we hadn't crashed that hard, the car still functioned, still pumped out heat, keeping us from shivering. But my teeth were chattering, and I didn't realize until headlights swept over the snow that it was nerves.

Jeremy climbed out of the sedan and found his footing in the deep snow, going out to greet Elijah. I could see him in the side mirror, though he looked crooked. Could see when Elijah's boots touched the ground. Could see him ignore Jeremy completely, stride straight up the side of the car, and—

The passenger's door popped open, catching on the bottom of the ground and digging into the snow. Elijah bent down in front of the doorway to look at me, eyes meeting mine. They were lit from somewhere deep inside, the pupils large and swallowing the irises. Something was etched into the lines of his face, into his forehead, around his mouth.

"Are you okay?" he asked in a low whisper, scanning every inch of my face as to discern the truth himself. He pressed his fingertips to my temple, a gentle kiss of skin against skin. His fingers were cold, and I shivered. "Are you hurt?"

"I hit my head on the window," I said, grabbing ahold of his fingers and drawing them away. "But I'm okay."

"You hit your head?" Concern crossed his gaze as the wind tugged at his hair. "Remi, you already had a concussion, you—"

"I'm *fine*," I said firmly, breathing slow. "I just want to go home."

To go home, to get out of Jeremy's car, to never have to think about this night again.

Elijah watched me, held our hands together, as the moment charged even further. I pulled back to look at his fingers, skin tanned, rough from sculpting.

Suddenly, Elijah wrapped his arms around me, drawing me close, hugging me so tight that I could hardly breathe. I let his scent and body heat wrap around me, envelop me, disorient me. Let it wash away the touch and the smell and the taste of Jeremy. I melted into it. The way everything in me seemed to angle toward him, my heart, my mind. Like I was drawn to him. This was incomparable to the kiss moments ago, and we were only hugging. And this hug—I could practically feel the barrier between us begin to fade away, all the pressure on my chest that had been weighing me down begin to lift. I nearly choked on the feeling, clutching him as if my life depended on it.

"I almost didn't pick up Jeremy's call," he said as he hugged me, voice low. "I'm so glad I did."

"He said you were with Savannah."

He drew in a short breath, the hug turning stiff for a moment. "We were just hanging out."

A humorless laugh escaped me, swallowed by the fabric of his shirt, because I couldn't stop myself from being swamped with jealousy. I knew I needed to let go, to pull back. But I loved the feel of his body against mine, his scent mingling with mine, his heat warming me.

Despite my thoughts and the tightness of my grip, Elijah easily leaned away and I met his gaze. A handful more lashes on the right than on the left. In their depths held relief, warmth, and something else I couldn't quite figure out. "I owe you an apology."

"Yeah, no kidding," I said. "Your apology better be more detailed than that. Better than takeout Thai. I got detention for it. And grounded."

His lips twitched. "I deserve that, and every other scolding you've got. But why don't you yell at me from my truck?"

"Good idea."

Elijah grabbed both my bags, lifting them from the car and looping his arms through the straps. He offered a hand down to me.

As I got to my feet, my boot slipped on a clump of snow, and I fell against Elijah's chest. His hand tightened on mine to give me balance. But we were close. So close. Close enough for me to see that freckle on his brow bone, to see the slight curve to his nose. Close enough to stand on my tiptoes and meet his lips with my own.

Man, I wanted to do nothing more than just that. Miraculously, I held back.

Elijah jerked his head back as if he could read my mind— and maybe he could. He was my best friend, after all. The one who knew me inside and out. Maybe he knew exactly what I was thinking. But there was something so wide to his eyes, so pale to his cheeks, that I frowned. "What's wrong?" I asked, almost afraid to hear the answer.

He didn't answer at first, and the expression on his face didn't change. It was a look I couldn't recognize; I'd never seen him look so shocked out of this skin. As if he woke up from a dream, still wondering if he was trapped in its grip. "Nothing," he whispered eventually, voice hoarse. He shook his head a little, flicking the golden hair out of place from behind his ears. "Nothing."

We rounded the back of the car and made it up onto the road, where Jeremy stood huddled in his jacket.

"Where's your hookup?" Jeremy asked Elijah from the edge of his truck. "You can pull me out, right?"

"I would, but Remi said she hit her head," Elijah said, ghosting his hand over my shoulder. "We really should run her to the ER to make sure she's okay."

"She did? Wait, can't you pull me out first?"

I thought about how I hit the window, wondering if it'd been as loud of a sound as it seemed. "Haven't you heard of second impact syndrome?" Elijah demanded, glancing my way. "Her brain could swell, and she could die. We really should've called an ambulance—"

"No!" Jeremy said quickly, glancing at his car. "No, no ambulance, no police. Jeez, my dad would kill me if he knew I crashed this car."

"You're worried about your *car*?" The tone of Elijah's voice lowered, darkened, and he took a step toward Jeremy. "Are you kidding me?"

"Chill, Eli, she's fine."

"It's *Elijah*," I corrected him for what felt like the billionth time, wondering why it never got through to him. "And he's right, Elijah, I *am* fine."

But he wasn't convinced, and the tension in his shoulders didn't loosen. "I should leave you here. Your car's running, and you've got heat. Since you're so worried about your car, you should keep it company."

I reached out and grabbed one of Elijah's hands, which was fisted at his side. I pried his fingers apart.

"It was an accident, Elijah," Jeremy said. "We parked for a minute, and the car just slid off the road when I tried to go again."

"You *parked?*" Elijah's expression got murderous as he dropped one of my bags against the cool, hard ground. "What'd you go and park for, Jeremy? What were you expecting to happen?"

Jeremy's eyes narrowed. "What does it matter what I expected? Why do you care?"

Was this seriously happening right now? "Because I'm her best friend, idiot, and she's not some girl you go off and *park* with."

It was seriously happening right now. Fantastic. "You know, you sound like her dad right now. Or a jealous boyfriend."

"Both of you, cut it out," I told them sternly, jerking Elijah's hand. "It was just a kiss. Go get the car strap and I'll put my bags in the back." With my free hand, I swiped up the duffle from the ground, hauling it over my shoulder. "I'm sorry again, Jeremy."

It was a pathetic apology, but he graciously accepted it with silence. At least he didn't try to jot down my insurance information, make me pay for his dented car.

Looking at him now, standing off to the side of the road, I wondered what life would've been like with him. If I *had* kissed Jeremy that night in the closet. If it *were* Jeremy I'd dreamed about, and not Elijah.

I popped the back door of the truck, shoving my bag in. Elijah's voice came right above my ear. "You kissed him?"

My eyes slipped shut for a second, and I braced myself on the edge of the truck, turning to face him. The emotion on his face was limited, the only clear indication of his frustration the spark in his eyes. "Yes, I kissed him," I said, propping a hand on my hip. "That's all that happened, though, so chill. You don't have to intimidate him because you're my best friend. You can take your big-brother pants off."

A muscle twitched in Elijah's jaw, and I fought the urge to reach out, to trail my fingertips along his skin. I wanted to tease him, say "well, don't actually take your pants off, of course," but the words wouldn't come. Looking at him made me realize what was missing with Jeremy. The sun was missing from the sky earlier, but now it stood before me, with wheat-colored hair, eyes as brown as chocolate, lips as soft as a cloud. Before me, tempting me, something I could never have. And without him, everything would just be cloudy and gray.

"I did kiss Jeremy," I said, voice barely audible, but the words wouldn't stay trapped within me. They were exhaled into the air almost as if of their own accord. "I kissed him, and I...I thought of you. I mean, I thought about how you were right. I—I don't like him."

I would've expected Elijah to chuckle, say "I told you so," but he didn't. When he spoke, his voice sounded strange. "I'm glad."

"Glad?"

Elijah reached out and smoothed his fingers over my hair, curling several strands behind my ear. I forced myself not to shiver, not from his touch and not from the intensity of his gaze. I wanted him to just tell me what he was thinking, to tell me all his secrets, but he didn't. His other hand curved behind me, causing my heart to beat faster, his body inching closer and closer. His scent invaded my senses, swirling my mind.

"You're too good for him," Elijah said finally, softly, barely audible. And he leaned one more inch forward, his arm brushing my hip. He was a magnet, pulling me to him. And I held my breath, waiting for—

Him to grab the tow strap on the seat, dragging it out from behind me, his hand falling from my cheek. "Hop in. We'll pull him out and then we can go," he said, before turning away, leaving my furious heart tremoring in protest.

Later on that night, Dad and I sat in a curtained space at the St. Joseph's Medical Center, listening to a song attempting to filter its way out of the crappy speakers. The entire place smelled too clean, like bleach and antiseptic, and that alone would've given me a headache if I didn't already have one.

I'd promised Elijah that as soon as I made it up to Dad's apartment, I'd tell him about what had happened. Dad had immediately grabbed his keys. This was the last thing I wanted to do right now—honestly, going back to his apartment and just sleeping was so, so tempting. Yeah, making sure my head wasn't cracked like an egg probably was important, but I just wanted to be by myself.

I'd seriously better not be concussed again—my annoyance would go through the roof.

Dad patted my knee. "The results will be back soon. How do you feel?"

"The headache's still there," I told him, trying not to squint against the bright lights. "I'm sorry that I interrupted Harmony's bedtime routine."

"Clarabelle can handle it. This is more important."

I closed my eyes and dug my fingers into the hospital bed underneath me, feeling the paper crumple from my touch. "You got out of coddling last weekend, but it looks like you'll have to coddle me anyway, huh?"

"Don't act so sad about it. I make a mean chicken noodle soup. Although, it *is* your mother's recipe, so that's probably cheating."

Dad wasn't a prier like Mom. He didn't ask a thousand questions, didn't give forehead kisses, didn't overuse hugs. He enjoyed the quiet and personal space as much as I did, enjoying being left with his thoughts. Although right now it was a little tough for me. Being alone with my raging thoughts almost hurt.

The curtain slid to the side as the doctor came back with his clipboard, positioned just enough to obscure his nametag. I couldn't remember his name—something with a K?—and hoped he wouldn't ask. "Well, Remi, from the tests we've run, it doesn't look like it was a second concussion."

"But she's got a headache," Dad piped up, pulling on his parental jacket. "Is that normal?"

"She was in an accident. Even though it was minor, the shock of that event will cause a flood of stress adrenaline, which runs out. Headaches and fatigue are normal. You did good coming here, though. It's always better to double-check when it comes to head injuries."

I felt my shoulders droop a little bit. Not in disappointment, but in annoyance. This *had* been a waste of time.

"Anything we can do for her pain?"

"Acetaminophen should help curb that headache, but no aspirin." The doctor smiled at me. "And you might want to invest in a helmet."

Ha-ha. Doctor No-Name was a part-time comedian.

Dad signed the discharge papers and wrapped his arm around me as we made our way back to the car, as if afraid to let me walk on my own. He must've read the expression on my face. "I've learned that you and winter don't mix well, Remikins."

"Yeah, no kidding." I guess everyone had been right when they called me clumsy.

"Did you have anything you wanted to do tomorrow? We could go get lunch at that restaurant you like up here. The one with the mind-melting pot pies?"

The idea alone made my mouth water. "I have a school project I need to work on, but that sounds great."

When we got to the car, Dad pulled his cell out of his pocket and began to type out a text. I tried to read his screen. "Is that Mom?"

"And Elijah. We made a group text."

Elijah had a group chat with my parents? I tried to not let that idea weird me out. "What are you telling them?"

"What the doctor said."

"Is Mom freaking out?"

Dad sent the message and turned to me. "Just about as

much as I did when you asked to go to the hospital." He started the car, kicking the heat into full gear. His hand wavered on the shifter, though, and he didn't immediately put it into gear. "Your mom called me the other day. She said that you two were fighting."

I closed my eyes and groaned. "This is between us, Dad. You don't need to get involved."

"Normally, I'd agree, but she said you told her that you wished you weren't the only person in her life. We didn't raise you to talk to people like that, did we?"

Ugh, I *had* said that. From him, it sounded horrible. "I've just got so much going on, Dad. You have no idea. I—I was just stressed. I didn't mean it."

"Just because you're stressed doesn't mean you can lash out at people and get away with it. And just because I'm not at that house anymore doesn't mean I can't discipline you for what goes on there." Dad's expression was as cross as I'd ever seen on him, voice stern. "Fighting and not getting to the bottom of things is like throwing a rock at a window. It may not break the first time, but eventually it will."

"How long did it take for you to come up with that?"

His lips twitched. "Listen to me. I'm wise. What are you stressed about, anyway? I thought your teenage life was supposed to be exciting and *totally amazing*?"

"Ew, don't ever say it like that again. And it's a bunch of things." For a moment I wanted to lie to him, or just not say anything, but I couldn't. "Elijah and I have been...at odds."

"What does that mean? I thought you loved Elijah."

"I don't love him!" I nearly shouted, causing Dad to jump. *Way to not draw suspicion, idiot.* I forced myself to lower my voice. "We had a fight a few days ago, and I guess I'm still a little on edge from it."

I knew from looking at Dad's face that he was no longer my father; Mr. Lawyer looked at me now, examining every piece of evidence given to him. "What did you two fight about?"

Now *that* I couldn't tell him. I couldn't tell him that Elijah had accused me of being a bad influence, that we'd fought about Terry. I couldn't tell him that I'd kissed Elijah and that had complicated things. A lot. I couldn't tell him that I hadn't been able to stop thinking about him since. That all my efforts to stop those stupid butterflies and dumb thoughts hadn't worked. Not even in the slightest.

"Can I ask you a question?" I asked instead.

"I'm not going to say the 'you just did' dad line, even though I really want to. Of course you can ask me a question, Remikins. I'll even let you ask me two."

"When you and Mom got divorced..." I paused and took a breath, trying to muster up the courage to look at his face, but my eyes kept gravitating toward the dashboard instead. "How did you know you made the right decision? I mean, I know you two always said it was because you fell out of love, but how did you know that you really loved Clarabelle after that?"

Dad didn't answer right away. "Where is this coming from?"

Where? *Oh, I'm just wondering if falling out of love is possible, or if I'm going to be stuck feeling this way about Elijah for the rest of my life.* "I—I'm just curious."

Dad leaned back in his seat and let out a breath, letting

the steady hum of the pumping heat fill the void of silence around us. "Remi," he said softly. "You know it wasn't because of you."

"I know that," I said honestly. "I just...how do you love Clarabelle differently than Mom? Not that I don't love Clara, I do," I rushed to add. "She makes you happy and she's amazing. I'm just curious. We've never really talked about it."

He glanced down at where his hands rested on the edge of the steering wheel, trying to find the right words. "Being with Clarabelle...it's different than being with your mother. The love felt different. It felt warmer, steadier—like I was free to take a deep breath again. Does that make sense? Not that I'm bashing your mother by any means—but it didn't feel like this. We were at odds a lot. Personalities clashed. She was more outgoing than me, lived life louder." Dad's lips twitched into a smile as a wistful expression washed over his features. "At first, Clarabelle didn't like me very much. We met at work, like you know, but it wasn't love at first sight. At least, not for her."

"Were you a lovesick idiot?"

Dad laughed. "Yep. I told myself that if I won her affections, I'd love her forever."

It felt a little strange talking about this with him, but not in a bad way. Just different. "And if you didn't win her over?"

"Then I'd love her forever anyway. I'd just have to try and not be creepy about it. You know, no following her home, no memorizing her commute times." He wiggled his eyebrows. "I'd love her, but I'd let her go and live her life."

"And you weren't willing to love Mom forever?"

That question sobered the conversation a bit. I could

practically feel the humor bleed from the car, my harsh-sounding statement hanging in the air. "It's not that I wasn't willing, Remi. Your mom and I grew apart for a while," Dad said after a moment, voice quieter. "She started her new career, and I got more and more cases at the firm. We just grew into different people. People change, Rem. Evolve. And that's not a bad thing."

I knew that part of the story. Both of them working more and more, losing enough time for each other. Falling out of love.

"Remi, whatever's going on, I think you know, deep down, how you're feeling. Don't think I don't know why you're asking me questions about love. I may not be the sharpest tool in the shed, but I know how to read people."

There was no objecting to it, so I relented. "What do I do?" I shook my head. "I think I know how I feel, but he doesn't feel the same."

Dad reached out again and pulled me close to him, an awkward hug in his small car. "You're young, and this is just a season in time."

My mind was at war as I settled into his arms. I didn't want this to be just a season in time—I didn't like the idea of Elijah and me eventually growing apart—but I also didn't want to feel this way forever. Like I couldn't ever take a deep breath. "What if he's my Clarabelle?"

I felt Dad's lips find the crown of my head. "Then I'll buy you military-grade binoculars so you can watch from afar. Or at least from across the street."

I smiled at that before the full realization of what he said hit me. Stiffening in his embrace, I pulled my head back just enough to look into his eyes. "How—"

Dad reached out with his other hand and tapped my nose. "I know how to read people," he said again. "And I know my daughter."

I settled back into his hug, clinging close, eyes aching. A wave of guilt crashed over me as I realized that this was exactly what Mom tried to do. Coddling was her way of comforting me. I truly was the worst daughter in the world, refusing her embrace but allowing Dad's.

Maybe it was because Dad's hugs weren't as frequent as hers were, since I lived with her for the majority of the time. Dad's hugs were a novelty; Mom's were customary. But no excuses. As I sat there, I tried to think of ways I could be better, make it up to her. She deserved better. Hopefully she'd forgive me for lashing out like I had.

"Uh, Remi?" Dad asked after a moment.

"Yeah?"

"Are you ready to go home now?"

"Yeah," I laughed and pulled back, wiping my fingers underneath my eyes. I hadn't even realized the pressure behind my eyes was tears. "I'm ready."

Dad and Clarabelle both offered to help me with the snowflakes, which I graciously accepted. To heck with Mrs. Keller's no-cheating rule. By Sunday afternoon, I had a total of sixty-one snowflakes completely finished, and all of us had glitter in our lungs. Dad gave me a zip-up bag to carry them home in, so the inside of his car wouldn't be Snowflake Dance-themed for the rest of its life.

My knees were drawn up and my feet rested on the edge of the couch, creating a nice little pocket of space for Harmony to sit cradled in my lap. She kept reaching out and running her fingers over the fringe of my bangs, her grip sticky. "Still no steps, huh?" I asked her, shaking my head. "And here I hoped you'd beat me."

"You weren't walking 'til fourteen months, so I heard," Clarabelle said from the other end of the couch, watching us with a small smile on her face. "I reckon there's still plenty of time for her to win."

"Shh, we don't need to talk about it," I cooed, smiling at the baby in front of me. Harmony blinked her big blue eyes at my mouth before stretching her own mouth to match, her tiny stub-like teeth adorable. "All we need to talk about is *her* walking. I hoped I'd get to see it."

Clarabelle reached over and patted my leg. "You will."

Dad entered the living room, stuffing his wallet in his back pocket. "Ready, kiddo?"

After giving Harmony a squeeze, I passed her to Clarabelle and stood. My insides felt calm for the first time in a long time. The conversation with Dad Friday night had opened my eyes to a lot of things, as well as the idea that peace could come from this situation. Though I felt like I still didn't fully understand love, I understood it enough to know that I would be fine. I didn't know what would happen, whether I would fall out of love or deal with this feeling forever, but I knew both of those meant the same thing: Elijah would stay in my life. That was the most important thing. Whatever happened, I could stick it out. It might be hard, but I could do it. As long as I didn't lose him.

"I had a great weekend, Dad," I told him as we settled into the SUV. Dad turned on the heated seats, and they warmed as we drove along. I juggled my bags closer, careful not to squish my snowflakes. "Thank you for talking with me."

"Always, Remikins. If you have any more questions, you can call me. You know that." Dad loosely gripped the steering wheel, his other hand resting on his knee. He looked so relaxed as he drove along, sun visor flipped down, sunglasses on. I didn't blame him; with all the snow, the sun reflection was killer. He caught me looking. "You know what you're going to say to your mother?"

Right. Mom. All weekend, I'd been thinking about a way I could make everything up to her. What to say, how to say it. I almost phoned her Friday night to apologize, but I knew something like this would go over better in person.

"She deserves a fabulous apology, based off what you said," Dad scolded, loosening the scarf from his throat. It surprised me that he'd kept it on for so long. "I should've stopped and made you get flowers from the supermarket or something."

I thought about what Mom could be doing right now. It was Sunday, so she probably wasn't at work, but she could've been in her office. Despite the fact that it was a job, Mom never treated it as such. She loved it too much, and the proof was in her homes. Especially ours. Even though she had an abundance of things—shoe racks, mirrors, empty vases—they had all been placed by a loving hand. That's what made them just *work*.

I couldn't remember if I'd ever told her that.

"It'll be okay," I said, finally answering his question. "She's not big on flowers."

"How's Kathleen doing?" Dad asked, setting our conversation on a new course. "She called the other day."

"Mom told me she wanted to talk to you about Terry." I pictured Mrs. Greybeck's face from the grocery store, pictured her slumped over her computer screen. "She asked about that, didn't she?"

Dad let out a little sigh, a crease forming between his brows. "She did. Everything was done by the book, though. Terry got a great deal, all things considered."

Yeah, being an accomplice to an armed robbery. "But?"

"I told her that it was time to wait now. Wait until his sentencing is carried out and he's back home. Eight months is long, but it could've been longer. *Much* longer." Dad settled deeper into his seat, shoulders slumping a little. "Fighting and digging for more information where there is none isn't doing anyone any good, and I told her that."

"Do you think you got through?"

"I don't know, Remikins," he said softly. "I just don't know."

Every single time Dad dropped me off at home, I always wondered whether it felt strange for him. Not because he'd have to see Mom—no, they loved seeing each other, and it was weird—but because he came to this house. His old home. This was the house he and Mom had bought together, fresh from the chapel. He helped Mom redo all the bathrooms, pulled up all the carpet to install hardwood floors, even built a shed in the backyard. He'd let Mom keep the house because —his words exactly—"she had more junk."

He'd lived in our house for almost a decade. Sometimes I still found stuff of his shoved between couch cushions or in small boxes. Even if it wasn't something he ever thought about, I always did.

Dad's brakes squealed as he pulled up to the snowy curb in front of the house. Though he put the car in park, he didn't reach for his seatbelt.

"You're not coming in?" I asked, looping my arms through my backpack straps.

"You need to do this on your own," he said, giving me a stern, parental glare. "You've been putting it off all weekend, and you don't need me to be another distraction."

He knew me so well. "I love you, Dad."

"Go, go, save your mushy-gushiness for your mother."

The snow had turned into slush near the road, and my shoes squelched in it as I hopped out. I made the trek to the house, heart pounding in anticipation. Words I should've said immediately sat on the tip of my tongue, ready to fly out the moment I saw her. She deserved more than I'd given.

I remembered to go around to the back door, leaving my boots outside on the welcome mat. "Mom?" I called, not seeing her figure in the kitchen or the open living room. "Mom, I'm home."

"In here," came her soft reply, and my backpacks thudded as I dropped them. Almost as an afterthought, I hoped that my snowflakes survived the fall.

I stopped in the doorway of Mom's office, coming to a

standstill. She had her hair wound up into a low bun with several strands escaping, giving it a crazed look. She was in sweats and didn't have any makeup on, but she looked beautiful.

Her dark eyes found mine. "How was your dad's?"

"I was a brat," I said immediately, the words coming out in a rush, mixing together. "No, worse than a brat. A jerk. I shouldn't have said those things to you, Mom."

Her eyebrows rose in surprise, lips parting. "Remi—"

"No, let me finish." I walked farther into the room until I stood on the other side of her desk, my puffy coat making scratching noises the entire way. "I'm grateful to have a mom like you. A mom who cares about me, who stops what she's doing to see if I need anything, who always puts me first." A burning sensation came alive behind my eyes, surprising me. "Even when I'm forty, I'll always need you to coddle me, Mom. No matter what I say, I don't want you to stop. And you know, if it's just you and me for the rest of our lives, then it's you and me against the world."

Mom's eyes were shining by the time I finished my speech, about to spill over. She stood and rounded the desk. "Well, good, because I intend to coddle you even longer than that."

For the first time in a long time, I reached out to her first, wrapping around her frame and holding her tight. My guilt was still there, but the fact that she so quickly forgave me made me realize how truly lucky I was to have her in my life.

Her chin nudged around my hair as she tried to get her mouth free. "Your cell phone is in your bedroom. It's been going off since you left."

"It can wait," I said, refusing to let go. "I love Elijah."

Okay, *that* hadn't been in the speech I'd been preparing all weekend, but as soon as the words slipped from my mouth, I realized they were true. I did love him. And maybe it was a love mostly fueled by our friendship—I'd loved him long before we kissed in that closet, just differently—but I knew now that I loved him on a deeper level. I didn't love him like a brother, but I loved him the way a woman might love her husband after sixty years. Steady, sturdy, unending. And confessing that to Mom was putting everything in the open, exposing the truth inside me. No more secrets. I didn't hold onto them anymore.

Mom tried to pull back to look into my eyes, but I held fast. "You love him?"

"I kissed him," I said. "We were at a party and blind-folded, so he doesn't know that it was me, but I kissed him. And I realized that even if he loves Savannah for the rest of his life, it'll be okay." I loosened my grip, allowing space to form between us, my stomach starting to ease. "You can still love them even if they're with someone else. As long as they're happy."

Her office filled with silence as Mom watched me, and I had a feeling that she saw this moment for what it was, too. The thought of confessing such a thing to her before would've sent me into a panic, hyperventilating as my honesty came out. Saying those kinds of things out loud to her would've seemed corny and cheesy, but now they felt right.

Her smile seemed a little sad. "That's a hard thing, though, to love someone who loves someone else."

"Good thing I've got a great mom to support me when I need it. One who knows how to piece me back together."

"You do," she agreed, pulling me back into a hug. "Yes, you do."

We stood there for a while longer, just listening to each other breathe, stuck in a hug that I never wanted to end. In the same weekend, I'd gotten the same strong hug from both my parents. If this was coddling, I would take it. Always.

"Remi?" She spoke over my shoulder, voice kind of muffled. "When, exactly, did you go to a party?"

Oh, *crap*. What had I just said about no more secrets?

Mom's calm voice came through my cracked door early in the morning, and it barely stirred me. "It's a snow day, sweetie," she whispered, as if trying to speak more to my subconscious. "You can sleep in."

The second time I woke up was the final time, and after breakfast, I dove headfirst into getting the snowflakes done. Around noon, Eloise asked if she could come over. If anything, I had ten more fingers to help make snowflakes.

But she sat on the end of the couch, flipping through a magazine, claiming that "glitter gives me hives." Honestly, I couldn't blame her. I sat at the kitchen table, gluing away. "Don't you hate that they've limited the number of quizzes they include?" Eloise demanded, rustling her pages. "Seriously. These things used to be filled with them." Eloise changed her seating position so that she sat on her ankles. "So no more Jeremy, huh?"

"No more Jeremy," I confirmed. "That ship has sailed." *Or crashed into a ditch.*

"What happened?"

"I kissed him," I said, trying to focus solely on my snowflakes so I wouldn't see her expression, "and there was no...spark."

Eloise leaned her head against her hand. "I'm going to play devil's advocate here, okay? Sparks only happen in books and movies, Remi. *Corny* books and movies. 'His lips felt like a firework exploding against hers' probably isn't realistic. If anything, it sounds dangerous."

I couldn't agree with her on that point. Okay, so maybe the fireworks analogy was a bit much, but when I kissed Elijah, *something* had happened. Some spark. And maybe it was the effects of the sensory game or whatever, but I'd felt a static charge between us then, and it gave me goosebumps. With Jeremy, there was...nothing.

"The ship's still left the port, Eloise."

Eloise pushed up from the couch and came over to the kitchen table, her high bun bouncing with each step. "It feels weird. After all this time you've thought about him, it's just...over."

I patted her on the arm, trying to fight a smile at her dramatics. "You should go for Jeremy. Although I will say, he calls his car *baby*, so that's a little weird. And he talks a lot. But I think you can handle that."

"Oh, no," she said at once. "I wouldn't dive into that shark tank. But, so," she dragged the word out, shifting on the couch. "How's Elijah?"

I stiffened, all over. "Good. He's good. Fine. I mean, I'm assuming he's fine. He's always been good at being...fine." *Cringe.*

"Have you two talked about—well, you know."

Well, you know. Heck yeah, I did. And heck no, we hadn't. "You mean about Jeremy? Yeah, he knows that we broke things off. He came to pick me up Friday."

Obviously, I knew that hadn't been what she was asking about, but I was too much of a chicken to delve into that conversation. Eloise was my best friend; she was the perfect person to talk about all of this with. I mean, we'd spent how many nights talking about boys before? But there was something strange about talking about Elijah with her. I couldn't put my finger on it.

Eloise, though, seemed to get the memo. She glanced at my art paraphernalia, lips twisting in disgust. "I can't believe you're helping out with the dance decorations."

"It's not really *helping*," I confessed to her, sifting through the half-cut snowflake designs. "I'm doing it so I can pass my senior year."

She looked at me for a moment. "Do I want to know?"

"Probably not."

"Are you going to tell me anyway?"

Aww, she knew me so well. I relayed to her the predicament I'd found myself in, my failing art grade, Mrs. Keller's last-ditch effort to extend a life raft. Now I just had to grab it.

"So that means we're going to be seniors together next year?"

"You don't have faith in me?"

Smiling, she raised an eyebrow. "Come on, Remi. We both know you're the queen of procrastination. You'll probably put this off and it'll be too late."

The scary part was that she was right. Or would've been

right. Because that was what I'd done for so long. Whenever I had a project in art, I'd spend the entire period doing something else—other homework, painting my nails, texting—and not working on the assignment. I'd put it off to the last minute, rush to get it done, and get a crappy grade. If I even finished it at all.

"This is going to be different," I told her, gripping my scissors tighter. "Too much is riding on this." If I got held back, no way I could show my face at Greenville High again. Mortification would kill me first.

"I'm here for moral support." Eloise patted my arm. "You're still studying for your midterm exams, right?"

"Here and there." Definitely not as much as I should've been. I was doing fine in my other classes, though. It was just art threatening to ruin my life.

We lapsed into a peaceful silence as she watched me work, lightly tapping her nails on the table. Having her here was good company—even talking about magazine quizzes and my possible failure. It felt good to have her to talk to, someone to confide a little in.

I wondered what she was thinking about: my grades, the fact that I'd said no to Jeremy, or the whole ordeal with Elijah.

"Elijah," Eloise said.

I jolted in my seat, freaked out. "What?"

She gestured to my cell, which sat face-up on the table. "He's calling you."

My heart fluttered as I picked up my phone, and miraculously, I managed to answer with a clear voice. "Hey."

"How are you doing?" he asked at once, his lilting voice

nearly making me break into a grin. "Your head feeling okay?"

"I'm in perfect health," I told him matter-of-factly, setting my paper down. "No headaches, no nausea, no throwing up."

"And no falling asleep and slipping into a coma," he added.

I nodded, though he couldn't see me. "Right. None of that. Though the doctor did suggest that I get a helmet."

"Probably a good idea, knowing you." Elijah hesitated on the end of the phone for a second. "I want to see you."

He hadn't said it strangely, no turn in his tone of voice, no change in volume, but my heart jumped anyway. "Eloise is here."

"Yeah, hi," Eloise said, loud enough for Elijah to hear her. "Is he coming over?"

"I don't have to if you don't want me to," Elijah said, and I wasn't sure if he was speaking to me or answering Eloise's question. "I can wait until she leaves if you want. I just... really need to talk to you."

Eloise must've heard him because she just gave me a knowing smile. "I've got to head out anyway. I'll give you two some *space*." She said the last word quietly, nearly a whisper, pushing up from the table. I didn't want to chase her off, but I was sure she knew how I felt, knowing that Elijah wanted to talk. She knew the truth. Her next words were so low that I knew Elijah couldn't hear. "You need to talk to him."

"I can't," I mouthed back. "Just drop it." And then, speaking at my normal volume, "I'll see you at school tomorrow."

"Yeah, yeah. Love you," she said as she headed out the back door, blowing me a kiss.

I pretended to catch it and press it to my heart. "She's heading home. You can come whenever you want. But come in through the back door. The front door still isn't opening right."

"Okay. I'll be right over," he said, and the call disconnected.

I immediately threw myself into overdrive. I ran to my room and tore a hairbrush through the rat's nest on my head, wincing as it caught in the tangles. My bangs were getting to the point where they were hanging way too far into my eyes, really needing a trim, but I couldn't worry about it now. The oversized hoodie I wore had a hole near the collar from years of wear, but it still looked kind of cute. I mean, probably cute enough. Not that Elijah would notice, anyway.

I got back to the kitchen just as Elijah passed the back window, and a second later he stepped over the threshold, pushing the door open. It caught on the collection of welcome mats Mom had; of course, she owned way more than we needed.

His eyes immediately found where I stood, and he drew in a breath. "Do I just leave my shoes on the porch?"

"Yeah, that's fine," I said with a wave of my hand, trying to hide how my fingers were shaking. With all the shoe racks Mom had in the front entryway, she had none for the back. "Didn't have anything better to do on the day off, huh?"

"I could say the same to you." Elijah tipped his chin at my arts and crafts project, slipping his jacket off and shaking his hair free of the collar. "A bummer they couldn't cancel last night so you could've stayed one more day at your dad's."

"Eh, he would've been at work anyway," I said. "How's your entry for the contest?"

He nodded slightly, making his way into the kitchen and draping his jacket over the back of a chair. "Putting on the finishing touches, actually. I'm hoping to be done by tomorrow. How are your snowflakes coming?"

"I'm not nearly as close as you. I still have eighty to do. So I need to make sixteen a day to finish on Saturday." The looming deadline made my head spin.

Elijah gave me an expression I couldn't quite read. "Well, wouldn't you have to finish by Friday so Mrs. Keller has time to hang them all?"

Ha, crap. Of course he was right. "You in the gluing mood?"

"Always." Elijah sat down at the table, swiped up the glue stick, and immediately got to work on covering a bare snowflake.

I sat down across from him, pulling my legs underneath me. I waited for him to start speaking again, but he practically threw himself into the work, lips unmoving. "So what did you need to talk to me about?" The strings of my heart tugged in expectation, my breath stalling while I waited for his response.

Elijah didn't lift his head, but let his hair fall into his eyes, shielding them from view. "I wanted to tell you that you were right."

"I often am. But about what?"

A gust of wind knocked into the side of the house, strong

enough to make the structure creak, giving Elijah a buffer before he answered. He drew in a slow breath. "Terry. You were right about Terry."

I didn't really know what I had been expecting him to say, but it wasn't that. Not about his brother. "How do you mean?"

"I never told you about that night," he said quietly, not looking at me. The lines of his shoulders were stiff and straight, discomfort a second skin. "The night he was arrested. I know I called you over, but I...I never really told you about it, did I?"

He was busy at work, but I was busy watching him and his movements. His opening up like this was similar to how I'd spoke with Mom yesterday. Monumental, significant, something that you had to put everything down and be in the moment for. "No, you never did."

Elijah still watched his fingers move, his attention completely captured by their calloused edges and bitten-down nails. I would've gladly taken both, his attention and his touch. "I always looked up to Terry, you know. He was my big brother. I just wanted to be like him." He tipped his head so I could see his mouth pull into an ironic sort of smile. "Even my parents wanted me to be like him. Responsible. Trustworthy."

"You're both those things," I said quickly, trying to mimic him and continue working through this serious topic. My brain, though, was hardly able to multitask. "And so much more. You don't need to be like him."

"I always wonder what would've happened if Terry told me what they'd planned to do."

I immediately thought back to the day Mr. Greybeck had driven me to school, about how he said things would've been different if Terry had confided in Elijah.

"If he'd told me they were going to rob those places that night. I would've tried to stop him, but would he have listened? Would he have done it anyway? Would I have called the police? Told my parents? Kept silent? The wondering killed me. Jeremy talking about it the day we went out just made me feel so...helpless. I couldn't stop Terry. I've always blamed myself for that." He drew a breath. "Other people, they didn't know him. Didn't know him, didn't know our home life. I guess that's why I didn't mind them talking about it, because they really had no clue. But you knew. You knew him, and you knew me. And that made me feel so...embarrassed."

When I tried to think of the last time I saw Terry, I remembered the week before everything happened. A black car had been parked on the curb by his house, and Terry ducked his head to lean into the driver's side window. I'd been outside mowing the lawn, trying to mind my own business, but I couldn't help glancing over.

The guy in the passenger's seat was cute, I remembered thinking that, what portion of his face that I could see from over Terry's shoulder. He had tattoos winding around his neck, his freckly face open and boyish. But when the driver looked over, I felt my insides run cold. Something in his gaze was...off. The mere way his eyes rested on me made me feel unsettled. Terry must've noticed the guy's divided attention because he'd turned and looked at me.

Terry hadn't waved, and I didn't either. He said something to the driver and backed away from the car. The driver pulled away from the curb and continued down the street, eyes lingering on me as the car inched away. By the time I turned my attention back to Terry, he had already disappeared into the house.

"You have nothing to feel embarrassed for," I said now, shaking off the memory.

"There was an anonymous tip to the police," Elijah said, drawing my attention back to the moment, pulling me from the memory. "It was Terry. After the first robbery, he made the call. He told my parents that, I guess, the first day they visited him a couple weeks ago, but...they never told me. I never knew." For the first time since he'd sat down, Elijah glanced at me, dark eyes partially hidden behind his hair. I surrendered to stillness. "I hated him for willingly going along with those bad decisions. But he knew. He knew what he was doing was wrong, and he tried to stop it."

Knowing that Terry tried to make things right made me feel a little relieved. "He made a mistake, Eli."

"And so did I. Yelling at you the other day—it wasn't you. It was a collection of everything—all the constant gossip, Jeremy asking about it—and I just took it all out on you."

I could still remember his anger, an emotion so unlike him. "You said it was because I'm a bad influence."

"You're not a bad influence, Remi. If it weren't for you, I probably wouldn't ever leave my house. I don't know who I'd be without you." Elijah squeezed his eyes shut for a moment. "I'm sorry. I'm making such a mess of things. And then seeing you with Jeremy, I just—"

I blinked. "What? What does Jeremy have to do with Terry?"

"Nothing with Terry," he said, shaking his head as if to clear it. He was quiet for so long that I thought he had finished speaking, and I almost opened my mouth, but he went on. "Mom's been asking me to go visit him. Terry. When she first asked, I didn't want to. I didn't want to see him. But knowing everything now, I think I need to, you know? I think I need to."

I squeezed his arm, his skin warm underneath mine. "I'll be here for moral support."

Elijah laid his free hand over mine, sandwiching my fingers. A charged emotion built between the two of us. "You're my rock, you know. Without you, I don't know what I'd do."

"What about Savannah?"

Ugh, it was stupid, stupid, stupid, mentioning his girl-friend while he was touching my hand, but the simple question needed an answer. I needed to hear it. I needed him to say her name or say "yeah, of course, she's my rock, too" to stop these thoughts from raging inside of me. Even though I'd accepted the idea of living my life loving him in silence, it still wasn't fair if I couldn't keep my thoughts reined in. So he just needed to say it, to assure that she'd be there, to assure me.

But Elijah, with his fingers still covering my own, said nothing.

"Oh, Elijah, I didn't know you were here."

That broke whatever our moment could've been in an instant, Mom sauntering into the kitchen to refill her water bottle.

Elijah expertly slid back into his seat, his fingers moving from mine. "I just got here not that long ago."

Mom glanced between him and me with an expression that was all too obvious, and I put my nose to my project. My face, though, was flaming, as if she'd just caught us making out.

"We're just working on some snowflakes," I said.

"And talking about Terry," Elijah added, causing my head to jerk up.

Talking about it with me was one thing, but confessing it to my mom felt like another.

Even she seemed surprised, eyes widening as she gazed at him. I knew where her mind was going. *This is progress —good progress,* she was probably thinking. *Maybe he'll ditch some of that baggage and be with Remi.* "How is he doing?"

"Good, I think. I...haven't talked to him in a while, but Mom was over at the facility on Friday and said he looked good."

"I've been meaning to stop over myself. I thought maybe a familiar face would be nice once in a while."

Huh? Mom had never confessed such a thing to me, but from the expression on her face, it was clear she was telling the truth.

The ironic trace of a smile Elijah wore earlier morphed into something warmer. "I think he'd like that. Seeing a familiar face."

Mom capped her water bottle and headed back toward the hallway. "Well, I've got a dining room to plan. My client wants to find a way to mix orange and hot pink into their color scheme. Can you imagine the nightmare?" She shuddered before lifting a hand in farewell. "If you need anything, just holler."

We watched her leave the room, both of us waiting to hear the click of her office door as it slid shut.

"How was your dad's, anyway? How was Harmony?"

I shook my head at him. "You just love Harmony. Are you sure she isn't *your* baby sister?"

His lips twitched. "Hey, I'm invested. I've always wanted a sister."

"Well, you've got me."

Simple words, but they cut open a torrent of problematic emotions. He looked back down to the snowflakes, fingers coasting over the edges of the paper.

I knew I had to open up a little to him, since Elijah had decided he wanted to be honest with me. Our silence lulled too thick, and I didn't want it to continue. "I'm not doing these snowflakes to just help out, you know."

"Yeah, I know. For extra credit, right?"

Well... "More like if I don't do them, I'll fail senior year."

Those brown eyes widened as my words washed over him. "*What?*"

My words came out in a rush, a dam broken. "I may or may not be failing art. It's funny, I'm acing calculus and failing art. Why art is a deciding factor for graduating, I have no idea. Mrs. Keller just hates me."

He blinked rapidly, like a little bug. It was kind of cute. "She's a teacher. Contractually, she can't hate you."

"Well, tell her that," I said, slumping in my chair. "She's the one making me do this. These snowflakes decide whether I get to wear a cap and gown."

"Why aren't you more freaked out about it?" he demanded, almost sounding incredulous. "Why are you going to parties and going on dates and not spending every waking moment getting these done?"

Okay, judgey. But I couldn't blame him. "Art is just not my thing."

"And procrastination is?"

Well. "Yeah."

Elijah buried his face into his hands. "Remi..."

I leaned my elbow against the table and dropped my chin into my palm. "I didn't want to tell you because I didn't want you to feel bad. Or be mad at me. I know how much art means to you and I didn't want you thinking I was being reckless." Even though I totally was. "You just had so much on your plate. I didn't want you to have to worry."

He parted his fingers to peek at me. "You should've at least told me earlier so I could've helped out more. We could've been done by now."

"Well, see, I'm not supposed to ask for help. At least, not your help. Mrs. Keller practically ripped me a new one over the whole papier-mâché drama. Thanks for that, loser."

Elijah's mouth tipped into a smile as he leaned back in his chair, stretching his arms over his head. "That was pretty good, wasn't it?"

I swatted at the air in front of him. "Uh, *no.* She almost failed me."

The table separated us, but I wished we could've gone back to the part where he touched my hand and I leaned closer. *Closer* was a good word for what I wanted, but I had to push it down. And that had to be okay because this was our normal. This banter, this conversation—this was us.

"Let's get to work, then," Elijah said, swiping up his glue stick. He pushed my piece of construction paper closer to me. His eyes seemed to linger longer than normal, but that was me reading into it, no doubt. "We've got a lot to get done before Friday."

This was us, and this was enough. For now.

"Remi?" Mom called to me later on that day, after Elijah had left. I'd been sitting at the table alone for a few hours, focused on these stupid snowflakes. "The snow finally stopped. Can you come help me shovel the driveway before it gets any darker?"

I set down the snowflake I'd been working on, looking at my glitter-covered fingers. "Yeah, let me grab my coat."

It was only a little after seven now, and the sunset shone in brilliant effect, casting the driveway in a beautiful glow. Quite a lot of snow had fallen last night, but throughout the day, it had been more of an on-and-off flurry. The driveway was untouched since Mom stayed home today, her SUV blocked in.

Mom offered the cold snow shovel to me, using her other hand to pull her hat lower over her ears. "It shouldn't take us longer than five minutes if we're both working."

"Thank God for small driveways," I said with a smile. I hadn't brought gloves out with me, so the metal of the shovel felt cool against my fingertips. My breath fogged in the air each time I exhaled. "Too bad it didn't keep snowing. I would've loved another snow day."

"Yeah, I bet you would've," Mom said. "You start down by the road, I'll start here."

After giving her a thumbs-up, I made my way to the end of the driveway. My boots slipped a little on the concrete, but I managed to make it to the roadside in one piece.

I glanced down at my laces. "Mom, I think maybe it's my boots. I think that's why I'm so clumsy. The tread is probably bad."

"Remi, each time you hit your head, you weren't even outside."

Huh. She had a point. When we had our heart-to-heart earlier, I'd come clean about hitting my head at Jeremy's party. "True...but can we still get me new boots?"

Mom smiled at me from the other side of the parked car. "You're ridiculous, you know that?"

I stuck the snow shovel underneath a clump of ice, pushing it horizontally across the driveway. As Mom and I worked, I thought about the snowflakes. I was getting so close to being done, so close to the goal. Things would be so much better as soon as I could put this behind me. I couldn't even believe I'd gotten myself in this situation in the first place.

"Oh, I've got to run inside real quick," Mom said, and when I turned, I found her looking down at her cell phone. "My client is asking me to resend the mock-up we worked on today."

"You're just trying to get out of work," I teased. "You can

stay inside, but only if you make hot chocolate for when I'm done."

"As soon as you're finished, it'll be ready for you. I promise." She started to head around the back of the house.

I truly didn't mind shoveling now by myself. And plus, if Mom went inside, I'd have a little pick-me-up when I finished. A win-win.

As I looked across the street at Elijah's house, the front door opened, and out walked Mrs. Greybeck. She had her head down, an oversized cardigan bundled around her. I watched as she headed down the driveway to her mailbox, putting something inside and flipping up the red arm.

When she turned, she saw me. "Hi, Remi."

"Hi," I returned, expecting her to start walking away. She didn't. "Something fun going out in the mail?"

"Oh, just a letter. I go and see Terry every week, but I think he still likes getting some mail."

I pulled the shovel up and gripped the handle. "How's he doing?"

Mrs. Greybeck pulled her cardigan tightly around herself, looking off down the street. "He's doing fine."

"How's Elijah doing?" I asked, wondering if her answer would be the same.

"Didn't you just see him a little while ago?"

"I did," I said. "I just wondered if you knew."

That probably wasn't fair of me to say, but a part of me couldn't help feeling a little resentful toward her. She'd left my mom hanging, and she didn't get how much strain she put on her family, on Elijah. I could still remember the way Mr.

Greybeck's shoulders had slumped in the car that day, as if the mere act of sitting was a relief.

Mrs. Greybeck's eyes narrowed at me, like she didn't quite understand what I meant. "Why wouldn't I know how he's doing?"

"No reason," I said glibly, offering a plastic-feeling smile. "I should get back to work. Have a nice night, Mrs. Greybeck."

She watched me for a moment longer at the end of her driveway, but I'd already gotten back to work, forcing myself to at least look like I was focused on shoveling snow. But all I wanted to do was tell her how much her dedication to Terry hurt Elijah, to shake her shoulders and tell her how much she hurt my mother. So much anger welled within me; I was surprised it wasn't melting snow.

Before my composure had the chance to shatter, though, Mrs. Greybeck turned on her heel and made her way up the driveway. A moment later, she shut herself inside the house.

I clenched my jaw shut, wishing everything wasn't so complicated.

I went into school Tuesday morning absolutely dreading it. Well, maybe not dreading the school day, but dreading seeing Jeremy. Neither one of us had texted the other since Friday, and I didn't know what to expect. But when I walked past him in the hallway, he looked up and offered me a smile. So maybe not the flirty smile he used to give, but a polite enough one. If I were him, I would've been giving me dagger eyes.

At least that I was one less thing to stress about, not that it lessened my caseload by much.

I'd been putting so much time into these snowflakes that I'd let myself fall behind on the sculpture project we were supposed to be working on. And it was due in three days. So during third hour, I begged and begged Mrs. Galvery, my English teacher, that I could go to the art room. I told her that my life depended on it. That was answered with a dull expression, but she did let me go ten minutes before the bell. Mrs. Keller let me sit at a table away from the other students in that period, giving me ample space to work.

The bell rang overhead, signaling the time when I should've been heading to lunch, but I didn't move.

"Remi?" Mrs. Keller asked, walking up to my table as students began filtering out of the room. She had a pink lunch bag in her hand. "I'm going to go on my break, okay? Feel free to stay in here if you'd like."

"Thank you," I told her, relieved she'd let me continue to work. I really had a lot to do.

The stupid clay wouldn't mold to my will. It was some sort of gray-brown material, gross and slimy, and totally not morphing into what I wanted it to look like at all. I'd been trying to create a simple heart-shaped lump—right now, points for creativity were the furthest thing from my mind— but it just looked like a gray-brown piece of poop.

"Are you struggling?" Elijah asked, coming up behind me and peering over my shoulder.

I'd done great ignoring his presence the entire hour, the amount of anxiety brewing within me more than I could handle. I still couldn't believe that I'd forgotten about this project. The final exam. In my period of art class, I'd worked on this sculpture project *some*, but it completely slipped my mind that it would go toward my grade. I'd put all my energy into the snowflakes. But the chances of me passing were riding on the snowflakes *and* this stupid sculpture assignment.

What Eloise and Elijah had said last night was totally true. Procrastination *was* my thing. It was so ingrained in me that I didn't even realize that I'd been doing it.

The chair beside me scraped as Elijah pulled it out, sitting down and watching closer. "What are you trying to make, anyway? A soap dish?"

"Don't make fun," I said, refusing to look at him. I didn't want him looking at this crappy thing in front of me. He's Mr. Pottery Hands, and has been working on his own art project for his contest for weeks now. In comparison, this was a pathetic clump of crap. "In fact, just leave. You're distracting me."

I still had so much that I needed to do. I needed to have it fully formed, make sure there were no air bubbles, get it glazed, fire it—and I hated it. Every minute of it.

Elijah stood and walked away, leaving me on the brink of a breakdown. I didn't blame him. I mean, I *did* tell him to leave. My face had to have been an icy mask of something scary. I wouldn't have wanted to be around me either.

But now that he was gone, all I could focus on was the weight of everything. I dug the heels of my hands into my eyes, my clay-covered fingers curling, pushing until stars popped behind my lids.

The table twitched as something clinked on top of it, and

I opened my eyes to find a bowl of water at my elbow. "Your clay is too dry," Elijah said, leaning against the table, taking my hands away from my eyes. He moved to dip my fingertips in the bowl. "You're not going to be able to shape anything the way you want to with it being so dry."

Elijah pressed my dripping fingertips to the lump of clay in front of me. "This is stupid. Art is stupid."

"Art isn't stupid," he responded, dampening his own fingers. "You just have to know the ins and outs of what you're working with. What are we trying to make?"

I tried not to let myself overanalyze the use of the word *we*. "The assignment is to make a vase in the shape of something. I'm doing mine in the shape of a heart."

"Anatomical?"

"Do you *think* I'd be trying to make an anatomical heart?"

From the tone of his voice, I could tell he was smirking. "If you want to make a heart, you have to help the clay out. It's not like dough. In this state, it's not so malleable. Water helps. And you make strips." He reached around me and pressed his slick fingers against mine, pushing harder against the clay. "You roll the strips together and then make your shape. You can't fire it when it's a mound or there'll be air bubbles. Air bubbles aren't good."

Sure, yeah, uh-huh. All viable options I could've said in response to him.

But don't worry. I said something much smoother.

"It's like we're making a baby."

Smooth, right?

Ugh.

Elijah burst out laughing behind me, leaning closer. "You're ridiculous, you know that?"

"Hey, my mom said the same thing last night."

Elijah took ahold of my fingertips and moved them to a different spot on the clay. I gave him full control. The water made our skin slippery, fingers sliding over each other against the firm piece of clay. The pressure of his hands against mine felt strange, as along with how his chest kept shifting against me. I never thought much about how our hands felt, pressing up against each other. Never, not once. But it was all I could think about now.

If moments like this kept happening, I was never going to get over this boy.

"Think you've got it?" he asked after a moment, words as soft as a feather's touch against my ear.

No, can you just show me for the rest of the lunch period?
"Y-Yeah, probably."

Elijah didn't move away. "Clay's my favorite. It's reliable. Forgiving. If you make a mistake when it's wet like this, it gives you a chance to fix it."

Why were we talking about clay again? We should've been talking about something else, something like how his hands were so soft against mine, how his chest brushed against my back, how I just wanted to turn around and tell him—

"There you are."

I startled at the sound of a voice, so harsh and intrusive. Elijah pulled away from me with one sharp movement. "Sav."

Oh, crap.

Sure enough, Savannah stood in the doorway of the art room, hands clasped together in front of her. Her expression appeared impassive. "What are you two doing in here?"

"Remi needed help with her technique," Elijah said, and I couldn't help but hear the undercurrent of defensiveness in his tone. "Figured I could lend a hand."

Literally.

"You're so generous," Savannah said with a smile, tucking a curl behind her ear. "Why don't you wash up and we'll go catch the end of lunch?"

Elijah didn't reply as he walked over to the sink.

Savannah took a step into the room, glancing around. "Where's Mrs. Keller?"

"She has lunch this period. She usually eats in the teacher's lounge." Elijah headed to the doorway, glancing at me, then her. "Are you coming?"

"We'll be just a second," Savannah said in a chipper voice. "I'll be right behind you."

Oh, no, don't leave me alone with her. Don't do it, Eli. But he only wavered for a moment before nodding. "I'll see you guys at the table."

I pulled my hands away from the lump of clay, feeling the material underneath my nails. As much as I liked Elijah, I seriously didn't relish in the idea of stepping on Savannah's toes. After all, he was her man—even though he was my best friend, I had no right. "Savannah, he was just helping me, it was—"

"He's such a helpful person," Savannah said while bobbing her head. "I'm so excited to go to the dance with him on Saturday. A bummer you don't have a date."

I clenched my jaw, looking down at my sculpture. "Yeah."

"Elijah and I picked out his tie the other day. It matches my dress perfectly. And Jeremy asked Haisley yesterday," she told me. "Of course she said yes. Who wouldn't?" She let out a breath, and I looked up to find her smiling. "Well, I'll let you get back to work. Looks like you've got a long way to go."

And with that, she walked out of the art room.

Safe to say, I didn't follow after them. I spent the rest of the hour in the art room, feeling a little sick to my stomach.

I hit snowflake 100 on Wednesday night, sitting at the kitchen table freezing to death. Elijah had to prop the door open while he attempted to fix it, letting in a stream of wintery air.

"Can you hurry up?" I called to him. "You're making my glue freeze before I can get the glitter on."

"If you *helped me*, I wouldn't take so long," he said evenly, and I turned just in time to watch him shake his head. "You can hand me nails."

With a sigh, I laid down my cold pair of scissors, huddling deeper in the blanket I'd wrapped around myself. heading down the hallway. "Have you been doing this for hours?" I called to him, heading down the hallway. "Because it feels like it."

Elijah threw a glare over his shoulder, but from the loose set of his shoulders, I knew he wasn't really offended. "I hope your fingers have frozen off."

I stuck my tongue out at him, reaching for the tin can full

of nails and screws. Elijah had borrowed a few of Dad's old tools from the garden shed out back, promptly getting to work when we got home from school. The sun was now falling out of the sky, leaving behind orange and red streaks. They cast a luminous glow against the door, against Elijah's cheeks.

"Here you go, sir, one silver nail for you."

Elijah snatched it from my fingertips and poised it on the sagging doorframe, getting his hammer ready. "This is by no means a facelift, but it should get you by 'til spring and give me time to research how to actually fix a door. Terry was the handy one, not me."

"I wondered why it was looking rough."

"You are just full of wisecracks today."

"I'm just a witty person, what can I say?"

Elijah had his gaze on the doorframe, but I saw the amusement flicker over his features.

I wrapped the blanket tighter around my shoulders, as if that would replace the longing that festered inside me. I could pretend that the tightness of the blanket was like a hug, strong arms wrapping around me, holding me close. Sounded unhealthy. Probably was. But if I closed my eyes, it was a warm image in my mind. Almost enough to chase away the chill. Almost.

A different image filtered through my mind then, of Savannah watching the two of us with narrow eyes. Thinking about it still left a pit in my stomach. I knew if I were her, I'd be ticked too that someone was cozying up to my boyfriend. But it was like I couldn't help myself—these situations kept coming together and I had no power to stop them.

When I opened my eyes, I found Elijah looking at me

with an expression so open that it made my heart jump. He never looked at me like that. "What?" I demanded.

"What...what?"

"You're staring at me."

Elijah blinked, looking away to squint at the jamb. "Oh. I was just thinking. About the door."

"Do you love her?"

A scoff ripped from his throat. "Yes, this door and I are having a torrid love affair. Don't tell my girlfriend."

"That's what I mean. Your girlfriend. Do you love her?"

The question came from a place in my subconscious that hated me, I was sure of it. Otherwise, why would I have ruined a perfectly great moment with something so personal? It wouldn't have been weird before, asking him about his love life, but it felt weird now. And I wasn't sure I wanted to hear the answer.

Elijah clearly thought it was weird too. The look he gave me was pure alarm, and a strangled noise came from his throat. "What?"

"Do you love her? I've never heard you say it."

"I *haven't* said it," he said, holding his hand out for another nail. His voice was lower than it'd been a moment before. "I don't—I don't know, Rem. We haven't been together that long."

I placed the cool nail in his palm, my fingertips brushing his skin. He jerked away at the touch. "I wasn't trying to pry."

"It's payback, I guess, for me being so involved in your love life."

No, get involved, please. Get involved, be a part of my love life. Be in this with me.

I opened my mouth to say something—hopefully not to voice my thoughts—when my ringtone cut through the air, chirping from back at the table. "It's probably Eloise," I said, moving toward it. "She's probably going to ask the answer to a homework problem or something."

When I picked up my cell, though, I saw that it was Dad wanting to video chat. I pressed accept. Dad's face filled my screen, his smile wide. Judging from the background, I could see that he stood in the living room, but the phone was so shaky that I couldn't tell if anyone was with him. "Okay, okay, look!"

When he flipped the camera view, I saw Harmony leaning on the couch, staring up at Dad with her tiny eyebrows pulled together. Dad called her name, and I could hear Clarabelle chiming in as well in the background. "Come on, Harmony, walk to Daddy. You can do it."

"No way," I gasped, pressing one corner of the soft blanket over my mouth.

Harmony's lips twitched as she heard all of our voices mixing together, and she pushed off the couch and stood still for a moment. And then, slower than a turtle, she lifted one little socked foot in front of her and took a step. And then another. Another.

"She's doing it!" Dad said through the phone, and I could hear Clarabelle clapping.

"What's going on?" Elijah asked, coming up behind me. "Is she—"

"She's walking!" I told him with a laugh, holding my cell so that he could see the picture. "Elijah, she's *walking*!"

"Oh my gosh," he breathed, reaching around me to wrap

his arm around my shoulders. I could feel all five of his fingers weigh down the blanket, could feel his hair brush against mine. "Look at her. Go, Harmony, go!"

Mom hurried into the hallway, scanning until she found us huddled together. "What's going on? What happened?"

"Harmony's walking," I repeated, gesturing to the screen of my phone. "Dad's video-chatting me."

"Ooh!" Mom closed the short distance between us, coming up to my other side, and peered at the screen. She immediately smiled, the kind of expression everyone got when looking at babies. "Oh, she's getting so big!"

The five of us cheered on the little baby, all of our voices mixing together as we watched Harmony take another step, and then another. I leaned closer to Elijah, his warmth and his scent wrapping around me, and I knew this moment would be embedded in my brain forever. Even if things were complicated—at least on my end—it felt fitting that he was seeing this, too, that he was part of this moment. No matter what, he was family.

My parents' divorce could have made this moment strange. I knew a lot of couples never spoke again after a divorce. But Mom cheered on Dad's baby with another woman with tears in her eyes, cooing at the screen.

Mom and Dad always said they fell out of love, but at that moment, I knew that wasn't true. Maybe they fell out of romantic love, but they never truly fell out of love. Because with Mom, Dad, Clarabelle, Elijah, and me all cheering on Harmony, I had never felt the love between all of us more.

For some reason, it made me think of the boy beside me. I always thought of Elijah as my Clarabelle—my deep breath of fresh air—but maybe that wasn't quite right. Because I could see myself in this moment, further in the future. Watching him and Savannah grow up and marry and have a daughter about to take her first steps.

I thought of Mom, falling out of love with Dad, watching him live his life with someone else.

In the scenario with Elijah, who was I—Clarabelle? Or Mom?

Thursday, Savannah was absent from the table at lunch, leaving me alone with Elijah and Eloise. I was in the process of quizzing her for her history midterm when Elijah set his tray down with a small clatter, and I immediately cut off my question. "Mom said thanks for fixing the door."

Eloise flipped over a card. "Finally. That thing was practically falling off the hinges."

"Eh, I didn't really *fix* it so much as just jammed it back into place," Elijah said, settling beside Eloise. She scooched her cards over into a pile before her, giving him room. "I'll have to really fix it once it gets warmer. Or maybe I'll convince your dad to."

"Mom said that if you fix the door, she'll reward you with her homemade chocolate pie. That's your favorite, right?" I unwrapped my peanut butter and jelly sandwich, wiping the excess oozing off the side with my finger and licking it off.

"Also, I'm going to be able to swing by the library tonight. Seven, right? I can get some snowflakes done in detention today, so I can spare an hour tonight. Only an hour. But I have it on my calendar and I'm *going* to be there to see your super-secretive sculpture, okay? Elijah?"

Elijah didn't respond, and I looked up to find his eyes resting on me so intensely that I had the urge to glance over my shoulder, almost positive he was staring at something else. I couldn't even describe how he looked at me.

No, not at me. At my...mouth.

I licked my lips. "Did I get peanut butter on my face or something?" I hadn't even taken a bite yet.

Elijah blinked his eyes up to mine before they fell to his tray, hand on the table twitching into a fist. "No, I was just thinking. About your mom's pie." He stabbed his salad with his fork. "Uh, yeah. It's seven."

"Where's Savannah?" Eloise asked, passing her cards back toward me. Her lips were kind of forged into a smirk as she glanced between Elijah and me. "I would've thought she'd been here by now.

"Don't know," he said, not glancing up from his lunch.

We ate quietly for a little while, me quizzing Eloise between mouthfuls of sandwich. While Eloise studied another card, I took that opportunity to just watch Elijah. It sounded creepy—probably because it was—but he sat on the other side of me, so that was where my eyes naturally fell. On his curling hair, and how it had grown just a touch too long. With his head bent like that, peering over his lunch, the broken curve of his nose was obvious, and I liked the idea that he would forever hold a memory of me.

Ew, okay, yeah, that sounded creepy.

He took a bite of pasta and licked his lips, completely oblivious to my cataloging of every feature. Before our kiss, I had been able to look at him and see him as cute—it was almost impossible to ignore that he was cute—but looking at him now, electricity became a constant presence, transforming the bland "cute" into...sexy.

Eloise kicked me hard underneath the table, causing my knee to slam on the underside, jarring the surface. It made Elijah's juice almost topple over, and he looked at me.

Eloise's eyebrows were raised, as if saying *could you be any more obvious, Remi?* Answer? Yes. I probably could've.

"I meant to ask you, Elijah," I said, trying to play off what just happened, even though both my ankle and my knee ached. "Can I hitch a ride with you Saturday? To the dance? I would ask Mom to drop me off, but I don't want her to make a big deal of things like she totally would, you know?"

I could see the exact moment Elijah's shoulders stiffened, as if every single one of his bones transformed into rock. "Um, Savannah's friend, Haisley, is getting ready at her house, so she and her date are just going to carpool with us—"

"You mean Jeremy?" I clarified, my eyebrows drawing together. It wasn't so much jealousy, but I almost felt betrayed that Elijah was still speaking to Jeremy. Ridiculous, sure, and totally horrible, but it stung all the same. I tried to not let it show on my face, but Elijah had always been able to read me. "You're giving them a ride to the dance?"

"He's having a party after the dance, did you know that?" The falsely hopeful tone to his voice hinted that he wanted to just brush past what he'd just said, but it wouldn't work. His face pinched. "Remi—"

"Hey, guys," Savannah said as she slid into the seat beside Elijah. She didn't make eye contact with me. "I saw Mrs. Keller in the hallway. She said she wanted to speak with you, Remi. About the snowflakes?"

I tried to steady my breathing, tried to ignore Eloise's and Elijah's gazes. *It's not a big deal. It's not a big deal.* "Okay."

Elijah reached out as I stood, his hand cupping my wrist. "Don't be mad."

"I'm not mad," I lied, and hated myself for it. I didn't want to be mad. It wasn't fair. "I just have to go."

"Remi," he said, softer now, his hold unrelentingly gentle. I could've broken free if I wanted to, but the warmth of his skin against mine coaxed me into a halt. "Please."

I didn't even know what he was asking, why he said "please," why he looked so...distraught. I should've sat back down. I should've asked. But I didn't.

"Elijah, let her go," Savannah piped up on his other side, opening up her lunchbox. "Mrs. Keller is waiting on her."

I pulled my arm free and crumpled my lunch bag into a ball, my half-eaten sandwich inside. "See you guys later."

Before storming out of the cafeteria and being reported by the cafeteria monitor again, I made sure to ask for permission to go see Mrs. Keller. When I glanced back over my shoulder, I saw Eloise slumping her hand against her chin and Savannah looking at Elijah, who watched me go with the same intense expression.

When I got to Mrs. Keller's classroom, I found her desk vacant. "Mrs. Keller?" I called, searching for her. The lights were on, and from where I stood, I could see her computer screen was lit up, but no one was in sight.

Savannah said she'd seen Mrs. K in the hallway—maybe if I hung around for a minute, she'd show up?

I glanced around the empty space, inhaling the scents that I always associated with Elijah. Creativity radiated from every corner of the room, from sculptures to paintings to drawings, all hung up for students to see and draw inspiration from. The room had never felt inspiring to me, the hodge-podge of colors and mediums overwhelming, but there was something about the space when it sat empty.

I wasn't an artist by any means, but looking at so much inspiration and hard work sparked something in my chest. Something like creativity. Strange.

A sculpture Elijah made earlier in the year sat on the other side of Mrs. Keller's desk, atop a table near the chalkboard. Made from clay, of course—his favorite medium—half-painted a baby blue with the bottom painted into a wispy grass field, swaying in the invisible wind. The sculpture itself had been morphed into the shape of a car wheel, with the rims and tread standing out. A golden sun hung in the upper right corner, whitish-yellow, and it dripped toward the grass. But not dripping paint—it dripped *words*, white and scrawled so minuscule that it was nearly impossible to read them.

Seeing this sculpture sent a flood of warmth to my chest. This was what Elijah loved doing, sculpting. Even sculpting things that could've been more creative, could've been better. This wasn't his best work, not in my opinion, but it had to have been something if Mrs. Keller had placed it behind her desk.

The county art contest awards were tonight, and looking at this sculpture now made me wonder what his new one would look like. If it would be small, big, clay, cardboard. He'd kept everything about it so under wraps; I had no clue what it was.

I tapped my fingers against the sculpture once more before turning to head from the room, feeling a bit better after having gotten a moment alone. I'd have to make sure to find Mrs. Keller later.

It was unexplainable, but the feeling that washed over me was similar to the peace I'd gotten from Dad's house, the feeling that even though some things were glitchy, life still was good.

"I like the way you cooked the chicken tonight, Mom," I told her as we sat down for dinner. "It's kind of spicier than you normally do it."

"I used red pepper flakes tonight. Something different, that's for sure." Mom smiled as she dabbed at her lips with her napkin, ever and always the picture of manners. "How are your grades, sweetheart? I know tomorrow's the last day of the semester, but I've just been so busy. Everything holding up okay?"

I told myself that there was no reason to stress her out now; might as well save it for when report cards were emailed out tomorrow evening. At least then she'd have the entire weekend to melt down. I waited for Mrs. Keller to call me up to her desk during my fourth period with her, but she never did. She worked on her computer all hour, hardly looking up. She must've figured out whatever she needed from me, so I left her be. "Yeah, everything's going good."

"You have to get started on some college applications," she continued, cutting her piece of chicken smaller. "I know you want to go to the community college in Addison, but it might be nice to try some other places."

"As long as I'm not far from you and Dad. I want to see Harmony grow up."

I knew some kids wanted to get the heck out of dodge once graduation came and went, but I was quite fond of the idea of sticking around, staying in or near Greenville. Maybe even Bayview, with its views of the ocean. But I loved the security of coming back to a place that would always be home.

"It's crazy how close we're getting to you being finished," Mom said. "I mean, you're already going into your last half of senior year. Time just flies, doesn't it?"

She could say that again. It felt like just yesterday Elijah and I rode our bikes up and down the cul-de-sac, or banging my soccer ball again and again against his garage door. A similar sense of nostalgia had washed over me when Terry graduated, a strange sort of panic at the idea of growing up.

"Yeah. It does," I said. "Has Elijah's mom tried to get in contact with Dad again, do you know?"

"I don't think so. She's doing better, I think. I saw Alan outside the other day and asked him how everything was going. I guess Terry and Kathleen had a conversation about his time in the facility." Mom took a bite of food and chewed it. "Terry told her that he's making the most of his consequences. He's taking some online college courses. It sounds like he's shaping up in there."

Elijah had looked up to Terry, and probably in many ways still wanted to—it was a relief that after he'd messed up, Terry could see the wrongs of his actions. That was the Terry that I knew—who owned up, who did his best. I was happy to see that that side of him was making a reappearance. "That's really good. I'm glad that he's making the most of what happened."

We passed the conversation along as we ate. I asked her about her work and she asked me about my snowflakes and Elijah. No change on the Elijah front. As for the snowflakes, I only had fifteen left to do tonight to hit 150. *If I never see another paper snowflake in my life, it'll be too soon.*

But I still had to go to Elijah's contest. If I was there for an hour, I'd get back by eight. I probably wouldn't be able to go to sleep until two in the morning, but it would happen. I would finish. I would pass my senior year.

"I'll be back around eight," I told Mom as I shrugged on my jacket. "Elijah's thing should only be about an hour."

"Okay, I'll work on some snowflakes while you're gone," Mom said after she cleared the table, sitting down and tapping her fingers along the surface. "I've seen you do it a dozen times; I'm sure it'll be okay. Probably."

The "probably" didn't instill the most confidence. "You don't have to help," I told her. "It's kind of messy."

Mom raised an eyebrow at me. "Remi, my job is practically one big arts and crafts project. Plus, I'm sure I can do a better snowflake than your father. Did you want to take my car?"

"No, that's okay." I grabbed my boots and hurried past her toward the back door. The library wasn't a far walk from our house, and I was being a little manipulative. If I didn't take Mom's car, Elijah would no doubt offer to drive me home. Sneaky, right? "I won't be long, I promise."

It was a little after seven o'clock, so the sun that had been hidden behind the clouds today was now completely eclipsed from view. Snow fell as I hurried down the street, flipping my hood up. Despite the wintery chill, it was a beautiful night to be outside. The streetlights guided me to the library, flurries from the snowbanks catching in the wind.

The scene was something from a movie, because at that moment, everything just felt *right*. My snowflakes were almost finished. I'd finished my dumb clay sculpture for my final exam in art. Mom and I were bonding much more. Elijah and I were finding our groove again, more or less. Lunch earlier today was just me being a brat—he had the right to hang out with whoever he wanted, Jeremy or not.

There were a few cars parked outside the library when I walked up to it. The brick structure glowed from within, like a candle lit to a flame. People flickered around that flame, moving in front of the windows, along the stacks of books. A sign was propped in the library's front yard: FENTON COUNTY ART CONTEST.

It smelled like warm sugar and old paper as I pulled open the door, revealing the people and setups within. A table stood right at the front door, offering cookies and punch. Though they were tempting, I shrugged off my jacket and made my way farther inside, eyes peeled for a certain shock of blond hair. A wave of anticipation went through me at the idea of finally getting to see his sculpture. The theme was "Family," and I couldn't wait to see what he crafted.

"Hello," the librarian greeted as she walked up to me, her lips curved into a wide smile. "Are you here to vote in the contest? You're just in time if you'd like to. The voting ends in five minutes, and then we'll count them."

Voting? Elijah hadn't said anything about voting—he'd mentioned the contest, but I just assumed there would be judges. If I'd known it was a voting contest, I would've sung his praises to everyone I knew. "I absolutely want to vote. Where are the sculptures?"

The librarian steered my shoulders. "We have five entries over this way, behind the History section. There are papers in front of them that you can write the sculpture name on and stick it in the jar."

I rubbed my chilly fingers along the thighs of my jeans as I walked farther into the depths of the library, trying to rise to my tiptoes to see over the shelves of books.

The displays were arranged in a straight line. Three of the five sculptures were made of clay, fired and glazed different colors, but clay nonetheless. I glanced at the name cards. *Tonia, Ron, Clayton, Audrey—*

I looked at the final sculpture posed on the table, taking a long moment just to figure out what sat before me. What I was looking at. The card held Elijah's name, scrawled in his usual messy handwriting, but the sculpture...

It wasn't made of clay, and that must have been what threw me the most. No, the material was papier-mâché, sturdy and thick, painted a pale color, shaped into a human figure. There were two legs, about as thick as a baby's fist, poised on the cardboard platform. One foot wasn't really taking a step but caught midway through the act.

The sculpture wasn't just legs, though. The papier-mâché was a human figure, yes: a small baby, just beginning to walk. And it was titled, *Help in Harmony*.

I felt my fingers against my lips. *His sculpture is of Harmony walking.* All of the times Elijah had asked about Harmony these past weeks came rushing back to me, tickling my mind. *This was why he always asked about her.*

"You like it?" A familiar voice asked from behind me, and the breath I drew in faltered. "It took me a while, and it was so hard to hide it from you. But I knew your face when you saw the finished product would be worth it."

Elijah stood with his hands in his pants pockets, his pale thumbs poking out against the dark fabric. He'd pushed his hair out of his face for tonight, kept it behind his ears. The shirt he wore was one I'd never seen before, a button-up that made him look different, older. Like Terry. I looked toward his hands again, noticing how he hid them. I would've bet money on the fact that there was still clay underneath his nails, paint smudging his cuticles or something, and he felt embarrassed by it. By how he could never get them quite clean.

His expression looked guarded, nervous. "Well, Rem?"

"You did a papier-mâché of Harmony," I said slowly, softly, turning back to the sculpture. "Why—how—"

"Funny story, I actually was originally going to sculpt something else, something clay. The night Terry was arrested, I...I broke it." His lips curved, but his cheeks pinked with heat. I remembered that night, finding him in his room, with the unfired clay pieces scattered around his room. Ends gnarled as if he'd ripped them apart. "It took me a bit to figure out what I wanted to sculpt, but I took my inspiration from you."

Why does my chest feel so tight? "And Harmony."

"And Harmony." He shifted on his feet, withdrawing a hand to gesture at the sculptures. "Everyone did a really great job, though."

"Why didn't you tell me that it was a voting contest?" I asked, turning back to the Harmony sculpture and grabbing a sliver of paper, ready to write down the name. "I would've been putting out social media ads like crazy."

"I wanted it to be just about the art. At least on my end. Mrs. Keller stopped by earlier, though. My parents, too, on their way to a date, strangely enough. It's the first time since Terry."

"That's good, right?" I glanced over my shoulder. "That's progress." A part of me felt bad that I'd called out Mrs. Greybeck the other day, but maybe it had encouraged her to get back to her life. Imagining that made me feel a little bit better. "Did Savannah stop by?"

"No," he said. "She didn't."

Now I turned around fully, the piece of paper crinkling between my fingers. "What?"

"She didn't come. It's fine." Elijah frowned a little as he looked at me, something passing over his expression. "We fight a lot, about a lot of things. Stupid things, really. So it's okay that she didn't come to this."

My eyebrows came together. "I've never notice you guys fighting."

"We don't fight in public. God forbid anyone thinks we're not a 'good couple.'" Elijah's chest lifted and fell harshly, the movement prominent enough for me to notice out of the corner of my eye. "I just...I don't know if we're right for each other."

A part of my brain wanted to rally behind that sentiment, scream, *yes, dump her! Date me!*

But, amazingly enough, I held back. I leaned against one of the display tables, making sure not to put too much of my weight on it. "Maybe you just need to talk it out, or...I'm not the best in the realm of relationship advice."

"Yeah, but you're smart. I don't know how you're failing art, because you're just so smart."

"You don't have to be smart to be good at art," I said, glancing at his sculpture. "I mean, look at you."

He made a choking noise, and even without looking, I knew it was a laugh.

It felt easy talking to him like this, with neither one of us facing each other. Maybe it was because like this, in this secluded corner of the library, it almost felt like I was speaking to myself. And as I spoke, my chest no longer felt pinched or heavy, and though the weirdness of the past few weeks still existed, in this moment, it didn't feel nearly as impossible to overcome.

"Terry would've loved this," I said. "He always loved it when you got into art shows and stuff like this. Remember that one last year at the street fair? How he told everyone who walked past to come check out your sculpture?"

"Remi," Elijah said as if I hadn't spoken, taking a step closer. His feet were soundless on the carpet. "I need to talk to you about something."

"I'm not mad about you taking Jeremy and Haisley," I told him, knowing what his serious tone was about. "I know I was being a brat about it earlier, but I'm not mad. I mean, I'll get over it. And I'll get a ride with Eloise, which will be better because she's going to do my hair anyway. It'll be fine."

"Remi." His mouth was tight around the edges, more serious than I thought.

"Elijah," the librarian called as she walked into the History section, bringing a trail of voters behind her. I stepped out of the way to let them look at the sculptures. "There's an art professor from Fenton County Community College out front. Would you like to come speak with him?"

"I'll be right there," Elijah said, reaching to touch my arm. "Don't leave, okay?"

I made a face at him. "I'm not going anywhere." He was my unofficial ride home.

It took him a moment to draw away from me, and at that moment, I couldn't help imagining him drawing me closer, closer. But he didn't. His lips twitched a little bit, but he turned away.

The people that had come into the section to look at the sculptures lingered, chatting about which they thought was best, which they thought took the longest, which might have been the hardest. I stood off to the side, eyes trailing over and over Elijah's piece. This was his best work by far. And maybe I was biased, but I couldn't deny it was the best one tonight.

And according to the people who flocked to his sculpture and copied down *Help in Harmony*, they thought so, too.

"This was a terrible idea."

I grinned, reaching down for the lever underneath the seat to propel myself forward, feeling the car hum. "It's a *brilliant* idea. I told you, I'm fine. It's been two weeks since the concussion. I can drive."

"You don't even have your license."

"I do too have a license."

Elijah raised a skeptical eyebrow from the passenger seat of Terry's truck, looking nervous. "On you?"

Ha. Well. "It's only, like, three blocks. I'm not going to get pulled over in three blocks."

"Great. You just sealed your fate."

I reached over and clicked my seatbelt into place, touching the brake experimentally with my foot. "I haven't driven in forever."

"Could've kept that to yourself," Elijah muttered as I grabbed the shifter, slipping it into reverse.

It wasn't that Mom never let me use her car; it was just that she needed it almost every day, so I never bothered paying for a parking pass at school. That meant even on the days she was working from home and not using the car, I still couldn't take it.

That explained the wide, almost manic grin on my face as I eased the truck onto the roadway. "Are you excited that you won?"

Elijah glanced down at the golden award in his lap, turning it over and over. "Golden" only because it was painted that color; the thing rang like hollowed plastic. "It's fun. I didn't participate to win, though."

"Blah, blah. You *can* be excited, you know. I'll be excited with you."

"It's not that I'm not happy. I'm just...thinking."

"I wondered what smelled like it was burning."

I watched as Elijah's lips quirked, like an electric shock jumping the thin line and forcing it to twitch into a smile. It didn't last long, though.

For some reason, his face made me think of that night so long ago. The night Terry had been arrested. I could still hear Elijah's voice trembling over the phone. *Can you come over? Please? I just...I need you. I need you.*

"Your sculpture *was* pretty epic," I told him, flipping on the blinker as I stopped at a light. "Papier-mâché was different from everyone else's. And the subject matter—I know I'm biased, but that was pretty impressive."

"That's what the art professor said."

The tires skidded a little as I put too much gas in the acceleration, and my fingers tightened on the worn steering wheel. "Why did you choose Harmony as a subject, anyway? What's the meaning behind that?"

Elijah shifted in his seat and turned to me, his face

bathed in the dashboard lights. I tried not to keep track of his movements, tried to focus on the road, but I couldn't help but be hyperaware. "You said once that Harmony kept falling but she kept getting up. It took her time, but she learned to walk because she kept getting up. I...I really understood that. On the level with Terry. With me. And I realized how much your life affects mine."

"In a good way?" I sounded hopeful.

"In the best way," he returned, his voice lower than it usually sounded. I flipped on my blinker and started down Grisham Street. "Never question that, Remi. Always in the best way."

"Beanie," I said.

"What?"

I glanced over at him as we passed underneath a street-lamp, watching the glare of yellow streak across his face. "You don't call me Beanie anymore. You haven't called me Beanie in a while. Why?"

Elijah blinked once, twice, as if trying to remember the last time he'd said it. "I didn't realize I'd stopped."

I eased the truck down the road to Elijah's driveway, twisting the wheel. The tires bumped as they met the divot in the sidewalk, jostling the two of us in the cab. Once we were at a complete stop, I slid the gearshift back into park, pulled the keys from the ignition. The chain Elijah kept them on rattled, and I looked to find the bracelet I'd given him still on a ring. BFFs FOUREVER was stitched into the bracelet, right beside my name. My seven-year-old self totally was unaware of how to spell. Seeing it, though, made me smile as I remembered all the past we had behind us.

"There, see? I told you everything would be fine," I said, unclicking my seatbelt and turning to Elijah. "Thanks for letting me drive. I'll have just enough time to finish my snowflakes." I wondered how many Mom had finished since I'd left. Maybe one or two? It sounded simple, but that'd be a big help.

Elijah unlatched his seatbelt too, but his movements were slow. He didn't reach for the door but merely sat still, gaze on his hands. Something was bothering him, different than things had been between us lately. Everything felt *strange*. Off.

"You wanted to tell me something?" I asked. "Earlier, at the library?"

He rubbed at his mouth, and even in the darkness, I could see that there were dark smudges along the sides of his fingers. I'd been right before, guessing about his hands. His hands were always like that. Stained. Dirty. Hinting at signs of previous creativity. Either from clay, graphite pencils, paint, glaze—always. He scrubbed and scrubbed, but it was never enough. Always a trace remained. "I—I don't remember what we were talking about."

"We talked about you fighting with Savannah." I sat back in the seat, looking at the front of Elijah's closed garage door. "What do you and Savannah fight about, anyway? Let me guess—you didn't like the tie she picked out for the dance."

In the journey from the library to his driveway, the truck hadn't had time to properly warm up, so the chill of winter hung in the air. "We fight about you."

Ha. Okay, I hadn't expected *that*. "Is she trying to pressure you to stop being friends with me? Is it because I take you shopping with me? Because I can stop, I can—"

"Did you know that Savannah and Jeremy used to date?"

I blinked again, struggling to keep up with the subject change. "Uh, yeah. Yeah, I knew that." Jeremy always found a way to bring her up.

"Sophomore year. Seems like forever ago. I didn't know about it until Savannah told me last Wednesday. That they used to date, I mean."

Last Wednesday—that was the day we went on our double date. Was that why they'd acted so strange when they picked me up? I stared at his hands, struggling to figure out what he was getting at. "And that bothers you?"

"No." His laugh sounded hollow, disappearing into the quietness of the cab. "Not a single bit."

"I guess I don't understand. If it doesn't bother you, why are you bringing it up?"

Elijah raised his eyes to mine. Their brown centers were warm and melty, focused on me. In this light, though, they almost looked black. "My point," he murmured, his voice dropping so low that the sound itself sounded like a prayer, "is that if I didn't care about Jeremy being with her, why did the idea of him touching you nearly drive me mad?"

Everything stopped.

If I could've collected all the times my stomach had dropped over the course of the last two weeks and combined them together, it wouldn't have even come close to the feeling that washed over me. Like I'd hit my head all over again, but instead of pain pulsing through my body, it was something else. The butterflies in my stomach spread to every inch of my body, filling me with heat and a fluttering sensation.

It felt like my last remaining brain cells had jumped ship. I was stupefied that I could open my mouth, let alone form a coherent word. "What?"

Elijah scrubbed a hand over his face, as if that could erase the trace of his words. "See, Remi, *that* is what we fight about. Not about dresses or shopping or ice cream. We fight about you because she knows how I feel."

She knows how I feel.

And, you know, how was that, exactly?

He kept his hands pressed against his eyes. "It's all I've been thinking about. Nonstop. Jeremy with you, Jeremy touching you, Jeremy kissing you. Like my brain's on a loop, never-ending."

I wanted to pull his hands away, but I couldn't bring myself to move. I'd morphed into the truck seat; we were both frozen.

"I know it was you I kissed at Jeremy's party," Elijah said simply, quickly, as if tearing off a bandage. "I didn't know it at first. Not until last Friday, when I took you to your dad's. Not until I helped you out of Jeremy's car. You—you smelled the same. The same as you did at his party. It all snapped into place."

The world was off-kilter, abruptly turned on its side. I was walking in a dream, fully convinced of its reality, only to wake up and finding everything different. The perfume. I'd worn the same, spicy perfume because I knew Jeremy liked it. And that was the only reason Elijah knew.

"I didn't know it was you when it was happening." The

volume knob on my voice broke, and my words were quiet. "I thought—I thought you were Jeremy."

The words weighed strangely on my tongue. After fantasizing about kissing him all this time, confessing the truth sounded strange. I *had* thought that Elijah was Jeremy. But it didn't feel right anymore. It was hard to believe that a time existed where the mere idea of Elijah's mouth against mine would've caused a whole hodgepodge of disgust in my stomach. Things had changed so drastically.

Elijah's cheeks were flushed, either from the cold creeping in from outside or from the moment between us—I had no way of knowing. But I entered his personal space, his breath warm against my skin. A handful more lashes rimming his right eye than his left. A freckle below one eye. A beautifully crooked nose. A face I had memorized.

"I thought you were Savannah. She wanted to play that stupid game, wanted to do something fun."

One beat passed, then two. Long enough for me to wonder if he'd ever speak again, or if I was going to live sitting here in this cab, watching Elijah's mouth in fear I'd miss any words falling out.

And then he did go on, speaking fast. "I knew you hit your head, and I...I thought about it being you in the closet. I entertained the idea. I think because deep down, I already knew. But I couldn't stop thinking about it. What if it had been you? Not Savannah. *You.*" Elijah did this little thing with his mouth then, lips twitching as if he was about to smile but then thought better of it. "What if it'd been the best kiss of my life and I'd been kissing *you*?"

I was outside my body, experiencing everything second-hand. His words were the ones I'd been waiting to hear, aching to hear, and my insides twisted as they finally, *finally* were spoken aloud. The emotion was so overwhelming that I closed my eyes.

Elijah reached around me to brush his fingers over my hair where I'd hit the shelf. The touch was hesitant, as if nervous, unsure of himself. A cool shock ran down my spine at the touch, causing me to shiver. My body swayed toward him, the desire to reach for him unbearable.

"I'm not Jeremy," I heard him say, the words achingly soft. It was almost like I could feel him, inches away from my face, the heat of his lips close to mine. It was a sixth sense. When he spoke next, I felt his words *everywhere*. Under my skin, inside my bones. "It's just me."

And then Elijah kissed me.

I'm dreaming, I'm dreaming, I'm dreaming. I had to be dreaming.

Because Elijah Greybeck—*Elijah Greybeck*—was kissing me out in the open. No blindfolds, no dark closets.

Instinctively, I grasped the edges of his coat and pulled him to me, so afraid that at any second he would break it off and walk away from me, from us, forever. That made no sense, though, because the gentle hand at the back of my head guided my mouth to his.

I pressed closer, over the console of the truck separating us. We met each other halfway, jackets crinkling as they touched. He might not have played sports, but he had an artist's hands, oh so gentle with the work they praised and adored. I savored the touch, skin zinging with an electricity that only built and built.

Elijah's hand struck at the console until it flipped up, exposing the extra seat in the front. He pulled me closer and I moved willingly, leaning further, further, closer, until there was not even an inch separating us. All the hardness of him, his angles and his muscles, pressed into the softness of me. I kissed him deeper, my teeth slipping against his bottom lip in my desperation to get closer. It was more of a need than a want. A desperate, desperate need.

"Rem," he gasped against my lips, the word so low that I wasn't even sure it counted as a word at all. One of his hands grazed the skin underneath my jacket, five cool fingers on my fire-hot hip. A flame in the snow.

There would never be a time or place that I could get enough of this—I was drowning in his touch, in this moment, gasping for air and just barely getting enough. I was a snowflake caught in a snowstorm, blown around in the blizzardy wind, destined to finally fall and melt into everything else. I was lost; I was found.

This kiss—it was so incomparable to the kiss with Jeremy, so much better. Each nerve tipped on its end and frying, splitting into two and reconnecting. So good that it was nearly painful.

Yeah, so much for thinking that our previous kiss was just a fluke.

I couldn't help but smile against his mouth as he broke away, my lips tingling and aching and swollen. My fingers curled through his hair, my other hand at the back of his neck, not letting him stray too far. "That was—I don't—"

"Yeah," Elijah breathed, offering a gasping chuckle. A whisper of a touch trailed its way down the side of my cheek, a streak of cold against hot. My lids fluttered closed for a moment. "I think we agree."

My brain still stirred, dwindling down from the high that

I'd dragged it upon. The high that included Elijah's hands, his lips.

Nobody pinch me.

Elijah's lips broke into a beautifully carefree smile above me, teeth shining and all, and it nearly busted my chest apart to see it. I realized how incredibly rare it was to see a grin like that from him, and I'd never noticed until now.

He pulled back to trace a fingertip across my temple.

"I can't believe this is happening," I admitted a little breathlessly. Man, Eloise was going to flip when I told her. I could practically imagine her eye roll and "I told you so!" I ran my free hand through my hair, feeling my fingers shake. "Why didn't you say anything sooner? We could've skipped all of this back-and-forth nonsense."

"This isn't entirely my fault," he protested, flicking my nose. "You could've said something. You've known longer than me. Since that night, you've known. You should've told me."

I laughed a little bit, and it sounded crazed. Like I was drunk. Like I was high. Maybe I was. Maybe kissing him was my drug. "Yeah, right. Your girlfriend would've strangled me." No way I could've risked it, made a fool of myself by confessing my feelings and watching him still choose her.

A sudden stillness worked through my body, stopping my racing heart, cooling my skin. The haze that had been clouding my vision dissipated in a slow ebb, in a way that almost felt like I was waking from a dream.

Elijah's knuckles brushed along my jaw. "Why did your face get so serious?"

"Why are you telling me this now?" I asked slowly. "Why

now, why not yesterday, last week? If you've known since then, why now?"

Elijah's eyebrows pulled down a little bit. "I—I don't know."

"Are you only telling me this now because of what happened with you and Sav?"

It was a dark place my mind went, that he was only kissing me since things with his girlfriend were on the rocks. But I couldn't stop the thought from repeating itself once it popped up, and there was no way I couldn't *not* ask.

I stared into his eyes, waiting for his rosy lips to part and words of affirmation to come out. Heck, I would've even taken him teasing me.

The coldness in the cab became frigid at once, like Mother Nature had turned the temperature dial to negative seventy, leaving us to freeze. I realized then that my breath had begun to fog in the air. Elijah opened his mouth, but no words came out.

"You're only telling me this because you're fighting with Sav," I whispered, horror, pain, humiliation, all bundling together to break apart my chest. Tears clouded my vision, causing the image in front of me to blur. "Because you're mad at her. You're only doing this because—"

"No," Elijah said quickly, eyes widening. He readjusted his grip on my fingers, preparing for me to pull away. "No. It's—that's not—that's not why, Remi. Not completely."

I felt like I was going to be sick, right there in front of him. Sounded an awful lot like *it's not what it looks like.* Wasn't that the cliché saying?

For a moment, everything was frozen. In the next, I moved.

I ripped my hand from his and scrambled for the driver's side door, hopping out as quickly as I could. For once, my shoes were sturdy against the ground.

"Wait—Remi!" he called just as I slammed the door shut, probably clambering after me, but I started running. "Wait, please—"

Whether Elijah followed me, I didn't know; I didn't turn around to check and didn't hear him continue calling after me. I hurried onto my front porch, putting all my weight behind pushing the door open.

I felt the door break before the chunk of broken jamb fell to the floor, clattering at my feet. The door swung inward with tremendous ease. From where she still sat at the kitchen table, Mom jumped, gaze flitting up at the commotion. She immediately took in my expression and set down the snowflakes.

"What's wrong?" She got to her feet. "Remi?"

It was one word—my name, my simple name—but that was all it took for me to let loose a strangled sob. The reverberation cracked from my chest as the reality of what just happened set in, and I hurried over to her, tracking snow and water all over the floor.

Her arms wrapped around me as I collapsed into them, unable to hold anything back.

My dreams were soundless and empty, and when I awoke, I felt much of the same. The inside of my chest held a hollow hole where my heart used to be, and the pain came back in an almost instantaneous wave.

After everything registered, panic set in.

I kicked off the covers and stumbled to my feet, nearly falling to my knees in my haste to get to the hallway. My jeans felt tight on my legs, the waistband eating into my stomach from sleeping in them all night. "Mom!" I called, voice still rough with sleep. "Mom, how did I fall asleep?"

As I reached the hallway, I saw her. She was slumped at the kitchen table, her arm knocking over a container of glitter, spilling it onto the table. Dozens of snowflakes lay scattered around her, some even on the floor. Her eyes were shut in a blissful state of sleep.

Now my heart ached for an entirely different reason. As I counted the snowflakes, I found she'd finished the number I needed. With all the ones I'd completed and the ones Mom had finished last night, I had a total of 150 glittery, sparkly, wintry snowflakes. Perfect decorations for a snowflake dance.

"Thank you, Mom," I whispered, bending down and pressing my lips to her forehead, something she did to me many times before. "Thank you, a million times. I love you."

I ran back to my room to get ready for school, my heart thumping heavily in my chest.

Even though I'd woken up without my alarm clock, I made it to the bus stop just as the yellow slug pulled to a stop, its doors opening wide. I stumbled on, my stack of snowflakes pressed securely against my chest. Nothing would happen to these babies. For so long I'd called them "stupid snowflakes," but not anymore. I'd give my life before I let anything happen to them.

And no, that wasn't too dramatic.

Grisham Street was one of the first stops in the morning, so the bus was relatively empty. As I settled into my familiar section in the back, the one with doodles carved into the seat in front of it, I found myself unable to sit completely still. This was the seat Elijah and I used to share before he started using Terry's truck. It made me feel even worse.

The nerves that stewed in my system had my stomach churning. I pressed my cheek against the cool glass of the bus window, not caring how unsanitary it might be. It felt grounding, and that was just what I needed.

Even though I had my snowflakes done, I knew this day was going to suck. I'd have to walk into school and sit next to Elijah in homeroom, pretending like nothing had happened.

But *everything* had happened. And I didn't know if I could look at him ever again.

I leaned harder against the window, rocking as the bus ran into potholes, using the pain to distract myself from crying.

I stopped by Mrs. Keller's room first to give her my snowflakes personally, but she wasn't there. Instead of risking leaving them on her desk—this was my green light for graduation, after all—I sealed my snowflakes in my locker and went directly to my first period class fifteen minutes early, keeping my head down. Though I so badly wanted to find Eloise, I wasn't going to risk running into Elijah in the hallway, walking in with Savannah.

Though the noise rose to its peak that morning, no one spoke to me in the hallways, which was a blessing. As I settled into my usual seat and laid out my pencil and school planner, I felt the nervous jitters of my pulse begin to pick up.

Time slowly passed and more students filtered into the room, finding their seats. He was going to walk in any second. Until, that is, Mrs. Maples called my name. I felt like I was about to have a panic attack. "Remi?" she said, and I looked up to find her hanging up her phone. "They want you in the office."

Me? What did they want me for? And before school even started? My mind raced with possibilities. Maybe Principal Martinez saw how poorly I was doing in art and she just wanted to go over my grade. She probably just didn't know about the extra credit assignment.

I gathered my stuff, trying to slip out as quickly as possible, but couldn't manage to get my heartbeat under control.

As I made my way down the hall to the office, I kept my head down, knowing that he could walk past me any minute. Had he told Savannah about what happened? Was he even going to?

"Hi, someone wanted to see me?" I asked the secretary as I came up to the desk, glancing around.

She had her glasses propped on her nose and had to tip her head down to look at me over them. "Have a seat," she said in a firm voice, turning back to her computer. Totally unfriendly. Although the last time we interacted, I *had* lied to her. I couldn't blame her for giving me the cold shoulder. "Principal Martinez will be with you shortly."

I sat down in one of the stiff green chairs pressed against the wall, where the misfits sat when they were waiting to get a "stern talking-to" from the big gal in charge. I felt out of place among the chairs. Even though detention and I weren't strangers, I was never there for behavioral reasons. My detentions were almost always because I was late.

Seriously, all this anxiety had to be shaving years off my life. I was going to sue.

Principal Martinez's door opened and she came into the office space, her eyes immediately finding mine. Her expression wasn't at all friendly. "Miss Beaufort," she said curtly, causing my heart to sink further. "Come inside."

I rose on wobbly knees and walked inside the office, a place I'd only been a handful of times. To my surprise, Mrs. Keller sat in one of the two chairs placed on either side of the principal's desk, not meeting my gaze. Was this where she'd been this morning when I went to drop off my snowflakes? What was going on?

I glanced between the two ladies uneasily. "Is this about my grade? Because I know it's low, but Mrs. Keller and I worked out a way to raise it so I could graduate."

"Sit down, Miss Beaufort," Principal Martinez said, her voice, like the secretary's, unpleasant and commanding. It sent me to the seat without another word. She sat at her own desk and folded her hands on top, watching me. They both were quiet for a long time, and it almost felt as if they were waiting for me to speak first. "Miss Beaufort, do you know why you're in my office?"

"No," I answered honestly. "I mean, is it about my grades?"

"It is about your grades. About your art grade, to be more specific." Principal Martinez glanced to my side. "Mrs. Keller spoke to me of the arrangement you two had made to gain some extra credit."

I glanced to my right, confused why Mrs. K still wouldn't look at me. "She's saving my senior year, honestly."

"She attempted to," Principal Martinez said, "at least, until you tried to take it into your own hands and change your grade."

My eyebrows slammed together. "Whoa, wait. Excuse me?"

"Yesterday, while Mrs. Keller went on her lunch break, your grade was altered. Someone went into her grade book and changed yours." She pulled a sheet of paper from the edge of her computer and handed it to me. "From a fifty-six to a seventy-two."

The two grades were circled in red ink, as if I wouldn't have been able to notice the giant jump in numbers. I blinked at it, trying to comprehend what I was seeing, what Principal Martinez was saying.

"The time it was changed was eleven-oh-two," she went on, "precisely your lunch hour. I spoke to the cafeteria monitor, and she said that you requested to go to Mrs. Keller's room halfway through the period."

Now my head jerked up. "I thought you wanted to see

me," I said, adding emotion into my words. I turned to Mrs. Keller, trying to catch her eye. "I didn't change my grades."

She pursed her lips. "Elijah comes into the art room sometimes to work during his lunch period," Mrs. Keller said, not speaking to me but to the air. "I leave the art room open for him and any other students during that time. Remi knows that."

The crappy thing was that I *wouldn't* have known that, not before Tuesday when I hurried to finish my sculpture last minute. But she'd seen me stay in her room when she left for lunch. "I know it looks bad," I said, folding the paper, the numbers starting to make me feel sick, "but I swear it's not like that. I have all 150 of the snowflakes finished. They're in my locker, I can go get them—"

Principal Martinez cut me off by lifting her palm. "I've already been informed by several of your teachers of your love for tall tales, Miss Beaufort. We have a zero-tolerance policy for cheating, especially of the lengths you went to. There is no excuse."

This is not happening.

This is so not happening.

This is so totally not happening.

I turned fully in my chair to face Mrs. Keller, my lungs seizing on the air they were trying to draw in. "You believe me, right? I wouldn't jeopardize my ability to graduate. I *wouldn't.*"

Mrs. Keller finally turned to look at me, and the disappointment in her eyes nearly killed me. I never would've thought her approval meant so much to me, but seeing that hope so cruelly dashed to pieces cut a new wound into my chest. "I'm sorry, Remi," she said, truly sounding regretful. "I wish you'd chosen the better path instead of trying to cheat."

"But I *didn't*—"

"We've called your mother," Principal Martinez said. She didn't want to hear me out; that much was clear. I could see everything slip away from me in an instant, swirling down the drain. "She didn't answer, but I left a message. You're suspended from the rest of today's classes, as well as from the Snowflake Dance tomorrow. We'll have a board meeting on Monday to discuss your situation, which you're welcome to come to and plead your case."

Plead my case. Like I was on trial. Like I was Terry.

"If you're not going to listen to me now, what's going to be different at a board meeting?"

Principal Martinez's face tightened and she leaned forward, the harsh lighting sending her shadow across her desk. "I suggest you change your tone, Miss Beaufort, for additional consequences won't be as forgiving."

"Forgiving? You're failing my *senior year!*" I'd have to repeat the year, stuck in high school while everyone else moved on. While Elijah moved on.

"And whose fault is that?" No compassion.

I dug my fingers into the knees of my jeans, hardly feeling the pain. The pressure was the only thing that kept me from spouting off a sarcastic comment.

"That's all. Please have your mother call us when you get home." Principal Martinez turned back to her desk, and Mrs. Keller glanced away from me. A clear dismissal from both of them. My speaking role was over; cue my exit stage left.

I got to my feet, my jaw aching from how tightly I'd been

clenching it. When I reached the door and pulled it open, meeting the prying gaze of the secretary, I couldn't keep a final retort from slipping out. "This must stink for tomorrow, huh? Can it really be a Snowflake Dance without any snowflakes?"

Before they had a chance to answer, I slammed the door behind me.

Mom was furious when I told her the story of what happened, but not at me.

"What do you mean they wouldn't hear you out? They said you tried to cheat? Well, then, can they explain why you slaved away at those godforsaken snowflakes for the past two weeks? Why I have glitter on every surface imaginable in my kitchen? Where's the cordless? I'm going to give that school a piece of my mind."

That piece of her mind involved a lot of passive-aggressive sighing, a little bit of yelling, and her hanging up in an angry huff. Principal Martinez had told her, apparently, that since all evidence pointed to me, I must have done it. Guilty until proven innocent.

I had to admit, it did look pretty incriminating. But it had been raised sixteen percentage points—even I wouldn't have been that stupid. If I'd done it, I'd only raised it by four points. Just enough to pass.

"You're not *really* suspended, right?" Eloise said as soon

as she picked up the phone. I called her after school let out, not feeling like summarizing everything into a text. "That's just a rumor?"

Ugh, it was already going around? "No, I'm really suspended," I told her, grunting in frustration as I flopped onto my bed. My ceiling held no answers and didn't even attempt to soothe me. "They think I hacked into Mrs. Keller's online grade book."

"That's a load of bull!" Eloise shouted over the phone. "Don't they know you?"

I snorted. "I'm not like you. I'm not Miss Goody Two-Shoes."

"Still. You're not a *delinquent*. And Mrs. Keller believed you cheated, too?"

"Wholeheartedly. In her defense, though, Elijah did cheat for me on the papier-mâché project, so," I said, dragging the word out, "it wasn't much of a stretch for her. Suspended from school, can't go to the school dance. Not that the stupid thing would've been fun anyway." Watching everyone dance with their dates—watching Elijah dance with Savannah—yeah, no thanks.

"Well...crap."

I scrubbed a hand over my face, over my mouth, trying to wipe away the memory of a certain pressure. "In other news, Elijah and I are over."

"What do you mean, *over*?"

"We're done. Not friends anymore." Not *anything* anymore. Not anything ever again. "So let's not mention his name anymore, okay?"

I waited for Eloise to say something on the other line, for

anything to filter through, but there was only silence. And then—"Remi, there is no *you* without Elijah. You're best friends. You can't just break up."

"Well, we did." My elbows dug into my mattress as I sat up, grinding my teeth. "Just wanted to update you, but I've got to go."

I hung up without letting her reply, dropping my cell on my bed and flopping back down. If I listened closely, I could hear the wind pushing up against the windows and hear the heat hum through the air vents. And listening closely was the only way to get my brain off everything falling apart.

My life sucked.

Let's review.

I had a best friend, one who knew me probably better than I knew myself, and I loved him. He kissed me and everything had been perfect—until I realized that he'd only told the truth because he and his girlfriend had a falling-out. I was his backup plan, and it *hurt*.

I spent who knew how many hours cutting and pasting and glittering 150 snowflakes for a dance for a school that had convicted me of a crime I didn't commit. A school that refused to let me graduate with the class I'd grown up with.

And now I had those 150 snowflakes for no reason.

The Snowflake Dance was in eight hours, but no way in hell was I going.

So...yeah. My life sucked. Monumentally.

Mom had been on the phone with Dad all morning Saturday, trying to come up with a game plan for "defending my innocence." Because that was what we had to do, apparently, which was so messed up. At the moment, Dad planned to come down to Greenville on Monday and go to the stupid meeting himself, intent on defending his daughter from the horrors of the district court. Or, well, the Greenville School District court.

This was literally a horror movie. A low-budget one.

I sat on my bedspread with my bag full of snowflakes, staring at them with such a dark hatred that I was surprised they didn't shrivel up into nothing but dust and glitter. How could something so dumb be my downfall? These stupid pieces of paper belonged in the trash. The only good thing about them being in my hands meant that Mrs. Keller and Principal Martinez didn't have them, and that meant their stupid dance would just be a Snow Dance. In their faces.

But the disappointment in Mrs. Keller's eyes was something I wouldn't be able to erase from my memory, not anytime soon. It sank my stomach, a rock floating to the bottom of a riverbed, and not even the strongest of currents could move it. She had been counting on me, and in her eyes, I failed her.

I pulled a snowflake out of the bag, careful not to flake any glitter off. These things were a true nightmare, a symbol of everything in my life that had imploded. I would never be able to look at the shape the same way.

Desperately, I wanted to just text Elijah. He would say the right thing; he always did. He'd say something so ridiculously positive that I'd have no choice but to believe him. A part of me hoped that he would text me first, maybe after hearing the rumors around school. He never did. Our silence didn't stop me from peeking out my bedroom window a few times, checking to see if his truck was in the driveway.

It was, and covered in snow.

Mom's voice leaked through the door, rising higher as she grew more flustered. I couldn't believe I'd allowed myself to get into this position, failing a class and dooming my senior year. Worse yet, I'd dragged my parents into this when they had their own lives to worry about.

My fingertips tangled with glitter as I thought about how different life had been two weeks ago.

These things might be a nightmare now, but I thought of all the times they'd brought me closer to someone. To Elijah, to my mom, to my dad, to Clarabelle. Even to Eloise, for a minute. Although she hadn't helped, she'd been moral support. These stupid snowflakes strengthened my relationship with all those people.

I thought about Mom, staying up all night and finishing them. What would've once felt overbearing had saved me in the end—her constant protectiveness helped me cross that finish line. It made me hate myself for ever yelling at her. No wonder she was as upset as I was. It meant the world that she was willing to stay up all night to help me, even when she thought they were for extra credit. Since all this went down, I had been forced to tell her the truth.

Report cards had been sent out last night, and mine had a brilliant, whopping F next to Fine Arts, accompanied by a tanked GPA.

I slipped the snowflake back inside its plastic bag and I got to my feet, grabbing my coat. "Mom?" I called, finding her on the couch, still on the phone. "I'll be right back. There's something I need to do."

It wasn't too bad of a day out today. The sun partially hid behind the cloud cover of winter, but my breath didn't fog in the air as I walked up to the building. Spring was still a ways away, but days like this made me anxious for warmer weather.

I could've driven myself, but it was a nice day, and I needed more time to think.

The school's gymnasium had been decorated quite well for the limited budget Mrs. Keller talked about. Various shades of blue streamers and ribbons were strung around the room, weaved in and out to create an intricate-looking pattern. A roll of blue fabric lay along the floor in some places, looking like a carpet movie stars walked down. White cotton batting lay torn apart along the ground, attempting to look like piles of snow.

But with all the decorations, there was not a single snowflake in sight.

"Remi."

I turned at my name, finding Mrs. Keller emerging from behind a photo booth.

Her features pressed into a frown, her eyes steely behind her glasses. "What are you doing here?"

"I wanted to give these to you," I said, holding out the bag of snowflakes. Her eyes fell to it, but she didn't immediately take it. "I didn't lie to you; I did make the snowflakes. All 150 of them. And I didn't change my grade. If I was going to change my grade, I wouldn't have been spending hours working on these dumb things." I added, "Do you know how annoying glitter is?"

She hesitated. "I do. That's why no one would take that job."

Ha. Of course. I got the worst job available. "Well, that's the only reason I'm here. I wasn't going to do anything with them, and I didn't want them to go to waste. Plus...I wanted you to see the truth, even though that doesn't change anything."

Mrs. Keller took ahold of the bag, turning over the snowflakes as she examined the glitter. "And you did these all yourself?"

"No," I answered honestly. "My dad and stepmom helped me, and we laughed around the table for hours. My mom helped me finish them. That's why she didn't answer the phone yesterday; she was asleep after staying up late. Elijah..." I cut myself off with a hard swallow, straightening my spine. "No, I didn't do these by myself, but these snowflakes made me realize how something small can have a big impact. Because these snowflakes will tie everything together."

Surprise rippled through me when Mrs. Keller broke into a laugh. "It's like you said. You can't have a Snowflake Dance without snowflakes." Her eyes met mine again. "I could see if Principal Martinez would let you come to the dance tonight, Remi. If you wanted."

Something moved in the corner of my eye, and I glanced over to find Savannah and a few other members of the student council carrying around a pillar and placing it near the bathrooms. From a distance, our gazes caught.

"Thanks," I told Mrs. Keller, backing away, "but I think I'm going to stay home."

My hands felt empty without the bag, a weight lifted from my chest. I'd miss that excuse to have something to do. Maybe it was time to pick up another arts and crafts hobby. *Ha, no.*

I stuck my hands into my jacket pockets as I made my way outside, feeling a little bit lighter.

"Remi!"

Savannah wrapped her arms around her middle as she came out of the building after me, her blonde hair flapping around her shoulders as she jogged over. *Great,* I thought, glancing around to see if anyone was here to witness this. *She's going to knock me out for kissing her boyfriend, isn't she?*

"Savannah, let's not do this, okay?"

"No, we're doing this," she said, stomping up to me. Her lips pressed tightly together as she looked at me. "I know what happened last night. And what happened at Jeremy's party. I know you kissed him, and I—"

"I'm sorry," I said, clenching my hands into fists in my pockets. "What happened shouldn't have ever happened. I shouldn't have kissed him; that was a seriously crappy thing to do. But don't worry, because it's not going to happen again." I couldn't stand to face her any longer, so I shifted my gaze to the sky. It hurt to look at her; it brought my jumble of emotions to the surface. "I know it was you who changed my grades, you know."

I saw her jerk—or maybe she shivered. "I didn't—"

"Just don't, okay? You came into lunch late. You told me Mrs. Keller needed to talk to me, and she wasn't even in her room. Conveniently, my grades were changed around the same time. Not exactly rocket science."

When I finally looked to Savannah, I saw that her eyes were wide, color draining from her cheeks. "You didn't tell."

I felt abruptly tired, as if all of my energy had been zapped, drained. "No, I didn't tell. Even though it's going to make me fail this semester. Fail my senior year. You know why? Because Elijah cares about you." The words ached a little to admit. "You only changed my grade because I kissed your boyfriend, right? I'm not trying to steal him from you, Savannah. He's yours. Just...promise me that you'll love him." My lips curved a little on their own accord. "You'll appreciate him for who he is. Accept him. Listen to his stories, be excited with him about his art, be a shoulder for him to lean on. Be there for him." *Because I won't be.* "If you can do that, I'll let this go. We'll be even."

"Fail your senior year," she said slowly, her expression twisting with a mixture of confusion and shock. "You'd repeat the grade instead of tell the truth and turn me in? You're going to fail your senior year just to make Elijah happy?"

Yeah, it did sound psycho, didn't it? Entirely psycho. Like I'd lost my mind completely. But Savannah, for whatever reason, was someone Elijah cared about. I wasn't going to stand in the way. I was going to do what Dad said: step back, let him live his life. Protect his happiness. Buy military-grade binoculars. Elijah was my Clarabelle, but I wasn't his, and that...that'd have to be okay.

I recalled the webpage I'd been looking on earlier from the school district's website. "I wouldn't have to repeat the whole grade, just the semester of art. I can take summer classes and graduate in the fall. And I love him," I told her, uncaring about how I was literally confessing my love to her boyfriend, uncaring about whatever expression crossed her face. I turned my back on her, muttering under my breath, "You do dumb things for the people you love."

Something about winter had me feeling different. Not good, not bad, just *different*. Maybe I could blame winter on everything falling apart, the skewed feelings—everything.

I always was a firm believer that things happened for a reason, but sometimes it was hard to imagine what that reason could've been.

I thought about Harmony, about all the times she'd tried to walk in the past but kept falling down, crashing, relying on someone to reach out and catch her. That was what Elijah had done his project on. I thought about Terry, a good kid who'd made some really dumb decisions, getting a second chance to restart his life. I even thought about Dad and Clarabelle, and how he'd gotten his second chance at finding his true love.

All of those things happened for a reason. Harmony had to fall to learn to walk. Terry went through his rough patch before coming out on the other side with a different perspective. And Dad, with his relationship with Mom—he learned how to love, to truly love, and he gained from it. He gained me and he kept a friend in Mom.

This had to be my "happens for a reason" moment. Even if I had no flipping clue how everything tied together.

I'd just turned down my driveway when I saw Mrs. Greybeck shut the door behind her across the street, bundled in her jacket, heading for her car. My steps slowed, and I felt torn between ducking my head and quickening my pace or raising my voice and saying hello.

The decision was made for me when she slipped on some ice and fell on her butt in the snow.

"Mrs. Greybeck!" I called, hurrying across the street. Even before I reached her driveway, I could hear her laugh, so light and familiar that it sent a tingle down my spine. Familiar like an old scent you hadn't smelled in years, or an image that tickled your memory but you couldn't place at first. It made my heart jump. "Mrs. Greybeck, are you okay?"

She was still laughing as I approached, reaching out for her hands. It was another thing that threw me for a loop, the sight of her grin. "Oh, I'm fine. I forgot how slippery the grass can be once the snow melts a little."

I helped brush the snow off the back of her jacket. "Yeah, winter is a notorious season for falls."

"So I heard." She looked up at me, her light eyes finding mine. "Elijah told me you hit your head a few weeks ago."

"Yeah, well, I'm just clumsy. Nothing to do with winter." I glanced at her purse, which sat in the crook of her elbow. She had her hair pulled back into a ponytail, her makeup done simply. "Were you going somewhere?"

"To the store," she answered. "I'm hoping to get a collection of fresh lunch meat. I thought maybe I could bring it over to you and your mother tomorrow, and we could have a nice lunch. I've been a little missing in action lately."

Her words were so surprising that a response eluded me. I felt something warm my insides as we stood in the cold together. It had been so long since our families had been together. After Terry, all their time and energy had been spent trying to keep their heads above water.

"I need to apologize," I said to her. "It was wrong of me to go prying into your life like that."

I felt her fingers touch mine before I realized she'd reached out, giving them a squeeze. "I'm glad you did. And thank you for being there for my son these past few weeks. I know how important you are to him, and I'm glad you were there for him."

"He's important to me, too." *More than you know.*

For a moment, I feared I'd spoken the last bit aloud, or that she'd heard my thoughts somehow, because she gave me a knowing look. "Elijah's good with his hands. Good with art. One thing he's not good with, however, is words."

I blinked at her. "What do you mean?"

"Just don't lose hope," she told me, squeezing my fingers one final time before letting go. She didn't give me long to think about what she meant, because she started to walk away. "Don't tell your mom about tomorrow. I want to surprise her, if you think that would be okay."

"Trust me, Mrs. Greybeck," I said, already anticipating Mom's enthusiasm. "She'll love it."

❄

Around eight o'clock that night, the doorbell chimed. The door opened with ease from when I'd busted through it the other night. Mom had shoved one of our end tables in front of it since it wouldn't properly lock now, and she'd already recruited Dad to fix it when he came to town on Monday.

I wrested the door open further, finding who stood on the other side. "Eloise. Hey."

She looked down at me with a relaxed gaze, eyes swiped heavily with eyeshadow, lips pink with gloss. She had on a leather jacket over a pretty top, her skirt riding up to her mid-thigh. "Hi. Are you going to let me in?"

"Why are you so dolled up?"

"Duh," Eloise scoffed. "We're going to a party."

I blinked at her standing on my snowy porch. "Do you mean the dance? Because I told you that I can't go."

"Not the dance," Eloise said, shoving me back so she could come inside. Though she was lean, she was *strong*. I shouldn't have doubted that; she did concuss a girl in volleyball this past season. Her strength was not something I underestimated. "A party. You heard that Jeremy's throwing one, right? After the dance?"

Only a beat passed before I burst out laughing. "You really think I want to go to Jeremy's party like nothing happened? Seriously?"

"You can't hide out in your bedroom forever. And no matter what you *want*, you can't just cut Elijah out of your life. Your souls are practically forged into one."

"This coming from a girl who thinks a spark during a first kiss is ludicrous."

Eloise slung her arm over my shoulders and began to

steer me into my bedroom. "Listen, REM-Sleep. You didn't get to go to the Snowflake Dance. That sucks. But you can go to Jeremy's party. And have fun, and pretend like your life isn't crashing down all around you."

Ha, no kidding. My life *was* crashing down all around me. I couldn't help but wonder, though, if this was how Elijah had felt those weeks ago. Terry being arrested, the sculpture project to work on, a new girlfriend. Everything complicated, coming all at once. "I doubt Jeremy would want me there."

"That's the beauty of a public party," Eloise said, turning to rummage through my closet. She threw a look over her shoulder. "Anyone can show up."

twenty-four

"I don't know about this," I said, digging my fingernails into my palms. Eloise had to park down the street since there were so many cars filling Jeremy's driveway, lining the road. "I mean, we could always just go home. Have a girls' night."

Eloise popped her car door open, giving me a look as the overhead light came on. Her eyeshadow glimmered just before she ducked out. "Don't be a party pooper."

Jeremy's party before had been a certain type of lackluster. The turnout was low, the beer was bad, and the music made me want to bang my head against the wall. But that party did have one thing going for it.

This one, though...this one was not like the other.

As I pulled myself from Eloise's car, music immediately curved over my ears, muffled by the walls of the house but still audible. I glanced around at the other houses along the street, wondering if someone was going to put in a noise complaint. If I could hear the music from outside, it must've been blaring. Through the windows, I could see bodies inside, shadows dancing along the walls, moving with the music.

I grabbed ahold of the porch banister, my boots slipping on the damp wood. "I guess everyone came after the dance, huh?"

"Looks like it. From what I can see," she said, nodding toward the window, "no one even changed. People are still wearing their formal outfits."

So I'd be the only ones in jeans, standing out like a sore thumb. Fantastic.

"You just need a drink in you," Eloise said, patting me affectionately on the shoulder. "Something to make you feel good."

"No alcohol," I said immediately, making a face. "Maybe just a glass of water."

Eloise snorted as we passed over the threshold, the temperature changing drastically as we walked inside. It was obvious why. I counted more than thirty people just in the hallway and pooling into the living room, talking, drinking, and dancing. Eloise took my coat from me, shoving mine and hers up behind a potted plant near the door, our secret hiding place.

Don't look around, I told myself, energy zipping along my skin. *Don't look for him. If he's here, you don't care.*

"Come on. Since you're going to be sober, you can be the designated driver. I'm getting me a drink." She wrapped her fingers around my wrist, pulling me through the house.

There was a handful of people in the kitchen, lounging against the countertops, sipping from their cups. On the counter, multiple bottles of something were lined up, varying in color and size, with a handmade sign that read HELP YOURSELF.

"Pick your poison," Eloise said to herself as she snatched up a red cup, pulling it close to her mouth as she debated.

Suddenly, two hands touched my waist, fingers curling, turning me around.

Jeremy loomed tall above me, his dark natural curls slicked back and out of his face with some sort of gel. He still wore his white and black suit, a hot pink bowtie secured around his throat. "Remi. You came."

Instantly, I was thrown to another time, another party. A flirty banter that had felt so natural, so right.

It's a nice surprise to see you here, Remi.

Are you saying you didn't throw this party secretly hoping I'd come?

Man, am I that obvious?

He pulled his hands off my waist, holding one out. "Want to dance, Remi?"

It felt strange, looking at him now after everything had changed. Two weeks ago, this moment would've sent my heart swooning, all aflutter. All that I felt now was a bit rueful. I didn't ask him where his date was, didn't ask him how the dance was.

I just offered a polite smile. "I'm good, Jeremy," I said with a nod, Eloise glancing between us. "I'll see you around."

My words didn't cause the smile to fall from his face, but he just nodded, looking almost contemplative. "All right. Have fun tonight," he said, and then he turned away.

"What a bonehead," Eloise said, watching as Jeremy disappeared.

"He's not," I told them both, letting out a soft breath. "He's just a boy." Just the wrong one.

As I watched him go into the living room, my eyes were snagged by a pair that loomed in the distance, caught in the crowd.

I'd seen Elijah in a suit before—we'd had other dances, and our junior prom—but somehow seeing him in this lighting, dressed up, felt completely and entirely different. My heart lurched into high gear as our eyes tangled, and even over the distance, I could practically feel the heat of him pressing up against me.

His blond hair wasn't slicked back like Jeremy's but flowing loose over his forehead in a way that fit him perfectly. He wore a black suit with a black undershirt, his tie charcoal gray and tied expertly around his neck. His dad had knotted it most likely, since Elijah couldn't tie a tie to save his life.

I saw his lips move from across the room, and then someone crossed in front of him, shielding him from my sight.

All at once, everything rushed back into focus. The music, the noise, everyone around me—all of it had been muted, like I'd pressed the button on a TV remote and everything ceased to be except him and me. Now everything felt too loud, too much.

"I'm going to the bathroom," I told Eloise, not waiting for a response before I turned to edge down the hall.

If I thought the line to the bathroom was long last time, it was *huge* now, stretching nearly to the corner of the kitchen. People in dresses and suits shifted on their feet, waiting for their turn. The air still felt clogged in the hallway, those filling the narrow corridor taking in all the oxygen. I just needed space to myself, just for a moment, just to breathe.

Without really thinking about it, I made a beeline for the guest bedroom, hauling the door open and shutting it quickly behind me.

Like last time, the room itself was as dark as night, shadowy and hard to see properly. The humidity from the rest of the house hadn't reached this closed-off room, and the air felt a little bit lighter. I ventured further, eyes snagging on the closet pushed off to the side, door shut. It was just a closet. Nothing special.

I pulled open the door, finding the space empty. Since it was the guest bedroom closet, the interior was clean. Shelves lined the perimeter of it, but nothing sat on them except for slivers of dust, fingerprinted and smudged. I brushed the edge of the corner I'd hit my head on, surprised there wasn't a dent or divot in the wood.

My legs folded underneath me, and I sank to the ground, pulling my knees up to my chest and leaning my head against the wall. Though the music still boomed, echoing around me, peace settled over me as I sat by myself. Eloise was out there somewhere, Jeremy was out there, Elijah was out there. And I was in here, listening to myself breathing.

I didn't know how long I sat there, allowing my soul to settle inside my body, to take a deep breath in and let an even bigger one out. Long enough for the tracks to have switched out in the living room, the bass dropping loud.

Long enough that the door to the guest bedroom opened, a rectangle of light filtering across the floor.

I knew it was Elijah the second the shadow formed, even though I couldn't see his face. That dang sixth sense. He came closer, footsteps soundless over the carpeted floor, until he was in the doorway of the closet. Until he was sitting down across from me, exactly in the space he'd stood last time. All the air that I had been inhaling fled from my lungs in an instant, leaving me staring back, breathless.

For several moments, neither one of us spoke, the music from inside the only noise between us. "I saw you come in here," Elijah said finally, solemn expression unchanging. "Can we talk?"

I clutched my arms tighter around myself, as if the action alone would keep me from coming undone. It was two nights ago, but I could still easily recall the pressure of his mouth on my skin, could easily feel it. If I allowed myself to, I could've gotten lost in that feeling of fireworks and sparks and desire and electricity that had existed between us.

Elijah pulled one of his knees up to his chest too, dress pants riding up with the movement.

"You didn't change," I said, stating the obvious.

"I didn't. I brought Savannah here straight from the dance."

My fingers dug into my thigh. "The front door broke again," I told him, buying time, stuffing words into these spare seconds. "You have to fix it."

Elijah didn't answer; his gaze was so heavy on me.

I was grateful for the dimness, because even though I couldn't see his expression, that meant that he couldn't see mine either. We were both in the dark. But even so, I could *feel* his eyes tracing over me, and that attention had every nerve in my body tingling. Though everything had happened, it felt *right* to just sit there with him. It almost felt like old times. Just the two of us enjoying the other's company, listening to their breathing. A part of me wanted to just close my eyes and pretend that nothing had happened—that I hadn't actually made out with him in his brother's truck—but there was no going back.

And the other part of me, the larger, more dominant part, didn't want to go back. It just wanted to replay his touch and kiss over and over until the end of time.

"I'm sorry," Elijah said quietly, breaking up my rampant thoughts and the silence. "For Thursday night, for the night of the party."

His words rang through in my mind. He was sorry. He was sorry for choosing Savannah.

I leaned my head against the wall, the firmness grounding me from the sharpness in my throat, in my chest. "You don't have to apologize," I forced out, the words feeling gross and thick on my tongue. "It's fine."

"Remi—"

"Were the snowflakes at the dance pretty?" I asked, squaring my shoulders. "I ended up giving them to Mrs. Keller. Did they look nice?"

"They looked like stars." His words were vapor, bouncing against the walls of the closet, the walls of my brain. "Hung by strings, falling from the sky. They looked beautiful."

I pinched my thigh harder, swallowing hard.

"I heard about the rumors. I know you didn't change your grade, Remi," Elijah said in the gentlest tone I'd ever heard. "You wouldn't do that."

Bitterness ate at me. "Why not? I mean, I go around kissing other girls' boyfriends, so why wouldn't I change my grade? Why stop there?"

"Remi."

"Yeah, fine, so the two aren't really on the same level of severity, but they both suck," I went on, looking out toward the bedroom. Emotion crawled its way further up my throat, leaking out. "That's what bad influences do."

His hands cupped my elbows, warm fingers on cool skin, and he ducked his gaze to try and snag mine. "Remi Beaufort, I'm an idiot."

Despite the seriousness of his voice, the seriousness of the situation, I snorted. It was an ugly sound. "I already knew that."

But Elijah wasn't about to be deterred, and he swallowed, fingers shaking on my skin. "Being with you is the only thing that's ever felt right, Rem. I can talk to you about Terry when I can't talk about it with anyone else. Why do you think I did your papier-mâché for you, take you freaking panty shopping, spend entire nights talking to you on the phone? Because you're my best friend, and I'm yours, and I can't imagine living my life without you in it."

"You said *panty*," I told him, almost as an afterthought. "Those are the kinds of things you do with your best friends, Elijah. Those are things I'd do with Eloise. Shopping and spending time together—friends do that." Emphasis on the *friends* part.

Elijah scooted closer across the floor, the space between us no longer enough for one person. If I leaned forward just a smidge, I could've kissed him. "But I *love* those things. I love spending time with you. I just...crave it. When we're not together, I want to be. So badly. And it's always been like that —wanting to be with you—but I never really paid attention to just how much. Kissing you at Jeremy's party was an accident, but Thursday night wasn't. As soon as you showed up at the library, I knew, without a shadow of a doubt."

I sighed. "Knew *what*?"

"That I loved you," he said simply, surely. They were three words that felt like three punches against my ribs. A strong heartbeat, *boom, boom, boom*. Elijah let go of my arms and placed a palm on the ground beside me, leaning in, forcing me to tilt my head back to meet his gaze. "And I don't mean love you like a little sister or anything like that. I don't think it's ever been like that. You're this huge part of my life, Rem, but I never realized why. But then it—it was simple. Clear. A light filling the darkness in my mind, like the stars hanging in the sky. It was you."

I nearly choked on a breath of air I tried to drag into my lungs. "You chose Savannah."

"I didn't choose Savannah." He shook his head, his hair tumbling. "Though it probably looked that way. I took her to the dance, yes, because she asked me not to cancel last minute. But we're over. We were over when I kissed you, I promise. She never wanted *me*—she just wanted *someone*. And I just wanted you."

My heart raced, about to arrest in my chest and leave me dead in the middle of the closet. I wanted to look away, to take the intensity out of the moment, but I felt too connected to him. A pull that there was no escaping. And his words— what exactly did they mean? What exactly was he saying?

"I didn't tell you that I knew it was you because you were my second choice," he said quickly, almost desperately. "I swear. You were never a second choice. You were a first choice I was afraid to choose. So afraid, Remi. Afraid that you wouldn't feel the same way. That I'd lose the only person who truly understood me. You were obviously not saying anything about the party for a reason, and for the first time in forever, I couldn't figure out what you were thinking."

I looked at the fabric of his tie as his words trickled through my brain, like droplets of water running down a windowpane. We'd both been afraid of the same thing. It felt fitting, that he felt the exact same as I did. So many times we shared things—even ice cream. And now we shared that feeling, the fear of telling how we felt.

Elijah pressed his fingertips against my cheek. "I mean, come on, Rem. I knew your *bra size.*"

I snorted again, and the noise caused a wide smile to break across his face. Gosh, he was so handsome. And I couldn't just attribute it to the suit he wore. No, it was his crooked nose, the freckle underneath his eyebrow, his uneven eyelashes. It was the way he smiled when he sculpted, the way he drove with one hand always resting on the gearshift. It was his clay-covered fingers, the way he laughed, the way he loved. It wasn't just his looks—it was just *him*, all of him, making my heart pound a mile a minute.

"Give me a chance," Elijah said softly, ghosting one fingertip down the slope of my neck. "A chance to take you shopping, to get ice cream, to fix your front door, and to kiss you," he added with emphasis, "and kiss you, and kiss you. I think I'm getting pretty good at it."

To kiss you, and kiss you, and kiss you. I wanted nothing more. But something held me back. "What if it doesn't end up working? What if it just falls apart and is super gross and ruins our friendship, and then you stop talking to me and we have to awkwardly avoid each other for the rest of our lives?"

He blinked, probably because I'd spoken rapid-fire. "I've spent my entire life with you, Remi," he said. "If I stopped talking to you every time you did something gross, we'd have stopped being friends when you ate worms."

"And I'd have stopped being your friend when you spewed pop all over the cafeteria table in the sixth grade."

His lips twitched before faltering. "But you're still here, and I'm still here. For as long as you want me."

For as long as you want me. He said that—he really said that. When I looked up at Elijah's face, choking on the air that I tried to bring into my lungs, I nearly burst into tears. This was actually happening. I wasn't dreaming, and there were no rugs about to be pulled from underneath my feet. Elijah was here, wanting me, offering himself to me for as long as I wanted him. And I would want him, until the end of time.

To keep myself from crying, I leaned forward in the darkness of the closet and pressed my mouth against his.

His mouth was still as soft as I remembered, so perfect against my own. I felt his lips curve underneath mine as he reached out and pushed my hair back, fingers spreading across my jaw. I pressed closer, wrapping my arms around his neck.

This was our first kiss that wasn't all heat and passion—not to say that those weren't great—but this felt softer.

Sweeter. Less about need and desire, but steadier, filled with the warmth of love. My heart swooned in my chest, the happiness in my veins sending it into overdrive.

Elijah leaned forward to touch his forehead to mine. "I think I'm starting to get the whole appeal of this Lip Locker thing."

"I think this is how you're supposed to do it. You know, leave out the head trauma." I couldn't wipe the smile from my face, curling my fingers. "Kiss me again, Elijah."

His laugh sounded ghostly, slipping across my skin. Against my lips, Elijah murmured, "Don't mind if I do."

"Stop doing that thing with your leg."

My leg, which had been bouncing nervously up and down, froze. I glanced to the boy beside me. "I'm nervous."

Elijah placed his hand on my knee, either a show of support or to make sure I wouldn't twitch anymore. Amusement flicked across his gaze. "I can tell."

"We'll set the record straight," Mom said from the chair on my other side, her own legs crossed. She'd pulled her short hair back into a tight bun, making her look serious. Or so she said. Between that and her pantsuit, it looked like we were about to walk into court. "My little girl is no cheater."

The weekend had flown by. It felt like just yesterday Principal Martinez called me to her office and accused me of cheating, sending me home with a suspension and the dooming fate of missing graduation. Friday and Saturday held their own struggles as I tried to come to terms with my life falling to pieces, but Sunday had been a day that I needed. Desperately. Mr. and Mrs. Greybeck had come over and surprised Mom with an indoor picnic, Elijah in tow. I invited Eloise, too, since I felt so bad for ditching her the night before at Jeremy's party. By the time Elijah and I emerged from the closet, nearly everyone had gone home.

There had been a ton of "I told you so" phrases coming from Eloise, and smiles. Big, big smiles.

Elijah moved his hand from my knee to my fist now, unwinding my stiff fingers. "Want to go get ice cream after this?"

I almost asked him how he could think about ice cream at a time like this, but then I realized that he only asked to take my mind off the situation at hand. "I think I'll get chocolate this time, so you don't have to share yours."

A smile sprung to his lips. "I never minded sharing."

Dad leaned out from Mom's other side, catching my eye. "Does she normally make you wait this long?"

"Brian," Mom shushed.

"What? We've been sitting here for about ten minutes."

He barely got the sentence out before the door to Principal Martinez's office opened and she appeared. Her expression looked entirely different than it had on Friday; her mouth pulled up into a smile upon seeing my parents. She even showed teeth. "Mr. and Mrs. Beaufort, Remi, please, come in."

We all stood up, my grip on Elijah's fingers tugging him to his feet as well. I let my parents walk past us, looking up into his beautiful brown eyes. The deepness of them grounded me a little as I searched them. "Will you still love me if Principal Martinez makes me repeat my senior year?"

Because even though I probably could've only repeated the one class, I was preparing myself for the worst.

Elijah's eyebrows pulled down a bit, lips parting. "Remi."

"You'll be off at college seeing college girls and going to college parties, and I'll still be in high school."

"When did you become such a worrier?"

When? Oh, just over the past few weeks, when my life slowly and surely fell apart.

He placed his hands on my shoulders with a little pressure, grounding me. "You're going to go in there, and you're going to tell the truth. If they believe you, great. If they don't, then they're idiots, but it doesn't change what really happened. Either way, yes, I'll love you." He finished off his sentence by leaning forward and pressing a kiss to the tip of my nose before pulling back completely. "Go. They're waiting on you."

And they were. Dad poked his head out of the office. "You coming, Remikins?"

I nodded, seeing Elijah give me one last supportive smile before brushing past him into the office.

I jerked when I saw Savannah sitting in one of the chairs opposite of Principal Martinez's desk. She had her chin down, gaze averted, but the mere sight of her had me hesitating in the doorway. "Uh—"

"Sit down, honey," Mom told me, patting the chair next to her. Mom and Dad's chairs were positioned closest to the principal's desk, and they were waiting expectantly.

As I moved into the room, Savannah kept her gaze off mine, no matter how hard I tried to catch it.

Principal Martinez closed the door before making her

way to her desk, settling into the chair. She shuffled a few papers in front of her, as if taking that moment to orient herself. "Thank you for coming in, Mr. and Mrs. Beaufort," she began, still holding onto her smile. "I've dug into the issue a little bit more since we last spoke, Remi, and a few things have come to light. And a certain someone has something to say to you."

"I'm sorry," Savannah said from the other side of the room, finally glancing my way. She looked a little like she had Saturday afternoon. Her eyes were wide, the blood draining from her face. "I changed your grade, Remi."

No. No, no, that wasn't what I wanted to happen. I didn't want her to confess to anything. I mean, yeah, I didn't want to repeat my senior year or have to take makeup classes, but I didn't want Savannah to get in trouble for it. It *was* my fault, anyway. I'd let my grade drop lower than it should've. The entire semester, I'd blown off art class. I led myself down this path.

And I kissed her boyfriend. I deserved the consequences, the karma—not her.

"Savannah, you—"

"I was jealous," she said, cutting me off, voice shaking a little. "Of you and Elijah. I shouldn't have done it. I...I didn't realize it would be so serious. That you would fail the grade."

Mom glanced my way as Savannah spoke, eyebrows drawn together. "It was just a big misunderstanding," I said.

"One that almost kept you from graduating on time," Dad pointed out.

"I'm sorry I didn't believe you," Mrs. Keller said, and I had to turn a little in my seat to face her fully. Her face softened, expression as open as I'd ever seen it. A fist of nervousness finally started to unclench inside me. "You're going to pass this semester with a sixty percent, Remi. You made all of those snowflakes. As soon as you turned them in, I knew there had to be more to the story. It's like you said. Would you have gone to all the trouble with the snowflakes just to cheat? I'm just sorry that I didn't listen to you earlier."

She'd listened to me. I mean sure, it was a little delayed, but she believed in me. A huge wave of relief rolled over me, so painfully crushing that I almost burst into tears.

"That *we* didn't listen to you," Principal Martinez corrected her, "but we're listening now. And I hope you forgive us, and the school, when we say how truly sorry we are for this miscommunication. Although, Remi," she added, "I expect you to clean up your act, or more detention may be in your future. None of this would've happened if your grade hadn't slipped so low."

Yeah, yeah, rub salt in that wound, lady. "I know, and don't worry, I'll be better about it." After all this, no way was I going to let my grades dip past a seventy ever again. No. Way.

"Savannah, that will be all for now," Principal Martinez said to her.

Savannah stood from her chair on shaking legs, the quivering obvious. She glanced at me, at my parents, one final time before going to the door and letting herself out.

Principal Martinez shifted behind her desk almost uncomfortably, and normally I would've loved to see her squirm, but I couldn't take my eyes off the door. "I wanted to issue a formal apology, Mr. and Mrs. Beaufort, for our conversations last Friday. With so much confusion going on, it's easy to get caught up in the moment and—"

"I'll be right back," I said, not at all caring about cutting her off, rising to my feet. "Keep going, I'll just—excuse me."

Elijah looked up as I exited the office, expression all sorts of confused. "What was Savannah doing in there? What's going on?"

I hadn't told him about Savannah's involvement with my malfunctioning grades, so he truly wouldn't have known why she was in there. "I'll explain but—just—stay here."

I hurried from the office and out into the hallway. All things considered, it seemed like a fair boundary between her and I. I kissed her boyfriend; she tanked my GPA. Fighting her about it would've made me feel wrong, guilty. And now that I had her boyfriend *and* a fixed GPA, I felt even worse.

The halls were empty, which made finding the blonde girl walking away incredibly easy. "Savannah, wait!"

I almost wasn't sure she was going to stop, but she did. She paused long enough that I caught up with her. "We don't need to talk about this," she said as I got close.

"We do." I stared at her back, dropping my voice. "Why did you turn yourself in?"

"You know, I didn't like you. Before. And I didn't know anything about you, I just knew that you...you were a threat. In my mind, anyway. You could've done it; you could've taken Elijah away." Her hair moved back and forth as she shook her head. "I didn't even bother getting to know you before I decided I didn't like you."

I frowned a little at the confession, not sure where it was

coming from. "I'm really sorry about how everything turned out, Savannah."

At the sound of her name, she turned, giving me a full look at her face. She wasn't crying, but her nose looked red, as if she could've started. But her eyes remained dry. "I did do it. I changed your grade. I changed it enough that I knew they'd catch it. I thought, *maybe if I change her grade, she'll stop trying to steal my boyfriend.*"

"I wasn't—"

"I know. I know you weren't trying to steal him." She pressed a hand to her cheek, sighing. When her lips curled into an involuntary smile, I blinked, because it was the first real one I'd seen from her. I knew in an instant that it was genuine. "But I realized something after we spoke on Saturday. I realized I hadn't changed your grade to keep *Elijah.* I didn't do it because I loved him and because I wanted him. I did it because I just wanted *someone.* A boy to call mine. All this time I fought for him, and we didn't even work well together."

"You did think his art was an annoying quirk," I pointed out.

The smile grew until she let out a chuckle. "I *hated* his art. The impracticality of it. The pointlessness of it." Savannah looked at me for a long moment, the traces of humor fading from her face. "After we spoke, I realized that you weren't the bad guy, Remi. I made you out to be one, but you're not. *I* was the one standing in the middle of *your* story."

I was the one standing in the middle of your story. I wasn't sure I agreed with that—it definitely didn't feel that way. The fact that she thought that made me want to reach out and hug her. Which was a strange feeling, given everything that happened.

"Oh, don't look so guilty," she told me immediately, rolling her eyes. "We weren't dating that long, and we were both miserable. We were just on a different wavelength. And you were right. Elijah deserves to have someone to listen to his stories and be excited about his art. He deserves to have *you*."

"Did you get in a lot of trouble for coming clean?"

She waved her hand in the air, batting away the idea. "Don't worry about me. I really am sorry for everything, Remi. I had no idea that would keep you from graduating. Honest."

I believed her. When I told her before that I wouldn't be graduating, the shock on her face had been enough to make me pause even in that moment. I didn't doubt her now.

We stood together in the hallway for a beat longer, the silence between us thick. And then I spoke. "Do you want to go shopping or something sometime? Just hang out, talk. Be friends?"

Savannah raised her eyebrows. "Don't you think that'd be a little weird, all things considered?"

"Maybe," I said, "but I don't have that many girl friends. Eloise and I go shopping pretty often. We'd love to have you come with."

"You know, I did hear that Liv's is having a buy one, get one sale on tops and bottoms this week. We could start there."

I let out a little breath, my lips slipping into a smile. "Sounds great."

Savannah hesitated for a moment before heading off in the direction of her first period class. The lightness in my chest nearly had me laughing, a strange sort of feeling bubbling in my chest.

Elijah's knee was bouncing as I came back into the office, and it stopped when he lifted his gaze. "Everything okay?"

I reached a hand out to him and immediately he laced his fingers around my own. The warmth of his skin jumped onto mine, like a little shock. "Yeah," I said as I leaned into him, welcoming the heat his body produced. Surely the secretary was about to yell at us for PDA, but I was going to soak this moment up. I was going to soak *him* up. "Everything's okay."

And it was. In fact, it all had fallen into place. My grades, Elijah, my parents, Elijah's parents, Savannah—everything had reached its peaceful moment. I was a snowflake, falling, and I had finally landed somewhere okay.

Elijah and I were together—something that seemed so impossible two weeks ago. But there we were, hands clasped, gazes tangling up. In a way, it almost felt like nothing had changed. He was still my best friend; he'd always be my best friend. Only there was a depth to us now that left everything inside me feeling like a puddle of goo. And, you know, there was also the added perk of getting to kiss him whenever I wanted. I would take advantage of that every chance I got.

epilogue

Elijah's fingers combed idly through my hair, gentle when they snagged on a few tangles, massaging them out. I closed my eyes and leaned into his touch, a cat leaning into a scratch, a flower leaning toward the sun. The heat between our bodies had reached the point of sweltering, the blanket over our legs definitely not helping, but no way was I moving. Possibly ever.

"Did you fall asleep?" Elijah whispered against my temple, shifting ever so slightly beside me.

"Mmm, not yet, but I could."

We'd been curled up on the couch for almost an hour now, or maybe it just felt like it. The steady thumping of Elijah's heartbeat underneath my palm, as well as his deliciously soft fingers, had lulled me into a state of bliss. "You *can't*," he corrected, voice equally tender. "We've got to leave soon."

"Your mom isn't out of the bathroom yet," I protested, curling closer over his body. My foot slipped against the smooth material of his dress pants, pushing the fabric up until I felt his bare calf. "We'll move when she comes out."

Elijah laughed against me, drawing his fingers from my hair to graze my cheek. "I can't even dream about napping right now. It feels like I just drank three cups of coffee."

I pried my eyelids apart to find his deep eyes slipping over my face, a tenderness in their depths that still managed to render me speechless. It felt like just yesterday we were on the floor of Jeremy's closet, talking, confessing, kissing. But that'd been nearly two months ago.

I reached up and poked his cheek. "You're just nervous."

He tried to bite my finger, but I pulled it away just in time. "What if he's mad at me for not visiting sooner?" he asked, voice dropping to a worried pitch. "What if he's different?"

"He will be different." I moved to run my fingers through his hair, just like he'd been doing moments ago. "But he's still your brother, Eli. And he's probably over-the-moon excited to see you."

In the month and a half since the dawn of our relationship, it had been nearly impossible to convince Elijah to see his brother. He wanted to, I knew that, but his nerves won out every time. The idea of facing his brother frightened him, to the point where I wondered if he'd ever be able to go. But the facility that housed Terry was hosting their annual March Meetup, where families and friends could come by and see their loved ones, and with the help of his parents and my mom, we'd been able to convince him it was time.

"It feels like he's been gone forever, and it's only been a couple of months," he sighed, eyes slipping shut at my touch.

"I know it may not seem like it, but I *am* excited to see him. And nervous."

"It'll be great," I told him. "I'm proud of you. Are you taking your sketchbook with you? I think Terry would love to see what you've been working on."

"That's a good idea. I hadn't thought of that." His hand returned to my hair, and I settled back against him, relaxing into his warm body. I was made to fit there, listening to his breathing, inhaling his scent. His voice, so quiet it sounded gravelly, sending a shiver down my spine. "Thank you for agreeing to come with me, Remi."

I pushed myself up a little bit to press my lips against the side of his neck, the smooth skin there scented with his body wash, and warm under my mouth. "I'll always do whatever you need me to do."

Elijah's expression was tender and soft. "I just need you to love me."

Looking into his eyes, which were filled to the brim with warmth, I thought about everything. Everything that had ever happened between us. Us as little kids, running around town and playing make-believe. Me breaking his nose with that softball. Him inviting me to his first art show. Our first time playing the switch game with our ice creams. Our first kiss.

Two months ago, the thought of us together like this would've sounded crazy. I never would've been able to imagine it, not in a million years. We'd shared a couch before, but not like this, not with our legs entwined, not with his fingers caressing my hair. But now heat spread over me, those memories fueling it, and I couldn't help but trace my fingertips along his lips. So soft, so perfect.

Never enough. "I do love you," I whispered, moving to replace my fingers with my lips. "I definitely do."

If you loved this book, support the author by leaving a review! It helps more than you know!

Check out the next book in the Love in Fenton County series, my Fake Relationship Romance OUT OF MY LEAGUE!

Before You Go!

Reviews are so important for authors, especially for indie authors. If you enjoyed this book, please head over to Amazon and leave a review!

Sarah Sutton

ALSO BY SARAH SUTTON

__LOVE IN FENTON COUNTY:__

WHAT ARE FRIENDS FOR
OUT OF MY LEAGUE
IF THE BROOM FITS
CAN'T CATCH MY BREATH
TWO KINDS OF US

Out of My League

Fake dating the captain of the baseball team is all fun and games until someone catches feelings.

If the Broom Fits

How do you move on from someone you never fell out of love with?

Can't Catch My Breath

Can love break free from the past?

ACKNOWLEDGMENTS

The idea of writing a book seems so solitary, doesn't it? You're typing away at a computer—who's going to be by your side? Answer: a butt-ton of people. Seriously. *What Are Friends For?* was a dream forged into a reality, but it was not without the help from my army of supporters, those who waved flags of encouragement when my tank came close to running on empty.

And, of course, with the help of you! You picked up this story, you joined me on this rollercoaster of a ride, and for that I'm so completely and utterly thankful. I hope you enjoyed reading Elijah and Remi's story just as much as I enjoyed writing it!

Ariel and Sam, my two amazing critique partners, you really helped shape this book into what it is. Both of you have read that original draft—yikes—and both of you have been there since the beginning. Without your words of encouragement, and countless hours of conversations, I'm sure this would be a very different story!

To my amazing beta readers, L., Steph, Stacey, Alethea, Brandy, and Phoebe—you people rocked my world, in a good way! The beta reading process is always something that's scary, but you all held my hand and guided me through it.

To my AMAZING editor, Rachel, for really getting down to the heart of this story with me and making everything sound amazingly beautiful. You rock!

To my wonderful and loving parents. Mom, Dad—I wouldn't have been able to do *any* of this without you. Your love and support was never-ending. From the bottom of my heart, I am so appreciative of all you've done for me.

And finally, to the One who deserves credit for everything. These story ideas were put in my mind and my heart by You, shaped by You, inspired by You. I'm so beyond blessed to have Your hand in mine, walking along this journey with me.

ABOUT THE AUTHOR

Sarah Sutton is the author of YA Contemporary Romance books from a tiny town in Michigan. These standalone novels can be read in any order and are sure to leave you swooning. She's always loved the idea of falling in love; capturing the fall through words and heart-melting kisses is one of her passions! Meet-cutes? She'll take all of them! Accidental touches? She lives for them! First kisses? Yes, please!

To follow her on social media and learn more about her books, visit her website: sarah-sutton.com
Facebook: @SarahMaeSutton
Instagram: @SarahMaeSutton
YouTube: @AuthorSarahSutton
TikTok: @AuthorSarahSutton

www.ingramcontent.com/pod-product-compliance
Lightning Source LLC
Chambersburg PA
CBHW021105110726
47900CB00007B/2039